KU-762-291

# ELEVEN HOURS

**By the same author**

Tully

Red Leaves

# ELEVEN HOURS

# Paullina Simons

Flamingo
*An Imprint of* HarperCollins*Publishers*

637720
MORAY COUNCIL
Department of Technical
& Leisure Services
F

Flamingo
An Imprint of HarperCollins*Publishers*
77–85 Fulham Palace Road,
Hammersmith, London W6 8JB

Special overseas edition 1998
This edition 1998
1 3 5 7 9 8 6 4 2

Copyright © Paullina Simons 1998

The Author asserts the moral right to
be identified as the author of this work

A catalogue record for this book is available
from the British Library

ISBN 0 00 225718 1
ISBN 0 00 225723 8 (Pbk)

This novel is entirely a work of fiction. The names,
characters and incidents portrayed in it are the work of the
author's imagination. Any resemblance to actual persons,
living or dead, events or localities is entirely coincidental.

Printed and bound in Great Britain by
Caledonian International Book Manufacturing Ltd, Glasgow

All rights reserved. No part of this publication may be
reproduced, stored in a retrieval system, or transmitted,
in any form or by any means, electronic, mechanical,
photocopying, recording or otherwise, without the
prior permission of the publishers.

*For my third child*

# ACKNOWLEDGMENTS

I am gratefully indebted to Mike Johnson of the Plano Police Department for his invaluable advice and real-life flair. I'll never forget looking inside the trunk of your car, Mike.

To Bob Wyatt—the life I have is because you believed in me, for *Tully,* for *Red Leaves,* for this book, and the next. Thank you.

To Joy Harris, my ever loyal, hardworking agent.

To my husband, for choosing a new job as editorial director of Wishbone Books, which brought us all to Texas and made this book possible.

To my beloved children, thank you for letting your mom alone long enough in her hot small attic room to write her books.

*It was not you that sent me here.*

— JOSEPH TO HIS BROTHERS,
GEN. 45:9

# ELEVEN HOURS

**D**idi Wood was walking to the mall from her car when her pregnant belly began to tighten until it felt like a taut basketball. She winced through her discomfort and slowed down to a near halt; this contraction was particularly strong. She leaned against a minivan, rubbing her belly with one hand as she wiped her forehead with the other. Maybe she shouldn't go to the mall. But she had promised Amanda new alphabet blocks a few days ago, and she wanted to keep her promise. Also, she needed new face cream.

Didi thought it was a good day for the air-conditioned comfort shopping provided. Dallas was having a brief heat spell. It was called summer. She contemplated driving to Rich's office and spending the hour before their lunch date relaxing on his small sofa, but decided to stay. She'd be all right. It was only an hour.

She couldn't wait to get inside the mall. When she had left the house earlier for her doctor's appointment, the temperature had already been in the high nineties. A radio bulletin had informed her there was a heat advisory on—for old ladies, for small children, and for women in Didi's delicate condition.

Perspiring and uncomfortable, she waddled into NorthPark.

Estée Lauder had something for her at Dillard's. The last thing Didi needed was more cosmetics, but who was she to refuse a little gift from a big department store? She was offered moisture-rich black mascara, two lipsticks whose shades she didn't particularly like, a perfume sampler, a pocket brush, some hand cream, and a makeup bag. It was the makeup bag she wanted.

The gift was free—with a $17.50 purchase.

Didi thought it was uncanny the way Estée Lauder never priced her products at $17.50. Oh, there was plenty for $15, all kinds of lipsticks and eyeliners and mascaras. And there was plenty for $30, $50, and $72. Nothing actually for $17.50.

To get the free gift, Didi spent $108.75—plus tax. She bought a jar of Fruition face cream, a rose lipstick for spring, even though it was July, and a teal eye pencil for her brown eyes. While she was waiting to pay, Didi felt the Belly tighten again. She grasped the counter.

"Oh," the girl behind the counter said. "Not long now?"

Didi managed to nod.

"When are you due?"

The contraction passed, and Didi looked at her watch. "In about two hours," she said lightly.

After seeing the frightened expression on the salesgirl's pretty face, Didi said, "Just kidding. I guess you don't have any kids—two weeks."

The salesgirl breathed a short sigh of relief and smiled. "Whew," she said. "You're right, I don't have any kids. Not yet, anyway." Then, with a little nervous laugh, she asked, "You're not in labor, are you?"

"No, no," Didi said, outwardly smiling but inwardly fretting, wishing the girl would hurry with her receipt. She wanted to get to FAO Schwarz. She added, "I'm having these little fake contractions. Braxton

Hicks, they're called. They're a pain, but they're not the real thing. Believe me, they're nothing like the real thing."

The girl giggled. "Oh, gosh, I'm never having kids. It's just all so scary, the labor, the pregnancy." The girl handed Didi the receipt.

"It's not too bad," Didi said, signing her name. "It's really not too bad at all. You forget right away."

"Bet you don't," said the girl.

"No, you do," said Didi. "You have to. Otherwise we'd never have more than one baby."

"I guess you're right," said the girl, looking at Didi's face. "Your skin is so nice. Do you use any foundation?"

Didi pushed the signed receipt toward the girl and reached for her makeup, which the girl wasn't giving her. "I'm done here. Thanks anyway. Can I have my stuff, please?"

"Oh, sure, sure," said the girl, handing her the bag. "Well, good luck."

Didi smiled. "Have a nice day."


In FAO Schwarz, the matronly woman behind the counter complimented Didi on her sleeveless yellow sundress. "Banana Republic," replied Didi.

"Oh, I didn't know they did maternity," said the saleswoman.

"They don't," Didi said. "It's an extra large." She hated saying "extra large," but she didn't like being ashamed of her size either. The woman handed her the bags and said, "Are you going to be okay with these? They're kind of heavy."

"I'll be fine," said Didi. "I only have a few more stops to make."

She was glad NorthPark wasn't as busy as it was on Saturdays. She didn't like to push through crowds with her bags and the Belly.

In Coach, Didi bought herself a new leather purse. It was brown, medium-sized, and on sale for $60, down from $120. With the $60 saved, she bought herself a wallet.

"When are you due?" asked the lady helping her.

"Two weeks," replied Didi, holding on to the Belly. She needed to sit. Gravity was pulling the baby down. Didi needed him or her to stay inside for a few more weeks. She and Rich were planning an escape to Lake Texoma in Oklahoma the following weekend.

"Do you know what it's going to be?"

Didi shook her head. "We want to be surprised," she said.

"That's nice," said the lady. "I couldn't do that. I wanted to know with my two kids. I have two boys."

Didi smiled, signing the American Express receipt. "That's nice. We have two girls. Do you like having two boys?"

"Oh, yes," said the lady. Before Didi had a chance to reply, the woman said, "They're a handful. But I wanted to try again for a girl. My husband said no more. What if we continue having boys for ten years? Two's plenty, he said. Who am I to argue, right? He pays the bills. I only work to make myself a little extra for the holidays, you know?"

Didi smiled and nodded knowingly. "We would like a boy," she admitted. "But it doesn't matter. Boy or girl, we're done after this one."

"I hear you, sister," said the saleslady.

Didi laughed. "I'm sure your boys must be wonderful," she said.

"Oh, no, they're terrors," said the lady. "Five and seven. Absolute terrors."

As she walked out of Coach, Didi smelled something sweet and delicious. She looked at her watch. 12:20. Lunch with Richie in forty minutes. She remembered their fight last night and sighed. No. She was meeting Rich in forty minutes, but that didn't mean she would be eating in forty minutes because there would be more arguing, recriminations, and apologies before food was ordered and served. Didi thought it could be as long as an hour and a half before she saw actual food. That was just too long to wait. She had a hankering for something now, something that didn't include bickering. A sweet pretzel would do nicely.

Didi headed for the Freshëns Yogurt stand, which also sold pretzels. She knew she had only two speeds—slow and very slow. Weighed down with thirty pounds of baby and baby nesting plus Dillard's, FAO Schwarz, and Coach shopping bags in her hands, she felt as if she were moving only through inertia, which dictated that bodies in motion stay in motion. She wished she were a body at rest.

"Could I have an almond pretzel, please?" Didi asked the teenage boy behind the counter. The words came out softly between short breaths.

"Sure. Would you like any topping on it?" he asked her.

"No, thank you. Just a pretzel." A second later, she said, "Make that two. And some water, please."

"One pretzel for you, one for the baby," a voice next to her said. She turned her head to the right and found herself face to face with a young man. He had a wide friendly smile on his face. She smiled back, but—something in his face thinned her own smile. A small pit opened up inside her stomach. The feeling reminded her of high school days when she'd meet someone cute and her heart would fall a foot in her chest.

The falling didn't come because he was cute, and her heart didn't skip because she was excited. Her heart skipped because the man was looking at her with a warm smile of familiarity, with the smile of someone who'd known her for ages. Didi was sure she'd never met him.

There was something else odd about him, something she couldn't quite put her finger on.

Reluctantly, she acknowledged him. "No, actually. One for me, one for my husband. The baby eats plenty as it is."

"Yeah, those babies can get mighty hungry," he said. "My wife had a baby boy a little while ago."

"That's nice," she said, turning away from him. "Congratulations."

"Do you know if it's a boy or a girl?" asked the guy behind the counter, handing Didi a white paper bag with two pretzels in it.

"No. It doesn't really matter," Didi said evasively.

"Oh, you say it doesn't matter," the friendly man beside her said. "But you know it matters a lot. We all want what we want."

"No, really," Didi said, wishing he would stop talking to her. "As long as the baby's healthy." She studied him briefly. He was somewhere in his late twenties, clean-shaven, neatly dressed, thin, and of medium height. His light brown hair was carefully trimmed above his ears. He had blue or green eyes; Didi couldn't be sure in the artificial light of the mall and didn't want to look at him that closely. Underneath his navy nylon jacket he wore a white shirt. He wasn't bad-looking.

"Bet your husband wants a boy, though," the man said.

He doesn't know I have a husband, Didi thought, and then remembered mentioning that one of the pretzels was for her husband. She was instantly upset with herself. Why am I being unkind to him? she thought. I'm being unkind and unchristian.

"Bet your husband wants a boy, though," the man repeated evenly.

"If he does, he isn't telling," Didi said quickly. She took out three dollars and paid for the pretzels.

Taking a gulp of water, she gave the cup back to the salesclerk to throw out. She didn't have a free hand to carry a drink. Throwing the change inside her purse, Didi said in a friendly voice, "Well, have a nice day."

"Yeah, you too," said the guy behind the counter.

The man followed her as she walked away from the store. Didi tried to speed up but realized it was impossible. He came up beside her and said, "Hey. Do you need help with those bags? They look so heavy."

Didi tried to speed up again. Did she look as if she was languishing? "They're fine, not too bad at all," she said. "But thanks. Have a nice day, okay?"

"You sure? I don't mind helping. Don't have much to do right now. Really."

She tried not to look at him. A troubled feeling settled on her heart—no, she thought, she was being silly.

She saw a Warner Bros. store. "Really, I'm fine," she said, moving away from him. "Thanks anyway."

She walked into the store without looking back, but the heaviness didn't leave her chest.

Didi went toward the children's section and looked around, putting down her bags and taking a few bites of the pretzel.

Suddenly she was no longer hungry and had lost her desire to shop. Deciding to call Rich, Didi pulled the cell phone out of her handbag. The cell phone was defective, with the number seven missing because little Reenie had eaten it on one of their weekend trips to Lake Texoma. It was time to get a new one.

What was odd about that man aside from his open smile? He acted as if he knew her, but that wasn't what was odd. Something else. She wanted to cross herself. *What's the matter with you, Didi?* she whispered, intently studying the plush Tasmanian Devils. *Why are you being so uncharitable? He was just trying to help.*

Her husband wasn't picking up. What else was new? His message machine answered. "It's just me," Didi said after the beep. "Calling from the mall, hoping I could meet you a little earlier." She paused and thought about turning around. "It's okay. I'll see you at one, I guess. Bye."

She picked out a couple of T-shirts for her girls and turned to walk to the cash register. She saw him immediately. He was near the Tweety Bird clocks. He appeared to have forgotten her completely.

At the register, Didi took out cash to speed the transaction.

"Linda, look!" the salesgirl exclaimed to another salesgirl. Then to Didi, "Wow, you're really pregnant."

"Yeah," said Didi, smiling as kindly as she could. "I'm also in a real hurry, so . . ." She slid two twenties across the counter, but the money didn't impress the salesgirls.

"When are you due?" Linda asked, looking warmly at her.

"Just a few weeks," Didi said, chewing her lip. The salesgirl scanned the T-shirt tags with near-deliberate slowness. Didi thought of walking out, but she didn't want the man to think she was nervous or in a hurry. She wanted him to think she had forgotten him completely, too.

"Do you know what you're having?" asked Linda.

"No, have no idea," said Didi.

"Don't want to know?"

"No, not really." Didi started tapping her fingernails on the counter. The nails were short, and the tapping wasn't satisfying.

"Oh, I'd want to know," Linda said.

Didi pushed the twenties so far to the edge of the counter that they fell to the floor. The salesgirl said, "Oh, look—your money." And for some reason she found the falling cash amusing and laughed. Linda chuckled with her. Didi tried to smile.

Suddenly, Didi sensed someone standing behind her and felt afraid.

She willed herself to turn around. An elderly gray-haired man in a suit nodded politely to her. The man in the jacket was still near Tweety Bird. Didi felt both relieved and silly.

Linda moved to help the elderly man, while Didi's salesgirl looked for a bag for the T-shirts. "The total came to twenty-eight seventeen," she said cheerfully. "Did you only give me a twenty?"

"I'm sorry," Didi said. "Two twenties fell on the floor. Listen, if it's too much trouble—"

"No, no, of course, two twenties." The girl bent down, picking up the money. She keyed forty dollars into the register. "Your change is eleven eighty-three," she said, taking the money out of the drawer. "That's twenty-nine—" giving Didi the change, and then counting the paper money—"thirty, and two fives makes forty."

Didi could not help snatching the money. "Thank you," she said. "Have a nice day."

"Yeah, you too," said the girl, and yelled after her, "Good luck with the labor and everything!"

Didi cringed.

After she walked out of Warner Bros., she wasn't sure what to do next. She glanced back. He wasn't there anymore.

Should she go to her car? Yes, yes, she should. No, wait. She wanted to make a quick stop at Victoria's Secret.

She looked over her shoulder to see if he was following her. This is ridiculous, Didi thought. He seemed a perfectly nice man.

A few days earlier she and her girlfriend Penny had been at the Collin Creek Mall when a man who looked a little like this one offered to take Didi's bags to the car. He didn't even offer. He just picked up the bags and carried them, saying, "Let me help you with these." Didi thanked him, got in the car, and went to the movies with Penny. It had been raining, and Penny commented what a nice man he had been to help them.

Didi felt better with this recollection as she walked into Victoria's Secret.

"Hi, can I help you?" An attractive thin girl walked toward her. Didi always noticed the thinness of other women when she was pregnant. Especially in a place like this. It made her feel self-conscious to ask for a negligee or underwear in extra large. The girls always went to the back of the store for that. Sometimes they loudly delegated the task to someone else. "Janice, can you go and check if we have an extra large in the red satin underwear, please?"

Glad to see there was no one in the store this afternoon, Didi asked for something silky and sexy for the hospital.

"I have just the thing for you," said the salesgirl. "When are you due?"

"Monday," said Didi.

"As in today, Monday?" The girl's eyes opened wide.

"Maybe not today," Didi said pleasantly. "But I'm hoping to have my baby on a Monday."

"Is Monday your lucky day or something?"

Nodding, Didi said, "It *is* my lucky day, I guess. I was born on a Monday. My second daughter was born on a Monday, and it was a pretty easy delivery, so that was lucky. Much easier than the first, which was on a Saturday."

"Maybe the easy labor was because she was second and all," the salesgirl said.

"You're right," said Didi. "But it's still my lucky day."

"Well, let's pray it's not today," said the salesgirl. "Let me show you what I've got for you." She had pretty red hair. Didi wondered if it was her natural color. Didi was proud of the fact that she had never colored or highlighted her own brown hair. She also didn't wear much makeup, though she bought plenty. Didi thought of herself as a person comfortable in her own skin. The salesgirl must have seen Didi looking at her hair, because she smiled and, touching it, said, "Best color money can buy. Do you like it?"

Smiling and secretly pleased, Didi said, "Love it. It looks very natural."

"I like yours," the salesgirl said. "Tell me, is it difficult keeping it that long in this heat and with being pregnant and all?"

Touching her hair, Didi replied, "It's not too bad. It's naturally straight, so I don't do much to it. But I can never cut it. My husband loves it long."

The girl found Didi a burgundy silk robe with a matching negligee, panties, and bra. The ensemble looked great on Didi, although the negligee was too small. It was the largest size in stock, and Didi had to hope that the Belly would not stay enormous forever.

"I'll take it," she said, walking out of the fitting room. From inside the store, she peered into the mall. Her heart beat faster when she thought she saw the back of the man. The person sitting on the bench was obscured by tall, leafy corn plants; it was hard to tell if it was he. She turned to the cash register.

"I'm sorry. What did you ask?" Didi said absentmindedly.

"Do you know what you're having?"

Didi smiled. "We're hoping for a boy," she confessed. "But we don't know."

"Hey, you got a fifty-fifty chance, right?"

"Not according to my husband," said Didi easily. "He's been wearing his *red* socks for weeks. He thinks that improves our chances to seventy-five–twenty-five."

"Red socks?" The salesgirl looked at her as if Didi were crazy.

"Hey, I'm not the crazy one," said Didi. "The same ones he wears when the Cowboys play. They won the Super Bowl once when he was wearing red socks and now he wears them every Sunday. I don't think he's ever let me wash them since then."

"Oh, dear," said the salesgirl, handing her a receipt to sign. "I hope you don't sit next to your husband on Sundays."

"I'm a football widow," said Didi, but it wasn't true. It just sounded funny, though she wished she hadn't said it. She loved football. She and Rich watched the games together when they could. It was true about the red socks. Rich believed in the socks even when the Cowboys lost. "Think how much they'd lose by if I wasn't wearing them," he'd say when Didi called the socks' dubious charm into question. Didi had no response to Rich's perverse logic.

"Good luck," said the salesgirl, tossing her red hair. "I hope you have your boy, and I hope your labor will be easy."

"Thanks." Didi smiled. "Have a nice day."

"Hey, and stay inside," the girl called after her. "It's brutal out there."

"Don't worry," Didi said.

She walked out of the store and looked at her watch. Five to one.

It was time to meet Rich. With luck she'd be only ten minutes late, but probably more like fifteen. She looked up and down the mall. Just a few shoppers. God forgive me, is everyone this paranoid at near term? Didi thought. Wait till I tell Richie.

Laden with bags, she walked back to Dillard's, made a left at the Freshëns stand and then a right, and walked out the mall doors. Outside was unbearable. The sun whipped her with heat. After taking a dozen steps, Didi was light-headed. She hoped she could make it to the car and not faint.

Putting her bags down on the concrete, she looked around, wondering where her Town & Country was parked. Slowly she took the pretzel bag out of one of the larger shopping bags, reached into it, and broke off a piece of a pretzel. She chewed and swallowed it. Looking at her watch, she saw it was already ten past one and tried to hurry. She picked up three bags with one hand, three bags with the other, and with her purse on her shoulder and the pretzel bag between her fingers headed up one aisle, swaying from side to side. Did she *have* to get those wooden blocks at FAO Schwarz? She struggled with the bags, setting them down again and wiping her forehead, wishing her hair were up in a bun.

Didi walked a few more feet but couldn't see the minivan anywhere. She put her bags down, sighed as loudly as possible to make herself feel better, and rummaged through her purse. She found her key chain and hit the alarm button to get her car to make its noise, but the alarm did not go off. Instead she heard the dull click of a door lock opening, and looked to her right to see her white van. She had pressed the wrong button. Thank God.

Relieved, Didi dropped the keys back in her purse and bent down to pick up her bags.

A voice behind her said, "You know, you really shouldn't be carrying those heavy bags. It's bad for the baby."

## 1 2 : 5 8   P. M.

**R**ichard Wood parked his Pontiac Bonneville in the Laredo Grill lot and looked for Didi's minivan. It wasn't there yet. He glanced at his watch and saw it was a little before one and he was early. That was okay. He sat in the car and listened to a Bad Company CD. Didi said Rich was forever stuck in the seventies, but he took that as a compliment.

The clock in the car read 1:17 when he decided to look for her inside the restaurant. Maybe she'd parked elsewhere. He hurried. He should have remembered that Didi sometimes parked in the adjacent Olive Garden lot to be a bit closer to the exit ramp for the highway home.

# 1 : 2 0 P.M.

**D**idi wanted to speak but found she was made speechless by her heart ramming itself against her chest. She didn't need to turn around. She recognized his voice. It was the man in the jacket. She felt slightly nauseated.

"Did you hear me, ma'am?" the voice said. "You shouldn't be carrying those heavy bags. It's not good for the baby."

Didi turned around.

The man was standing in front of her, hands in his jacket pockets. The heat index was up to 120 and he was wearing a jacket over his white shirt. The incongruity of the jacket hadn't registered in the cool mall, but now it seemed distinctly out of place.

She stared directly at him without averting her gaze. His upturned nose made him look petulant, as if he'd been waiting for a bus too long. His mouth was upturned too, in a semblance of a smile. It looked as if he was grimacing, stretching his thin lips upward, toward eyes that weren't smiling. They were blue and they were cold, and she saw that they lacked something essential. The expression in the eyes, like the jacket, did not belong in a mall parking lot on a hot summer day.

Didi held on to her bags as she and the man stared at each other. She tried to focus, but all she saw was dark spots instead of his face. Wait, wait, she said to herself, narrowing her mental vision. Think! It's not so bad. Maybe he is really concerned about the bags. *Remember? He said the same thing to me in the mall.*

Though now there was an edge to his tone, as if he were judging her. Didi knew the tone of judgment well enough. When her mother-in-law, bless her, would visit, she'd look at Didi and say, "You're not eating enough, Didi." It was the same tone, but Barbara was her husband's mother, and this man was a complete stranger who had followed her out of the mall.

Wait a second. Who said he'd followed her? Maybe he hadn't followed her. Maybe his own car was parked here and he was on his way home.

Didi had been silent too long. She tried to swallow, but her mouth was dry and her heart was beating too fast.

"You don't need to help me. My car is right . . ." She stopped, already regretting what she had been about to say. Take it back, fool, take it back. Why would she want him to know they were in front of her car?

The man said, "What I'd like to do is help you to *my* car."

Didi lost her breath and opened her mouth.

"I'd rather not do that," she said, her voice breaking. "I'm meeting my husband for lunch." Her knees began to shake. To steady herself, she leaned against the minivan.

The man stretched his lips sideways, exposing his teeth. "I think he'll be eating alone today," he said.

Didi hurriedly scanned the parking lot for a mother with a baby, an elderly couple, a man buying a present for his wife. Why was it that when she needed to adjust her underwear or scratch her inner thigh, the parking lot was teeming with people, but now when she needed someone more than ever, there was no one? Why was that?

Dumb luck.

No, it was karma, she thought, harking back to the fight she'd had with Richie yesterday. That's why.

Is this my karma? She thought. This young man in front of me, menacing me with his vagueness and his eyes?

She started to speak, but he interrupted her.

"Shh," he said. "Don't worry. I just want us to go for a little ride."

Shaking her head, Didi said, "I can't."

"Yes, you can," he said. "Please." And then added, "I have to insist."

He stood very close to her between the cars. He was invading her personal space, and Didi's knees would not stop shaking. She glanced this way and that. *Please, someone just come walking, get out of a car, something, somebody see us. Please.*

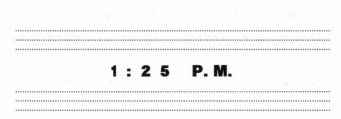

# 1 : 2 5   P. M.

**D**idi wasn't in the restaurant.

Rich thought there was nothing more pathetic than a man waiting for his late wife. Embarrassed, he straightened his tie and smiled politely at the hostess.

Finally he called the office for his messages and listened to one from Didi at 12:30 P.M., asking him if he could meet her a little earlier. There was something in her voice that he didn't like and didn't understand. There was an edge to it, and the pitch was higher than normal.

It was also an unusual call. Rich and Didi had been together for ten years. In that decade, Rich Wood had never known Didi to call from the mall and ask to meet him *early*.

*Late,* yes.

Honey, I'll be a few minutes late.

Honey, I'm stuck in line.

Honey, there is just one more stop I have to make.

Yes, yes, yes.

17

But honey, can you meet me *early?*

If she was at the Laredo Grill, then he could tease her about it.

But she wasn't there.

Rich knew there were many diversions between the mall and the restaurant. She could have stopped at the bookstore or the music store. Or the Container Store.

He waited awhile longer before calling his office again. There was nothing new from her after 12:30 P.M. If she had stopped off somewhere, she would have called. Didi usually was considerate about being habitually late.

At one-thirty, he glanced at his watch as a little worm of worry ate away at the empty stomach where hunger had been.

Thirty minutes was too long to be stuck in any line.

He dialed the number to her cellular phone. It rang the requisite seven times before an annoying male voice answered and told Rich that the cellular customer he had called was unavailable.

Rich wondered if Didi was getting back at him for the fight they'd had yesterday, to prove to him that all it would take was for her to be a little late and he would be concerned. Maybe this is payback time, Rich thought irritably, looking at his watch every thirty seconds or so.

Rich felt his throat constrict. It wasn't fair of her to be so late. She was exceedingly pregnant. Didi must know that Rich would immediately think she had gone into labor. Or had an accident.

He called his answering service for the third time and listened to her twelve-thirty message. *"It's just me,"* Didi said. *"Calling from the mall, hoping I could meet you a little earlier."* Pause. *"It's okay. I'll see you at one, I guess. Bye."*

He listened to it again, trying to read into the pause.

What was that in her voice?

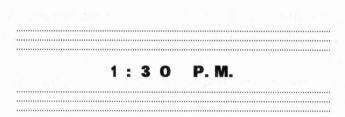

# 1 : 3 0   P. M.

**S**weat ran down Didi's cheeks. She hoped it was sweat and not tears. She didn't want to cry in front of this man. "Listen," she whispered. "Please."

He reached out and wiped her face. *He wiped the tears off her face.* "Just come for a ride with me," he said.

Where were her keys? Where were they? Where had she dropped them, ah, goddammit, in her purse! How would that work, anyway? Excuse me while I fish for my keys, let me rummage through my bag while you wait, just hang on a sec.

And what would she do with them? Hitting the panic button was a joke. It was the joke of parking lots, of streets, of urban living. Nothing was ignored with quite the same intensity as a piercing car alarm. What do we all think? We think, when is someone going to find his keys and turn that stupid thing off?

Still, she wished she could have her keys handy. Hit the alarm, startle him, get in her car, lock the doors, drive away.

She leaned against the car, not moving, panting, trying to steady her knees.

He moved closer to her and pushed her slightly with his body. "Come on. It'll be all right. I'm parked just over there."

Didi knew that in her condition she couldn't walk anywhere, she'd just fall down.

"Okay," she said, sniffling. "Can you carry my bags?" She thrust all the bags at him, except for her purse, and looked behind him, searching for other people in the parking lot. Didi cursed the day minivans became so popular. He and she were sandwiched in the three-foot space between her minivan and a small truck. Behind her was another minivan, and she could not see out. Worse, no one could see in. "Could you carry my bags?" Didi repeated, trying to sound calm. She just wanted a second to reach into her purse.

He chuckled. "No, I don't think that would be a good idea. But it's nice of you to ask me."

Moving off the car to stand on her own, Didi tried again. "You did say I shouldn't be carrying them. Could you help me out? They're really heavy."

He continued to smile peaceably. "Well, whose fault is that, now, ma'am? Is that my fault? Did I spend a half hour at Dillard's buying makeup? Did I go to FAO Schwarz and come back out with another bag? Did I go to Coach? To Warner Bros.? To Victoria's Secret? No, I didn't. I didn't buy anything. I'm not carrying anything. But you didn't seem to care then about carrying all these bags and hurting your baby. It's your fault they're heavy. Now come on. We're wasting time."

*My God,* thought Didi. It was clear he had followed her from her very first stop at NorthPark. For all she knew, he had seen her at the doctor's.

Why would he follow her? Why would he single her out?

She didn't want to turn her back to him.

Didi had thought that feeling fear was watching a scary Halloween movie with Rich, and when the teenagers were alone in the room and any second the vampires would appear, Didi would get a pit in her stomach, turn to Rich, and say, "I'm not watching this."

And that's what Didi wanted to do now. Turn away and say, "I'm not watching this."

"How's your wife going to feel about you taking other women for rides in your car?" Didi said.

She was instantly sorry. His expression lost some of its politeness. She saw him clench and unclench his fist, and his face struggled for control. He quickly regained it, and took her arm. He wasn't hurting her arm, but he wasn't letting go of her. Despite her brave tone, Didi thought any minute she was going to get hysterical.

He said coolly, "Why don't we make our first little rule, okay? You leave my wife out of this."

"I'm sorry, all right?" Didi said, in a pathetic low voice. "Listen— I'm going to have a baby."

He let go her arm and said, "Don't worry. I just want to take you for a ride, like I said."

Didi could do nothing to stop herself from sinking to the ground. She was shaking her head and saying, "I'm not watching, I'm not watching."

"What are you doing?" he said, pulling her by her arm. Didi dropped to the ground between the cars.

"What are you doing?" He yanked her again, careful not to raise his voice. Clearing his throat, he said huskily, "Could you get up, please, ma'am?"

"I can't." She panted. "I can't stand. Just leave me alone. I won't tell anyone. Just leave me alone. My belly hurts. My husband is waiting for me. Just leave me alone."

"Get up, I said."

If Didi could have gotten up, she would have. But she couldn't move.

She was still clutching the shopping bags. Letting go, she fumbled to get to her purse. Keys, keys, keys.

"I said, get up!" he said, bending down over her.

Didi opened her mouth to scream but didn't have the breath. It was as if she had just run a mile at full speed and was gasping for air. She bit her lip shut trying to breathe through her nose.

"Get up!"

She shook her head slowly.

No one could see them. Didi was still on the ground. Feeling herself about to cry, she covered her face with the white pretzel bag. She didn't want him to see her weakness. Then she tasted something salty in her mouth. There was blood from her bitten lip.

Knocking the pretzel bag out of her hands, the man grabbed her under her arms and lifted her to her feet. Didi had a second to feel his strength. This late in her pregnancy, even her husband had trouble helping her off the couch or up from the bed. If she was on the floor, forget it. Rich would need a car jack.

Didi's legs weren't making it easy for him, yet he yanked her up as if she were a stubborn weed. As soon as she got to her feet, she started to sink down again.

"Let's go," he snapped, shoving her lightly with his body. "Come on now. You may be pregnant, but you're not crippled. Not five minutes ago you were breezing through the mall, not a care in the world, bags and all. You can go ten feet now, can't you?" Staring at her, he said, "What did you do to yourself? Look." He wiped her mouth with his hand and showed her the blood. "Say something."

Didi tried to talk, but the words wouldn't come. Fear for her life, fear for her baby, fear for her family—all the fear in the world was in her mouth, and her mouth was bloody and mute. She felt as if her throat were filling with cement. Nothing was moving except her tongue, which labored to help her breathe. She felt nearly paralyzed when she thought of leaving what she perceived as the safety of her own car. She was at her unlocked door. If only she'd hit the panic button instead of the unlock. Maybe it would have scared him off. Maybe it would have. Is that what it all came down to? Hitting the wrong damn button on her key ring?

He shoved her again. Didi moved. She took a few tentative steps and walked out into the main row. A car drove by.

Suddenly hope sprang up inside her. Between cars she had no chance, but here in the open, maybe someone would see her. Maybe someone would see her running—

Running? Who was she kidding? Hadn't she just sunk to the ground faster than an anchor into water? She couldn't run, hadn't run in months. With the baby's head between her legs, pressing down on the blood vessels in her pelvis, she had to take stairs one at a time. She couldn't even pretend-run after her girls.

My girls. Didi gasped and dropped the bags.

"Could you pick those up, please, ma'am?" he asked.

"I can't," Didi panted. "They're too heavy for me." She wanted to leave a trace of herself behind.

"Pick them up, please," he said.

Shaking her head, Didi said, "I can't. Let's just leave them."

Bending his head to look at her sideways, he said, "Now, you know that we can't leave your bags in the middle of the parking lot."

"Forget it," she said, pretending not to understand him. She was trying to fight the fear that was pulling her down to the ground again. What could he do in the middle of a sunny parking lot, a hundred feet away from Central Expressway, in broad daylight?

She didn't think he'd do much, and that gave her a little bit of courage. She thought, he seems pretty calm. He is being reasonable, therefore he can't be crazy.

Bravely, Didi repeated, "Forget it. I don't want them. Really. If you can't carry them, just leave them."

"Oh, shit," he mumbled under his breath. He grabbed all the bags off the ground with his left hand, keeping his right hand on her. "I'll take your bags. Happy now? Come on, let's try to walk a little faster."

The man hurried, but she dragged her feet. "It's only a little further. Then you can sit down," he said kindly.

But Didi wouldn't hurry. She wanted to walk, to crawl, slower and slower, until she stopped and sat down, and had a drink and maybe some food, and stopped hyperventilating, and had her baby and woke up from a bad dream.

She promised herself she would never go to NorthPark again. Or any mall again without her husband, without a friend, or without a gun. A whole lot of good a gun would have done her here. Excuse me for a second while I ransack through my handbag so I can shoot you.

How long had it been? How was it possible that in the minutes since he had approached her, Didi had not seen anyone in the parking lot? Where was everybody?

She nearly yelped with joy and hope when she saw two women in the next row getting out of a car.

Didi didn't know if any sound would come out when she opened her mouth, but the terror that had made her weaker a minute ago when she saw no way out made her stronger now when she saw a chance for escape.

"Help! Help me!" she screamed, moving away from the man. He was fast. He dug his fingers into her arm.

Didi flung her free arm and hit him across the face. "Help!" she screamed. "He's—"

The women turned and looked at them.

And then he let go of her arm for a split second, just long enough to grab her around the neck, pull her to him, and kiss her hard on the mouth.

He pressed his lips to hers, blowing air into her throat and sticking his tongue into her mouth. All the while he never stopped walking. She tried to pull away from his face, but he was too strong. He held her painfully tight around the neck. If he were her lover, she could have said, stop, you're hurting me.

But he wasn't her lover.

She saw the women smile to each other, nod, and keep on walking.

He removed himself from her mouth, and when he did, she screamed once more. He pulled her to him again and pressed his lips on hers, but this time he bit her lip and clamped it between his teeth. "Stop it," he said to her through his teeth. "Keep walking."

Whimpering into his mouth, she ran in little steps alongside him.

Then he pulled away from her, and Didi whirled around to look for the two women. It was no use, because they were already inside the mall. The man stopped walking when they reached a beat-up beige station wagon. Clasping his right hand over her mouth, he dropped her bags and fumbled for the keys in his pocket. He opened the passenger door and sat her down in his car.

Didi screamed, for she had nothing to lose. Whatever his intentions were, Didi was certain they did not involve his giving her a lift to the Laredo Grill. Her day went gray, and she began to scream again, but no one could hear her.

He got in and started the car. "You know," he said, "you should really stop that."

They were racing through the NorthPark parking lot. The old car stank. Didi wondered for a moment if the stench came from her. Had she lost control of her bowels?

But no. It was an old, bad odor. The car smelled of sour, rotted food. She looked over at him.

He held the wheel tightly with both hands.

She wanted to say something to him. But what? What? To save herself, she would have said anything.

"What's your name?" she asked in her friendliest voice. Is that the best I can come up with? she thought. *What's your name?* What am I, a teenager at the school lockers?

He didn't answer her.

*Please show me the way, dear God, please show me the way out, for my kids, please hear my prayer.*

I guess it's really happening, she thought, starting to rock back and forth, it's happening. This man, he—I—I've been abducted. I've been snatched, stolen. He acts polite and tries to smile, but he's kidnapped me. How's Rich ever going to find me? And what could he want? Money? Of course, that must be it. He wants money. That's what all kidnappers want. He doesn't care about me. He saw me shopping at NorthPark and probably thought I was loaded.

What would it do to tell him the truth? she thought. And what happens to *me* when he finds out the truth?

Clasping her hands together, Didi tried to think of something comforting, but all that flashed through her was, *Am I going to die? Right here, in this man's car, this stinking car, die with a stranger? Is this how my life is going to end—*

My baby.

Why was she thinking about death, about stinky cars? She couldn't die, because if she did, her baby would too, and her baby could not die.

That was impossible.

The baby is counting on me not to let him die. That's my job as his mother—to keep him and save him from harm. What kind of mother would I be if I died on him? A bad kind, that's what kind. Gently, she stroked her belly.

Didi shuddered when she remembered the fight she had had with Richie yesterday. Poor Rich—he'll be thinking I didn't show up because I'm still mad at him. That stupid fight. It was just about this very thing—about harm coming to me and the baby. Rich got so mad he yelled at me that nothing was going to happen to the baby. He was angry at me for bringing bad thoughts into our house.

Didi herself had felt silly for fearing the worst.

Yesterday the worst had been some nebulous grief. She feared the baby might have two hearts, two brains, or not enough heart, not enough brain.

Today—well, she couldn't confront it.

Didi's hands were unsteady. Rubbing her belly gently, she looked out the side window.

She thought, is God punishing me? I haven't been penitent. I don't say my prayers and there are some Sundays I don't go to church and there are some I go and don't want to. Who said Christianity was easy? It's not like drinking water, accepting God into your heart. I've been remiss. And so have my children, and so has my husband. We watch TV, we make love, we don't pray. We fight, we curse. I've been feeling cocky and now God is about to show me who's boss.

They went through a stop sign. Keep that up, Didi thought, and a nice police officer will soon be stopping you himself. At the next stop sign the man slowed down and pretended to stop. Didi looked at the door handle. The car must have slowed to twenty, maybe ten miles an hour. All she had to do was open the door and fall out. She lifted her trembling hand off her lap and reached for the handle.

And stopped.

*The baby.* When Didi fell out, would she fall on her belly? Would the shock of hitting the ground burst her water, would it snap the umbilical cord? Would it break her baby's neck or crush its soft head?

She glanced over at the man. He looked tranquil. Would she be able to crawl away fast enough from him? Or would he stop, slam the car into reverse, and roll over her, killing her *and* the baby? And then calmly drive away never to be found, never to be seen again.

Didi knew one thing with absolute certainty: if she died, her baby had no chance. She closed her eyes briefly. *Baby Evelyn or baby Adam, anything your mom can do, she will do, God help her.*

## 1 : 4 5 P. M.

**R**ich called their hospital's labor and delivery ward to see if a Didi Wood had been admitted and was told no.

Finally he left the Laredo Grill. What mall had she been in? Was it Collin Creek right across the road, or the Galleria, or Valley View? NorthPark? She could have been calling from anywhere. She had had a doctor's appointment at eleven, so perhaps she was at Collin Creek, which was the closest to the doctor and to the Laredo Grill. Rich wished he'd gone with her to the doctor's as he usually did.

He called the doctor's office. The receptionist told him Didi had left at eleven-thirty after her routine weekly checkup. Then the doctor came on the phone and told Rich that Didi had dilated another centimeter to about two, normal for this stage in the pregnancy. Rich asked if Didi had mentioned where she might be heading. The doctor replied that Didi had said she might do a little shopping, but hadn't said where. Rich hung up.

Instead of going back to work, he drove to the Collin Creek Mall.

His Didi was nothing if not a creature of habit, and whenever they went to the mall—any mall—Didi always parked near Dillard's. He drove up and down the rows of cars, looking for their new white Town & Country—the Cadillac of all minivans, as the pamphlets had said.

He thought he'd seen the van several times, but he was wrong.

Remembering he had a meeting with marketing at three, Rich called his office manager and said he was tied up and couldn't make it in. She sounded nervous on the phone, and said, "But Rich, *your meeting.*" And he said to her, "But Donna, *my wife.*" And hung up without an explanation.

Then he called home. Maybe she wasn't feeling well and had gone home to lie down. Totally unlike Didi, but maybe.

No one answered. The babysitter must be picking Amanda up from school. Rich left a message for Didi to call him as soon as possible at the office. What could he do? He had to believe that Didi was still upset about the fight last night. It was the only explanation.

But he didn't believe that. It wasn't like Didi to pay him back for anything. Even when they fought, she still made him dinner, still went to sleep with him, and she never stood him up if they made plans to meet. Never.

Unprecedented events worried Rich. He remembered his dad, back in Chicago, every day for twenty-five years coming home from work on the 5:54 P.M. train. The train was sometimes late, but Richard Wood Sr. never missed that train—well, almost never. The day he missed the 5:54 was the day he died.

# 1 : 4 5  P. M.

**D**idi racked her brain to find something to say to stop the man, stop him before he drove his car out of the parking lot. Hope was a caged bird, and it was caged outside the NorthPark Mall. Once they were out of the lot and on Dallas streets or on the open road, the little bird called hope would flee this man's car. Didi had to try something now, while there was still a chance. Her mouth was dry and her heart was beating fast as she took a deep breath.

"Listen," Didi said. "We're not rich people, but—" She wanted to cry but wouldn't let herself. "Call my husband. I'm sure he'll give you money—"

His soft laugh interrupted her.

So he was listening. Her words were getting through. Heartened, Didi went on.

"I just want to say, I mean, if you—" She choked up. "If you let me out now, I'll walk back to my car and I'll never mention this to anybody. We'll never see each other again, but, please, couldn't you just . . . just let me go?'' Didi's legs felt clammy. Trying to ease the tension, she rubbed the Belly.

"Tell me, won't you be sad for us to part and never see each other again?'' he asked.

What is he talking about? thought Didi. It doesn't make sense. Maybe he's made a mistake. Maybe he's mistaken me for someone else. He acts as if he knows me. A crazy mistake but a mistake. He must think I'm someone who lives in Starwood or in Highland Park. I'm not, I'm not, she wanted to say.

"I'm sorry, do you know who I am?''

"Yes,'' the man said. "Fate has brought you to me.''

Didi felt sick.

Shaking her head, Didi said tearfully, "What does fate have to do with it?''

"Why, everything,'' he said.

"But my husband is waiting for me,'' Didi said. "If I don't come soon, he's going to get very worried. I know he'll call the police—''

"We'll be far away then, ma'am,'' he said.

Didi's heart expanded. It felt as if it were going to explode out of her chest. She put her hand over her mouth to stop herself from making a wailing sound.

So he seemed to have plans for them. He was moving along, traveling somewhere, and she was hurtling with him. By the time Rich was aware she was missing, *they'd be far away*. Sweet Jesus, what did that mean?

"He'll get worried right away. I'm never late,'' Didi said. "And if I am, I always call.''

"You're not near a phone,'' he said.

Didi almost mentioned her cell phone, but stopped herself. So the man hadn't seen her call Rich at the Warner Bros. store. She didn't want to alert him. Rich would definitely call her. Maybe there was a way to trace the cell phone to where she was. Maybe the phone had some kind of a Didi-homing device. The police could call the number and locate Didi. She kept quiet for a moment while sadness swept through her unsettled stomach.

"I just want to say," she tried again, "if it's money you want, I'm sure we can come up with something—"

He laughed softly again.

"Or," Didi tried, encouraged by his smiling. "You could let me out." She looked at him with hope. "There's no harm done—"

"There is already."

"No, not really," she said quickly, wanting to wipe her mouth. "I think you've made a mistake. You must think I'm rich, but I'm not really—"

"I don't think that, ma'am," he said.

She pressed on, "But if you continue, then you know, this will be a . . . a . . ." She couldn't get the awful word out.

"Kidnapping?"

"Yes," she said. "All you have to do is let me out right here. Please," she added. "Stop and think, think. Don't you know that kidnapping is a capital crime? In Texas, I think you get life for it."

"They'd have to catch me first," the man said.

"But they always catch the—" Didi wanted to say *the bad guy*.

"Not always," he said. "Let them try to find us."

Didi stared at him, wanting to argue. Not catch the bad guy? That wasn't possible. They always caught the bad guy.

Didn't they?

"What you're doing," she said, "It's—"

"Yes, I know," he interrupted, smiling coolly. "I'd better take care not to get caught then, hadn't I?"

Didi stopped looking at his upturned nose and faced the road. Her mind was frenzied. She tried to make her body outwardly still, but her legs from the knees down were uncontrollable.

Didi saw he was headed toward US 75.

As if reading her mind, the man said, "Hang on, baby. There is no looking back. Nice try, though. But we're in it for the long haul. For the whole haul," he said in his nasal drawl.

Didi put her arms around herself and stared ahead. Fear was invading her lungs from the malodorous car every time she inhaled. They made a right onto the expressway service road, and in a few seconds were on Central Expressway at seventy miles an hour, heading in the direction of downtown Dallas.

"Please," she whispered.

"I'm not even going to speed," the man said. "I'm going to take it nice and easy."

He was a man of his word, though Didi didn't think he'd meant to go quite *this* slowly. They were stuck in traffic. What had been a three-lane highway was now a single lane. The diamond orange signs warned of no quick resolutions to the traffic jam.

SLOW

MEN

WORKING

Didi's cool driver turned red in the face. His hands became jittery. He was past one exit, some indeterminate distance away from the next, and trapped with cars all around him. Pulling the cars in the left lane to the right, the orange cones were lined up alongside his station wagon. Up ahead, the yellow arrow blinked insistently. *Move over there,* the arrow seemed to say. *Now.*

The man turned on the radio and began humming to country music. Didi was about to try to engage him in some superficial conversation when suddenly her senses returned to life.

She thought there might be a way out of his car.

They were in the right lane. Next to her side of the car a low concrete divider ran as far as her eyes could take her. The car was stopped. Zero miles per hour. He was drumming his fingers on the wheel and singing softly along to the radio.

At zero miles an hour Didi could easily open the door and get out. However, the station wagon seemed so perilously close to the divider that Didi feared the door might not open. She was alive right now. What if she pulled a stunt like that and he killed her?

She placed her hands on her belly and then on her heart. It was beating too fast. He won't kill me, Didi thought. I have to believe that. He seems . . . almost *decent*.

## 2 : 2 0   P. M.

**R**ich called the office again and told Donna that he was expecting an urgent call from his wife. "Has she called?" he asked. Donna said no and asked if everything was all right. Rich didn't know how to answer that and didn't.

Then he called home again. Ingrid had come home with Amanda. No, Ingrid said, she hadn't heard from Didi. Yes, both kids were home and everything was fine.

"Daddy, Daddy." His five-year-old was on the phone. "Are you coming home early for dinner?"

"I don't know yet, honey. Maybe."

"Where's Mommy?" Amanda asked.

"I'm meeting Mommy for lunch. She'll see you soon, okay? How was school?"

"Good," said Amanda. "Mom has to see how much homework I have. I have to cut and paste a whole dinosaur."

"Mommy will be home soon, okay?"

"Okay. Love you." Her conversation finished, Amanda hung up.

Rich smiled, returning the receiver to the headset.

Yet the empty ache inside Rich would not subside. Where was his wife? Where was his ready-to-give-birth wife? He felt ridiculous, standing at a Mobil station on 15th Street in the broiling heat. He was going through the motions of his day without having the motion of a wife.

Realizing he was dying of thirst, he went into the Mobil minimart and bought himself a six-pack of Coke and some bottled water. The drink made him feel marginally better for a few seconds.

Then Rich drove to the Valley View Mall.

Up and down, up and down, up and down the rows of cars. If she was at this mall, he'd find her. And when he found her, lost at the hair salon and having forgotten to call him, he'd yell at her till her hair turned blue.

## 2 : 3 0   P. M.

**D**idi and the man sat in the car for ten minutes, moving a few feet a minute. The man seemed increasingly anxious. He kept turning on his right blinker and then turning it off again. Didi suspected he would get off the highway as soon as he could. She thought she heard her phone ringing, but the radio played too loudly to be sure. The phone was buried deep inside her bag. She listened carefully again but heard only the radio. Must have been my imagination, Didi thought.

Now the car wasn't moving.

It was time.

She grabbed the handle and swung open the door.

Didi had been right. The door was too close to the divider. It opened no more than a foot. The man immediately swerved to the right, scraping the divider and pushing the door shut.

"What do you think you're doing?" he yelled, pulling her by the neck away from the door. Didi cried out as he yanked her down on the seat, pressing his hand on her head to keep her down. She struggled to get up and bit his hand. She heard him muttering as he fiercely pressed her into the seat.

The car soon started moving, but in stops and spurts. It turned one way, then another. Didi tried to keep track of the direction, to no avail. She tried to sit up half a dozen times before the man told her to give up.

"Stay down, please," he told her. "You've caused enough trouble already. Stay down."

Did I cause trouble? Didi thought, uncomfortably scrunched up below window level on the bench seat. Have the police come? Have we been stopped? Am I with my husband? No, I don't think I caused much trouble at all.

Her eyes, level with the radio controls, darted past the glove compartment to the floor. She thought she heard the phone ring faintly again, but she couldn't hear above the country music.

Were they off Central Expressway? Didi thought so; she could see the tops of trees and houses. He must have got off and was driving through the side streets. Where was he taking her?

"Can I get up?" she asked.

He said nothing, but lifted his hand from her head, and she took that to mean yes. She got up.

"So what were you doing back there?" he asked. "What were you thinking?"

When Didi didn't reply, he said, "Look, I don't blame you. I'm not even mad." He smiled as if to prove that. "See? But you have to understand, it's useless."

She rubbed her head where his hand had been.

"Perhaps I didn't make myself clear. You have to behave. We're going for a little ride, that's all, but you're carrying a baby and you have to be careful. Do you understand?"

"Please let me out," Didi said dully. "I have a husband . . . children."

From the corner of her eye she saw a slight smile. He wasn't touched. He was just bemused.

Turning down the music, he said, "Look, I'd prefer not to argue with you. Don't get out of my car anymore. I want us to be friendly, but you have to show me I can trust you."

"Friendly?" she repeated, thinking she'd misheard. "Yes, of course. Friendly. Sure."

"Don't you think falling out of my car would have hurt the baby?" he asked.

"I wasn't going to fall out of the car," said Didi. "I won't do it again, I promise."

"Good. Then we won't have any trouble," the man said. "Now be a good girl and let me drive," he said. "We've lost over an hour because of the work on Seventy-five."

"Where are we headed?" Didi asked carefully.

"Mazatlán," he said.

Didi said nothing. She didn't want to know.

"Mexico," the man said.

*He told me anyway,* Didi thought, shuddering.

Didi again thought she could hear the phone ringing.

Soon she recognized the stark warehouse clubs and tattoo joints that defined Deep Ellum—the funky, loud, slightly dangerous boozing and dining section of downtown Dallas. There were a couple of interstates they could take from there. Interstate 30 to Houston, or Interstate 20 to Shreveport, or Interstate 35 to Waco, Austin, San Antonio, and eventually Mexico.

No one would ever find them—find *her*—in Mexico. Not Rich, not the police, no one. Mexico was where people went to disappear.

The prospect of disappearing—disappearing with him—dried up Didi's throat. She licked her lips and realized she had no spit in her mouth. For the first time since the mall she acknowledged to herself that she was thirsty.

Didi was about to ask him if the air-conditioning was on, and then she looked over at the dashboard. There was no air-conditioning. Oh, great, she thought, and for the next silent fifteen minutes, she obsessed about the fact that there was no AC in her kidnapper's station wagon.

No air-conditioning was an immediate problem. Didi was hot. Her own minivan had a gauge that told her, among other things, the outside temperature. However, his old car was not AC equipped. The dash clock was broken. The vent inside the car was blowing hot air, and the windows were closed.

Didi watched him get on Interstate 35E going south to Waco.

"We're going to Waco?" Didi asked.

"No," he said, his tone losing some of its earlier courtesy. "I told you where we're going. Now don't ask me again."

Didi sighed tensely, looking away from him. The road was hypnotic. It usually was so easy when Rich was driving to let her mind go blank and disappear into the road. However, not today. Not when she was this hot, this short of breath, this scared.

Didi reached over to roll down the window, and the man immediately lost his temper, shouting, "What are you doing?"

She gasped, stunned by his outburst, and said, "I'm hot. I was going to roll the window down."

"No," he said firmly. "No windows. Don't want you screaming again, do I?"

"Who's going to hear me here on the highway?"

"I said no."

"I won't scream," she said. "I'm just real hot. I need air."

"Yeah, well, you should have thought of that in the mall. Didn't need air then, did you?" he said coldly.

What was he talking about? And what's happening to him? Why did he sound so angry?

"I'm real hot," Didi repeated.

He swirled one of the central vents on her. "Here," he said. "Here's some air."

Didi sat back against the brown vinyl seat and closed her eyes. She wiped her sweating head, opened her eyes, and said, "Couldn't we stop for a drink? I'm thirsty." She was hoping to bring some of his earlier politeness back.

"No, we can't stop for a drink," he snapped. "What do you think this is? A trip to Disney World? Sit and be quiet. Please," he added, composing himself.

Didi had no choice about sitting, but she did shut up. He's moody, she thought. Is this ma'am and please thing just a facade? God help me if it is.

After a few moments, he said, "Look, I'm sorry, but we have to make tracks. I have to concentrate, okay? Don't want to go too fast, don't want to go too slow. We'll stop soon."

Oddly comforted by his courteous demeanor, Didi nodded and then said, "Don't you want to call my husband?"

"No!" His nasal voice was shrill. "Why would I want to call him?"

Beads of sweat ran down her cheeks. "To ask him for money?"

Shaking his head, he leaned toward her and touched her gently on the arm. "You're so naive. That's what I like about you."

Didi wiped her face and then licked her fingers. Ten minutes later, the salt in the sweat made her crazy for a drink, but she didn't talk.

What was her Rich doing? He must have realized by now she wasn't coming to the Laredo Grill. Where was he? Was he trying to call? Then she remembered her cell phone. She'd left it on standby at Warner Bros. after she called him. Could he have called already and she hadn't heard? Or was that the phone ringing?

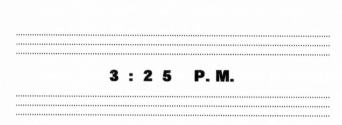
**R**ich Wood didn't find his wife at the Valley View Mall. He didn't find her at the Galleria Mall, either, though the parking there was more complicated.

Rich knew his wife liked to use valet parking at the Westin Hotel adjacent to the Galleria; Didi loved to just get out of the car and pay four bucks and not worry about parking space. So he drove over to the Westin and asked about Didi's van at the valet window. The valet, whose name tag read José, asked Rich to describe the van and Didi. Rich did. "Oh, jes, Didi, no, she no park here today. She have baby soon?"

José said that the last time he'd seen Didi was four days ago, and he always tried to park her car close for her because when she came out of the mall with the bags, "she no like to wait so much."

The fact that the valet knew his wife by name because she visited the Galleria so often amused Rich. Oh, you Didi. You lead a secret life

42

away from me. While I work, you're getting to know José. You never told me you were on a first-name basis with the Westin valet.

But he didn't have a wife to say that to just then. He didn't even have her van.

Before he left, he dialed her cell phone number again from the pay phone inside the Westin.

## 3 : 3 O  P. M.

**T**he light trill of the cellular phone was unmistakable this time. Didi didn't move. Glancing over at the man from the corner of her eye, Didi saw he was hypnotized by the road and the radio's loud music. He wasn't acknowledging the muffled ringing. She panicked, then became exhilarated.

The phone was buried deep inside her big black carryall on the floor between her and the door. Very, very slowly she reached to her right and in one motion stuck her hand in the bag without moving the rest of her body forward. The phone had rung four times. Keeping her eyes on the road, Didi hunted for the phone inside the bag. Please let me find the damn thing. Her other bag was so small, the phone always lay right on top—on top of her wallet or makeup bag or mail. The cramped bag had been so inconvenient—hence the new one—but now she would give away one of her cats to be able to reach the phone. Six rings. Maybe the man's hearing was bad, because Didi thought the phone sounded like a church's noontime bells. Finally, she felt the phone's smooth leather-covered exterior. Instead of taking the phone out, she flipped it open inside the bag. It stopped ringing. She waited. The man continued to drive, saying nothing. She was silent for a few seconds. And then Didi said, "Rich?"

The man came out of his torpor and turned to her.

"Rich?" she said again.

"Who are you talking to? I'm not Rich," the man said, looking suspicious and on guard.

"Well, what is your name?" she said. "You never told me." She was hoping Rich could hear her through the muffling effect of the bag.

"Why are you talking so loud?" he said. "I'm not deaf, you know." A pause. "And what was that ringing?" He slammed the radio power off. Didi's heart stopped. She couldn't answer.

"That ringing? What was that?" He looked over at her. Her hand was in the bag.

"Was that a phone?" he screamed. Falling sideways over Didi, he grabbed the bag away from her. The car careened to the right.

Didi heard honking in the distance. She tried to grab the bag, crying weakly, "No, no." And then louder, "Rich! Help me! Help me!"

The man hit her with the bag. He struck her again and again, making guttural sounds and barely keeping the car on the road. Passing cars honked.

Trying to shield herself from the blows, Didi turned away from him toward the door and saw a car in the right lane beside her. The driver, an old woman, was looking over at Didi with great concern. Didi put her hands together as if in a prayer and mouthed *help me, help me.*

Then the man, having thrown down the bag, yanked her head away from the window and down onto his lap. Didi fell over, hitting her nose on the steering wheel. She saw him floor the gas. Maybe the cops would stop him, Didi thought. Maybe Rich was still on the phone. Encouraged by his phone call, she forgot all caution. She screamed as loudly as she could, "Rich, help me, help me!"

And then the man brought his fist down on her ear.

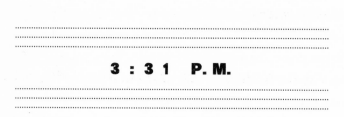

# 3 : 3 1   P. M.

The phone rang six times and then stopped. Rich listened intently and heard nothing, but as he put the receiver back on the hook, he thought he heard a very faint "Rich?"

By the time Rich thought he heard Didi's voice, it was too late. He had already begun hanging up; momentum carried the receiver the rest of the way. The receiver clicked on the hook. "Oh, shit," he said. Had he really heard her voice calling him? He picked the phone up again and got a dial tone. The first time he redialed the number he did it so fast he dialed only six digits. The second time the line was busy.

Busy again, a minute later.

And a minute later.

And another minute.

He waited five minutes and then called his office, thinking she must have tried to call him back. He hated crossed calls making both numbers busy.

There was nothing.

He called the cell phone again, and the useless message came on: "The AT&T customer you have dialed is not available or has traveled outside the coverage area. Please try your call again later."

He tried to remember what the "Rich" he thought he had heard sounded like. He couldn't recall. It was muffled and distant. He could have been mistaken. It could have just been a ringing in his ears and not his wife calling his name, whispering it. "Rich. Rich."

*He must be imagining things.*

Rich drove to the NorthPark Mall. If she wasn't there, he didn't know where she could be.

Dillard's at NorthPark was just off Central Expressway. He found two white Town & Country LXi minivans near Dillard's, but they weren't Didi's.

What was their license plate? TRX something. Or was it THX? No, THX was the sound system he was trying to talk Didi into buying. The license plate was TRX 6 something—or was it 7?

He saw a third Town & Country and slowed down. TJX 672. That was their car. He couldn't believe it. She was at the mall. He had been wrong about her. She was at the mall and had forgotten all about him.

Rich was first mad, then relieved, then mad again. He parked his car a few spaces away from hers and walked over. He opened the door to look in. The car was as they had left it last night after going out to Applebee's for dinner. Toys on the floor, newspapers, some shopping bags. Nothing new, nothing he hadn't seen before. The shopping bags were from last weekend's shopping expedition. Rich had been with Didi when they bought some clothes from Gap Kids.

He slammed the door shut and locked it. The car beeped once to let him know it was locked.

That's when Rich saw a white paper bag on the ground and bent down to pick it up. He thought it was something that had fallen out of the minivan when he opened the door, but when he looked inside the bag he saw it had one whole and one half-eaten pretzel in it. He felt the pretzels through the bag. They were soft, and this surprised him. He had expected them to be hard. This bag was not something that had been in the car for two weeks. The bag itself was ripped, with a chunk missing. Rich pulled out a receipt for 2x items at 1.19 ea., bought and paid for with $3.00 at 12:25 P.M. today.

He turned the bag over a couple of times and noticed brownish stains that could have been chocolate. He smelled them. They didn't smell like chocolate. They smeared onto his hands. But wait, was Rich going crazy? He put the bag to his face to smell it again.

He doubled over, feeling as if someone had punched him in the stomach.

The bag smelled of his wife's hand lotion. He knew the smell of her lotion very well. Didi wore it all the time, and the aroma would linger long after Didi had left a room. From Bath and Body Works—Sun-Ripened Raspberry. It smelled berryish and creamy—good enough to eat with a spoon. Rich had watched Didi put it on this morning after her shower and before they made plans for lunch. He had watched her spread it over her arms and legs and neck and remembered thinking how lovely she was with that belly of hers. Grudgingly realizing he wasn't mad at her anymore, he had asked her to have lunch with him after her doctor's appointment. Usually he went to the doctor's with her, but today he was interviewing a candidate for the southwest regional sales manager job all morning and couldn't make it. Why hadn't he gone with her?

It was her lotioned hands that had clutched the pretzel bag. Maybe another woman, wearing raspberry lotion on her hands, had bought not one but two of the sweet pretzels his wife loved only five minutes before Didi called him in a sharp voice, asking him to come to lunch early. And then dropped the bag right near their minivan.

Rich didn't believe in coincidences. This was his Didi's pretzel bag.

He was sure now it had been her voice he heard calling for him from wherever she was, connecting to him, and he had hung up on her and couldn't get her back.

Holding the bag in his hands emptied him of all feeling and then filled him with anger. She was at her car when she dropped the bag. She was heading out to meet him when she dropped the bag and vanished.

He grabbed his chest, feeling a nightmarish tightness. "God, Didi, Didi," he whispered, starting to pant and losing focus in his eyes. *What's happened?*

# 3 : 4 0  P. M.

**W**hen Didi regained consciousness, she wasn't lying in the man's lap, and her face wasn't squeezed between his abdomen and the steering wheel. She was hunched over on the seat, nearly falling onto his shoulder. She realized he must have pulled her up. Her head was throbbing, as if her hair were any minute going to be disconnected from her scalp. Squinting, she looked for her bag. He had thrown it down on the passenger floor.

She sat up straight and looked around, rubbing her belly. They were now in the right lane, going sixty-five. No more concerned drivers peering at her through the windows of their cars. Just Texas fields, a few shrubs, some houses off in the distance, a hazy blue post-zenith sky.

Didi moved as far as she could away from him and pressed her body against the passenger door. She wished she could become a liquid and pour herself into the door and disappear. There was obtrusive and persistent ringing in the ear where he had hit her. The radio was playing country music, and the man, cheerful and unperturbed, continued to hum to it.

Didi had to go to the bathroom. The baby's head was pressing too hard on her shrunken bladder. She had hoped she could just sweat out all the liquid in her body.

"I feel that we got off on the wrong foot here," she heard the man say. She could not believe the words coming out of his mouth. She wanted to say something nasty back, but her teeth felt too large for her mouth and her tongue too unhappy. So she said nothing and waited for him to speak again. Why did her tongue feel so swollen? She rolled it around her mouth. It hurt. Maybe I bit it when he struck me. Parting her lips, she let some air in. Maybe I'm just thirsty.

"Don't you think so, too?" the man said to her.

He'd asked her a question. What was she supposed to say to that? The Belly was locked in a Braxton Hicks. She held on to it for a few seconds and then said, shrugging lightly, hunched over against the door, "I guess so."

"No, no, we definitely did," said the man. "And it's my fault, and I'm sorry for that. We didn't have time to be properly introduced, and then I was so busy getting us out of Dallas that time just flew. You never even told me your name."

She opened her mouth to speak. His voice was gentle now, soothing, as if listening to soft country music had relaxed him and made him calm. Had it made him calm enough to stop the car and let her out here in the middle of the highway?

"When we were in the mall, I was trying to figure out what your name was," he said. "Did you try to guess what my name was?"

What was he talking about? She needed a drink. A sip or two of water. She was going to lick her wet-with-sweat hand again and then thought better of it.

"Uh-huh," she said, her mouth barely moving. She said it very quietly. "Is it John?"

"No, no." He laughed. "When I sat and waited for you to be done at Dillard's, and you did take a long time, you know, I almost left. But anyway, when I sat and looked at your back and hair and legs, I tried to figure out what your name was. Let's see . . . Ellen? Sonia? Maybe Jackie?"

He waited for her to answer him.

No, she said, or thought she said.

He nodded. "You don't look like a Melanie, I decided. My wife is a Melanie, and you look nothing like my wife."

Didi stared at her yellow sundress. She had felt so happy when she put it on this morning.

"Monica?" he continued. "No, that's a tall name, and you aren't tall. Annette? No. That's a short name, and you aren't short." He glanced at her, a smile widening his lips. "You are just right."

She looked away.

"You aren't blond like a Jennifer, or made up like a Jessica. You don't look smart like a Melissa, or lazy like a Megan. Am I right so far?"

"You're right so far," Didi said faintly.

He tapped on the steering wheel. "I'm having fun here. Right. This is tons better than working at some pathetic little job for a few bucks."

I knew it. He wants money, thought Didi.

He seemed to be enjoying himself. He was smiling and looked as if he hadn't a care in the world. The tension was gone, though he still kept both hands conscientiously on the wheel. "Hey, want to play a little game? Guess mine and then I'll guess yours." He almost giggled with delight.

"Listen," Didi said. "I'd love to play, but do you think we can get a drink somewhere first?" She thought that stopping would be preferable to being stuck in the car with him. There would be people, she might be able to get away, call for help, anything but sit in the car and sweat.

The man's smile dimmed a little. "What? And have you perform one of your little antics again? You're dangerous enough in a moving car. No, I'm going to take you to a safe place. Now guess my name." He paused. "Tell you what." The smile returned. "If you guess my name in three tries, I'll stop and get you a drink. Don't want to dehydrate a pregnant woman, do I?" His hand reached out to—oh my God, what was he doing? Was he thinking of touching the Belly? Didi was sitting too far away or he reconsidered, because he put his hand back on the wheel. "No, no, we certainly don't. But you have to play a part in quenching your own thirst. Is that fair?"

Is that fair? she thought. Up to one o'clock, the unfairest part of today had been the doctor telling Didi the baby might be too big and they might need to induce labor a little early to make sure there were no complications during delivery. And she remembered thinking to herself, God, it's unfair, to be penalized for having a big baby.

"Let's play," said Didi.

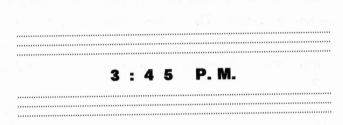

# 3 : 4 5  P. M.

**R**ich felt like bashing his head against the nearest car. What's happened to my wife? he thought, and then screamed. Screamed right in the middle of the Dillard's parking lot.

"Didi!" he shouted, and her name echoed amid the Toyotas and the Hondas and the Fords. "DIDI!"

A couple walking by turned to look at him and then lowered their heads and sped up. Rich ran after them.

"Have you seen my wife?" he said fervently. "My wife, five-seven, brown hair, brown eyes, very pregnant?"

They stared as if everything was not all right with him.

"Please," he said, in a lower, pleading voice. "My wife. Very pregnant. Have you seen her?"

The woman took her husband's arm. "No, sorry," she said and tried to push past Rich. The man followed, casting a sympathetic look at him. The man understood. But the woman shot him a frightened sneer; she must have thought Rich was crazy.

Clutching the pretzel bag, Rich ran inside the mall, heading straight for the Freshëns Yogurt stand. As he ran, he was thinking that perhaps Didi had been walking to the car, dropped the bag by accident, thought of something she'd forgotten to buy, and gone back to the mall. But he knew that made no sense. She went back and didn't call him? Her phone had been on, her voice whispering "Rich," when he dialed her number. She could have called him. But she hadn't called him. She hadn't got into an accident. The car was in the parking lot. Didi wasn't calling because she couldn't call, and the proof was in his hands.

A girl stood behind the Freshëns Yogurt counter. She smiled. "Can I help you?"

"I hope so," said Rich intensely. "I hope so. My wife—" He stammered. "My wife was here earlier today." He thrust the bag at her. She moved away. "My wife was here and bought these two pretzels."

"Wait, hold on, hold on, sir," said the girl. "I just came on. I don't know anything."

"Who worked before you?"

"Alex. He just left." Rich's face must have implied urgency, because she said, "Wait, maybe he's still in the back changing. Hold on."

She came back a few minutes later with Alex.

"It's your lucky day," said Alex.

"Somehow I doubt it," said Rich. "Unless you want to redefine the nature of my luck." He thrust the bag with the receipt and the pretzels at Alex. "My wife was here earlier. She bought these here."

Glancing at the receipt, Alex said, almost defensively, "Is something wrong with them?"

"No, but something could be wrong with my wife," said Rich. "She's disappeared."

Alex smirked a little. "Do you think it had something to do with the pretzels?"

The counter rattled when Rich slammed down his fist. "You think that's funny? Perhaps I didn't make myself clear. Let me explain. My wife, nine months pregnant, was here earlier today shopping. At twelve twenty-five she bought these from you. At twelve-thirty she called me and asked if she could meet me for lunch earlier than planned. At one o'clock she didn't show up, and no one's heard from her since. So now, tell me what part of that you find funny, so we can laugh together."

Paling, Alex said, "Hey, look, I'm sorry, I didn't do anything. What did your wife look like?"

"Pregnant. Extremely, inordinately, unbelievably pregnant. How many pregnant women did you serve today?"

"Well, one that I remember," said Alex grumpily. "But you know, the counter is high—I don't look over and check out my customers' stomachs."

Rich reached over and grabbed Alex by the shoulders, shaking him. "God, help me. Please," he whispered. "My wife is missing."

Immediately he let go; Alex looked noticeably upset. Rubbing his arms, the teenager said, "Look, I don't know anything. I just saw one pregnant woman here, long dark hair, carrying a lot of bags."

Rich brightened. "Yes?" he said. "That sounds like my wife. What was she wearing?"

"I don't know—oh, wait. A yellow dress."

Rich nodded. "That's my wife." Did that make him feel better? If it did, it didn't make him feel better for long.

"Yeah?" Alex said. "That's all I can tell you. She bought a couple of pretzels, I think. Paid. Left, carrying all her bags. A guy who was here buying a pretzel for himself caught up to her and asked her if she needed some help with the bags—"

Rich asked in a small, stricken voice, "What guy?"

"I don't know. Some guy. I'd never seen him before."

"No, of course not. Did my wife seem to know him?"

"No. He seemed nice, though. Kept asking her questions about the pregnancy, you know, when she was due, that sort of thing."

Rich stepped back from the counter. "This guy, what did he look like?"

"I don't know," said Alex. "I didn't pay attention."

"Please try to remember."

"I really don't know. Maybe your age." Alex looked Rich over. "How old are you?"

"Thirty-four."

"No. I don't know. He was older than me, that's all I know."

"Beard? Mustache?"

"No, clean-cut. Short hair. Taller than me."

"Taller than *me?*" asked Rich.

"How tall are you?"

"Six feet."

"No, I don't think so. Taller than your wife."

"Do you remember what he was wearing?"

"Listen, he was just a guy. There was nothing special about him. He was just another customer, you know?"

"You don't remember what he was wearing?"

Shrugging, Alex said, "No, not really." He glanced over at the sales-girl, who was listening to the conversation. She shrugged, as if to give him moral support. Alex turned back to Rich. "I think jeans, a jacket. But I can't be sure."

Rich was quiet. "You said he approached my wife and asked her if she needed help with the bags?"

"I think that's what he asked her."

"And she?"

"I don't know. They were, like, too far from me. I didn't hear her. I assume she said no thanks, because he lagged behind and she walked on by herself."

"When you say lagged behind—"

"What?"

" 'Lagged behind' implies he followed her. Or did he turn around and go the other way?"

Scratching his head, Alex said, "No. I think he lagged behind. I think he went the same way she did. I'm not sure. I got another customer, and stopped watching them."

Rich's hands were drumming on the counter. "Did you get a feeling about him?"

"No, I got no feeling about him," said Alex, for some reason sounding offended.

"Did you see him again?"

"No, I got busy. It was lunchtime. I didn't see anybody."

"Didn't see my wife either?"

"Uh—come to think of it, I did see him. I saw her too. She was walking back from over there." Alex pointed. "She had more bags in her hands. She looked tired, but was walking faster than before. Like she was hurrying, you know?"

"And when did you see him?"

Alex thought. "I don't know. I think after I saw her. He was kind of shuffling along."

"Was he going in the same direction she was going?"

"Well, I don't know if it was in the same direction." Alex pointed to the mall aisle. "You see, either someone is walking to the left or they're walking to the right. They either disappear behind the wall to the right or they disappear here to the left. Occasionally they may go into Dillard's or sit near the fountain. But that's it. I saw her going to the left, and I saw him going to the left too."

"Yes," said Rich in a raspy voice. "What time was that?"

"I don't know. Maybe a little after one. I went on my break at one-thirty."

"Alex, please take a ride with me, will you? To the police station."

"I'm not going anywhere," said Alex, looking nervous. "I'm not getting in a car with you. I don't know you."

"Okay, then can I use your phone? I have to call the police."

They let him call the police, and then they waited. Rich called home, found out that Didi had not called or returned. He asked Ingrid to call his mother and ask her to come and take care of the children for him.

"Is everything all right?"

"Yeah, sure," said Rich, closing his eyes as he leaned on the counter for support. "We're just—I'm just going to be delayed—listen, don't worry. How are the girls?"

"Hold on," said Ingrid. "Irene wants to talk to you."

Rich tried to put on his cheeriest voice. "Hi, honey. How was playgroup?"

Three-year-old Irene didn't want to talk about playgroup. "Daddy," she whined, "Manda won't share Sing and Dance Barbie with me!"

"It's okay, honey," Rich said. "Where's yours?"

"Mine broke and now she won't share hers!"

In the background, Rich heard Amanda's voice. "She broke hers and now she wants to break mine!" Then, "Give me the phone! I have to talk to Daddy too."

Rich took a deep breath. He heard the phone crash to the floor, followed by piercing screams. Ingrid picked up the receiver and said, "Everything is all right."

"Good," Rich said. "Please call my mother."

"If you want, I can stay a little later," Ingrid said.

"Thanks. I don't know how late we'll be, though."

"Is Didi having the baby?"

And in the background, Irene shrieked, "Mommy's having the baby! Mommy's having the baby!"

Rich tensely rubbed the bridge of his nose. All he wanted to do was hang up. "No, she's not having the baby. Just call my mom, Ingrid, please."

He had no stomach to call his mother himself. He had nothing to tell her, anyway. He just needed her help. His mother was going to lose it no matter what. Ingrid had never called before to ask Barbara Wood to come over and help with the children. Rich knew that talking to his mother required too much of him, and he didn't have the patience for it. Ingrid asked again if everything was all right, and Rich said yes, sure, but had to hang up. He could barely hold himself together.

Five minutes later the police arrived. There were two officers—Officer Charles, a man, and Officer Patterson, a woman. Patterson did not seem particularly sympathetic and Rich took an instant dislike to her. She reminded Rich of the disapproving older woman in the parking lot. Like, what's the matter, your wife is away from you for a few hours and you panic? What about when you leave us to go on your business trips and we can't get in touch with you? What about when you go out with the boys and say you're coming home at midnight and it's three and you're still not home? Don't worry, Officer Patterson's casual expression read. Your wife is probably at the movies.

Officer Charles was talking, but through the din in Rich's head, he could barely hear him. Then he realized the din was there just so he couldn't hear Charles speak, because Rich didn't like what he was hearing. Something about not jumping to conclusions.

Rich wasn't sure if he needed to respond to that or just get in his car and go home. He said, "I thought you came to help me. If you can't help me, then let me talk to someone who can."

The officers tried with little effect to be more helpful. "Could your wife have gone into labor?" said the woman officer. "Could she be in the hospital somewhere?"

Shaking his head, Rich said, "We're preregistered at Columbia Medical. If she was having a baby, that's where she would go, and they have my number. Also she has it. She's not there. I called them. And no one's called me."

"Could she have been in an accident?" said Charles

"Yes, yes, she could have," Rich said impatiently, failing despite his best wishes to talk slowly, calmly, reasonably. "No, absolutely. You're so right. She could have been in an accident." He paused. "But not in her own car. Because our car is parked out—" and he flung his arm for emphasis—"there."

Officer Charles stared at him. "Perhaps she had an accident in someone else's car?" he said.

"Maybe she met a friend and decided to spend the afternoon with him or her," Officer Patterson suggested.

Rich rubbed his eyes, shaking with frustration, and other things. "Oh, dear Jesus! We had a lunch date at one. She didn't show up. She has the cell phone with her—"

"Maybe it ran out of power," said Patterson.

"You mean to tell me that my wife decided to stand me up after calling me and asking me to meet her early?" he said loudly. He may have even shouted. The officers asked him if he wanted to go upstairs and talk to them privately in the security offices. Rich refused.

"Could she still be in the mall, maybe?" said Charles, while Patterson looked at Rich disapprovingly.

"Okay," said Rich. "She buys a pretzel from Alex at twelve twenty-five, at which point she's accosted by a stranger who offers to carry her bags. She refuses. He follows her—"

"He goes in the same direction she's heading," Officer Patterson corrected him.

"Of course, excuse me. At twelve-thirty she calls my office and asks me to meet her a little early for lunch. That's unique in my experience."

"Maybe you're prejudging your wife," said Officer Patterson. "There's a first time for everything."

Rich faced the male officer. "She shops for a little while longer, and then Alex sees her heading that way." Rich pointed. "Which is where her car is parked. I know because it's still there. The man is walking in the same direction she is. I know you say it's a coincidence, but how

**6 1**

many can we have in one day?" Rich could not stop moving. "If my wife met me for lunch, then I'd say everything's hunky-dory and isn't it all so coincidental. But she didn't meet me for lunch. No one's heard from her. Her car is still parked outside. Which means that my pregnant wife with all her shopping bags is still in this mall, because the bags are not in the car. Except for this bag, the pretzel bag. I found it next to our minivan. Look, there's a receipt in it, two pretzels, my wife's smell on the bag, and what to me looks like her blood. Look!" He shoved the bag rudely into Officer Patterson's face and then into Officer Charles's. "What do you think it is?"

"Listen, maybe her nose bled, and she decided to come back in," said Officer Patterson, a little more sympathetically. "Then she met someone she knew, and decided to spend the afternoon with them. That's likely, right?"

"Then why hasn't she called me?" Rich screamed.

They looked frightened of him. Frightened and concerned. As if they didn't understand what was driving him, what he was so upset about.

Am I crazy? Am I mad? Have I lost my sanity? Rich looked around him. There was the Disney Store, there was Dillard's, there was FAO Schwarz. He could see, he could comprehend. He wasn't insane yet. Rich concluded that police officers were trained to deal with robberies and homicides and rapes, but not trained to deal with fear.

"Tell you what," Officer Patterson said. "If she's in this mall, let's alert mall security. They'll call for her on the PA."

Rich threw up his hands. He paced furiously near the fountain in the middle of the mall, peering into strange faces walking past him while the officers went to talk to security upstairs. Rich was still hoping that somehow Didi would miraculously appear before him with a new hairdo. Within five minutes there was an announcement over the public address system: "Will Didi Wood please come to the security office on the second floor as soon as possible?" It was repeated twice.

Rich sat down, leaned his elbows on his knees, and held his head in his hands. Seconds later he was up and pacing again. Five minutes later—which seemed an eternity—there was another announcement: "Will anyone with any information about the whereabouts of a nine-month-pregnant woman with long brown hair and wearing a yellow dress notify the management or the security personnel as soon as possible." That message was also repeated twice.

The officers came back to Rich and flanked him as he walked back and forth. "Let's wait and see. Okay? Let's wait and see what happens," said Officer Charles.

They didn't have to wait long.

Rich saw two women walking alongside a security officer, and he immediately moved toward them. Charles and Patterson followed.

The young security officer said, "These ladies here said they might have seen a pregnant woman in the parking lot earlier today."

"What time was that?" Rich snapped.

Officer Charles put up his hand as if to stop Rich. "Wait a second," he said gently to Rich. He turned to the women. "What time was that?"

The ladies shrugged. They were short and chubby. The taller of the short women—bleached, heavy, and middle-aged—said, "I don't know. Maybe around one. We were just coming into the mall."

"And what happened?"

"We parked our car and started walking to the entrance. Then all of a sudden a lady started screaming."

An uncontrolled groan left Rich's throat. For a few seconds no one spoke. Rich couldn't even look up from the floor. He could barely stand.

"Go on," Officer Charles said quietly.

There were tears in the woman's eyes. "I feel so bad now, you know, because then we looked over at her, and she had a guy with her, and he smiled at us, wrapped an arm around her, and started kissing her—"

"Started what?" Rich said, horrified.

"Started kissing her."

He briefly felt relief. "Well, then, that couldn't have been my wife."

"Maybe not," she said. "But this woman was very pregnant and she had long brown hair. She was screaming, 'Help me, help me,' and then the guy kissed her and we just thought they were fooling around, you know? Didn't we, Debbie?"

Trembling, Rich clenched and unclenched his fists.

"This guy, what did he look like?"

Officer Charles extended his hand again. "Mr. Wood, wait." He turned to the woman. "What did this guy look like?"

"We didn't see him so good," she said. "We just saw them from the side, you know. She was wearing a white dress—"

"White?" Rich exclaimed, his heart pounding.

"Not white, Nancy," said Debbie. "It was yellow. Remember I said it was a cheerful color?"

"Oh yeah," Nancy said. "Yellow. And the guy, he was, I don't know—a little taller than her. Kind of thin, I think. Right, Deb?"

"Yeah, he was taller than her. He was wearing jeans and a jacket, that's all I remember. He was kind of nondescript, and we couldn't see them well."

Rich nodded in anxious agreement. "Nondescript—that's exactly how Alex described the guy who was hanging around Didi when she bought the pretzels."

Officer Patterson looked at Rich. He couldn't place the peculiar expression and thought maybe it was guilt for her earlier reluctance to believe that Didi was in trouble, but then Patterson asked, "Does the man sound like anyone you know?"

Rich wished Patterson was a man and not a police officer, because he wanted to hit her. "What the hell are you saying to me?" he said and didn't care how he sounded. "What the hell do you think you're saying? Does the guy sound like someone I might know? The guy who kisses my wife as she's screaming for help? You know, no one like that springs to mind at the moment." Rich glared at her. "You're saying, do I know if my pregnant wife has been fooling around behind my back?"

The officers looked ashamed, and the two women were downright embarrassed. "You just can't help yourself, can you?" Rich said to Patterson. "You just can't help saying the wrong thing."

"I apologize," Patterson started to say, but Rich cut her off. "Obviously you have a problem dealing with people, and I see that as a real detriment in your line of work, considering you pretty much have to deal with people all day long."

Disgusted with her, he turned away and spoke to Officer Charles. "Why are you looking for every possible explanation except the obvious? Her nose bled, she met a friend, the cell phone's dead, she forgot about our lunch date, blah, blah, blah. Everything. God, can't you see what must have happened?" He was choking on his words. "My wife is missing. My pregnant wife—she's probably been taken by force—" The words were larger than his throat. "What can we do now?" He looked around and walked back a few steps to sink into the wooden bench. "What do we do now?" he said and buried his face in his hands.

# 4 : 0 0   P. M.

**T**he man kept a steady pace on the road. They had just passed Midlothian, twenty miles south of Dallas.

"What are the rules of our game?" Didi asked.

"Rules?" Pleasure showed on his face. "Okay, how about this? We do it in three guesses and I give you three clues."

"Sounds good," said Didi, licking her lips. She liked it better when he wasn't sullen.

"My name," said the man, "is the name of a great country singer." She said, "Kenny?"

"Kenny?" he exclaimed. "Gosh, no! I said great, didn't I? Not a hack. No, a great, incredible country singer. Two more guesses left."

"Well, then," said Didi, "I need two more clues, don't I?"

He thought about it, saying nothing for a while. He drove. The sun beat hot on the car. Didi was panting. She needed cool air.

"Okay, how about this—he's tall."

Shaking her head, Didi said, "They're all tall, tall is not a good clue.

Sort of like, they're all men." She thought she'd gone too far. Like she was insulting his clues or something.

It was clear he thought the same thing, because he said to her, "Are you trying to get smart with me?"

"No, no," she quickly said. "I mean, maybe something a tiny bit more specific."

"I was married recently," he said, and Didi couldn't be sure if he was in character or talking about his own life. "And now I'm not anymore."

"Why not?" said Didi.

"Because my wife was a hopeless slut and wouldn't settle down," he said harshly.

She guessed he was in character. "Lyle Lovett," Didi said. "Lyle."

He looked at her sideways with amazement and maybe even admiration. "Wow. Two guesses. My name *is* Lyle. That's incredible. Very fast. Lovett is not my last name, though."

"No, of course not," Didi said. And then, "Lyle is a nice name." Sucker-upper, she thought. You'll say anything to save your life, won't you?

She must have looked stricken, because he said solicitously, "What's the matter?" and placed his right hand on her knee.

It was difficult not to cringe and pull away from him. Wiping her face quickly, she said, "Can I have that drink now? I'm really very thirsty."

"Well, hold on, hold on," said the man named Lyle. "I have to guess your name now, too, don't I?"

"I can just tell you my name," Didi offered.

*"No!"* He stuck out his hand. "I want to guess. Please. I was having so much fun with this at Dillard's. Let me see . . . what do I get if I guess in three?" And he leered at her, smiling suggestively and pursing his lips. She wanted to open the door and fall out of the car onto the embankment. She would have done so if she hadn't had a baby inside her.

"I don't know," she said helplessly. She did not add, *what do you want?*

"How about a little kiss?" he said, reaching out and placing his hand on her leg, just below her dress line. His hand on her bare leg made her emit a retching sound.

Lyle took his hand away. "Yes," he said, not smiling. "Maybe we'll start with a little kiss. Now give me the first clue."

She tried to swallow. Her throat was dry. She needed to swallow to ease her anxiety, but there was nothing to swallow with. The need, though, was great. She wiped her sweaty forehead and, panting, put her hand in her mouth. Unsatisfying, but better than the tightness that overwhelmed and paralyzed her. "Okay, first clue," she said huskily. "I was a major female character in an old, very famous play."

Lyle's brow furrowed. Suddenly he didn't seem to be enjoying himself. He obviously realized it was going to be harder than he had thought. "Play?" he said grumpily. "I don't know any plays. What do you mean?"

"Well, that's my first clue. If you want another clue, I'll give it to you, but then it will be two clues."

"No, wait. Let me guess." He looked pensive. "An old play?"

She was quiet, rubbing her sore right ear. "Yes, an old play."

There was an echo in her ear, and the ringing would pass through the canyon of her eardrum, bounce off, and ring in both ears. She was getting a terrific headache. Lowering her hands to the Belly, Didi felt the baby kick. In the first second it gave her comfort, in the second, anguish. *The baby.*

"I've never seen a play in my life," said Lyle.

"What about in high school?"

"Yeah," he drew out. "Maybe in high school. *Guys and Dolls,* maybe. *Sound of Music.* Yes! Your name is Maria."

"No," she said, and thought, *idiot.* Didn't I say an old play?

"No?" He seemed disappointed. He had looked so proud of himself when he said Maria. The baby kicked again. She closed her eyes.

"Another clue," he said.

"I was very much loved by one man," Didi said. "But another man hated him and wanted to do him and me harm."

"Loved by one man," Lyle muttered. "Another man hated me, wanted to do me harm." And then louder, "The clues aren't very good. They're too mysterious."

Didi watched the speedometer as the car slowed to forty. "Have a guess, and I'll give you another one." Didi was hoping he would continue to drive slowly and be stopped by traffic control for endangering public safety. Wouldn't that be a joke.

"Okay, lessee." Lyle's eyes brightened. Didi watched him carefully. "Maybe Charles Dickens, one man loved me, another—yes, yes, *A Tale of Two Cities*. Yes, but what was her name? What was the girl's name who was married to one of the twins?"

Didi wanted to say *A Tale of Two Cities* was not a play, but again she held her swollen tongue.

"Lucie!" Lyle shouted happily. "Lucie is your name!"

Didi shook her head. "Nice guess, though."

He snapped his fingers and clucked. He seemed extremely disappointed. "But the clue you gave, that was right. She is loved by one man, and the other wants to do her and him harm."

"No," she said. "Sydney Carton didn't want to do Lucie harm at all. He loved Lucie. He switched places with her husband so he could die instead of him. He died for her."

Lyle was frowning deeply. Now he was going over ninety.

Oh, to have the window opened, Didi thought. Oh, to have the police pull us over.

"I don't remember that about *A Tale of Two Cities*. I just remember she was deeply loved by one man, Miss Smarty Pants," Lyle added bitterly.

**6 9**

They were both silent for a few moments. Didi was recalculating her options.

He was still at ninety.

Didi was praying.

*Dear God. Whatever I've done in my life, forgive me, good Lord, and in Your infinite mercy, send an officer my way. At the very least, some water.*

He said, "Let's have the third clue."

*Lord, please guide Your servant Lyle out of the darkness he is in, guide him out, help him find the way, Lord, help him find the gate that leads into life.*

"Let's have it," Lyle said.

"Okay, third clue." Didi had hoped for more time. "How about if I give you the first initial? Would that be a good clue?"

"If I guess it, yes," he said, unsmiling. "If I don't guess it, no."

The words struck at her heart.

"Okay, here goes. Remember the other clues too, though. The initial is D."

"D," he said. "D. A famous character in an old play, loved by one man, harmed by another—was she harmed?"

"Yes," Didi said. "She was harmed."

Lyle scratched his head. He was still at ninety. Didi was still thirsty. Please, she was praying. A police officer or water.

She wasn't certain she'd opt for the police officer.

"Well, I don't know!" Lyle exploded, hitting his fist against the steering wheel.

Didi stared at him, her eyes widening.

"I don't know what you're talking about! I gave you a modern-day country singer, you're giving me some crap about a man loving her and harming her, an old play, I mean, what the hell!" He slowed down a little, both in driving and in language, and glared at Didi. "You're not giving me good clues," he said. "In fact, you're giving me very bad clues. And I think," he said slowly, "that you're giving me these bad clues on purpose, on purpose so I would lose to you, because you want to seem smarter than me."

She shook her head violently, pushing herself into the door. "No, that's not true. Look, I'll tell you my name."

He hit the wheel hard with his fist. She sucked in her breath, and for some reason that made him laugh.

"I'm glad you think it's funny," she said.

"Listen, it's funny that you think you're so smart." Now his laugh sounded hollow and miserable. "Hah! If you think you're so smart," he said, rubbing her thigh hard with his knuckle, "how come you're sitting here in *my* car then? What makes you so smart? That you know plays and I don't? Miss Smarty Pants!" Reaching over, he pulled her away from the door and closer to him. "Sit right here with me. I don't want you to sit so far away. We wouldn't want you to fall out, would we?"

"No," Didi whimpered, sweat running down her face.

"No, that's right. Now, you're going to sit right here, and you're going to give me clues till I guess your name. Okay?"

She adjusted herself on the bench seat and couldn't help but move slightly away from him. "Okay," she whispered. "It's just that I've never known anyone with my name, no one modern. It's hard for me to think of modern things. Listen, do you go to the movies?"

"Not much. Why?"

"Because there was a movie made of this play recently. Maybe a year or two ago. With Laurence Fishburne. Do you know it?"

"Who is Laurence Fishburne? Never heard of him. What was the name of the movie?"

"If I tell you, you'll know her name. That's like you saying who was Julia Roberts briefly married to. You'll know right away."

"That's okay. Give me the clue."

"Okay. The name of the movie," said Didi, happy to be ending the charade, "was *Othello*."

There was a silence. The engine sounded loud and unhealthy, going at eighty. A blue truck whizzed by. Didi noticed a barn and a blue sign that said, GAS-FOOD-LODGING. 5 MILES.

Lyle said nothing for several moments. And then he said, "*Othello*? What kind of a damn clue is that? I never heard of *Othello*."

"No? You'll never guess my name then. Never. It's the only clue I can give you. Let me tell you my name—"

"No!" he shouted. "I'm going to guess and I'm going to guess it right."

"Lyle," Didi said, trying to keep her voice on an even keel, and failing. He was unraveling right in front of her, and it was frightening to watch. "Trust me. If you've never heard of *Othello*, you will never have heard of my name."

"Try me," he said doggedly. "Go on, give me a clue. Tell me what it rhymes with."

Didi was crying openly now, tears mixing in with the sweat, running into her cheeks and into her mouth. "Please," she whispered. "Please. What do you want with me? Call my husband, please, ask him for whatever you want. Let's just have this over with. Why do you have to do this?"

He looked at her with a hurt expression on his face. "Do what? What are you talking about? I thought we were just having a conversation."

She nodded, taking a deep breath and pulling herself together. "Yes, yes, of course we are. Do you play these games with your wife?"

"I thought I told you to leave my wife out of this!" he snapped. "But yes," he added. "We do."

"Lyle," Didi said, "please let me go. Please. Stop the car, let me out. I won't tell anyone about you."

"You promise?" he said sarcastically. "You swear?"

"I swear."

"You swear on your unborn child?"

"I swear on my unborn child," Didi repeated.

"Bullshit!" he yelled. "Bullfuckingshit! As soon as you get out of my car, you'll be bleating like a lamb all over Texas. No, I can't let you go," he said, quieter. "Besides, I'm not done with you. You know that. Now, continue. Give me a clue."

"So call my husband and tell him what you want. Why have we been driving for more than two hours and you haven't called anyone?"

"Give me a clue, I said."

She wiped her face and licked her hand. Yes, salt, but salted *water*. "My name rhymes," Didi said slowly, trying to calm down, "with 'Arizona.' "

"Arizona, Arizona," he said. "I can't think. No, nothing is coming. Another one."

"It rhymes," she said, "with 'my bologna.' "

"Hmm. Arizona, my bologna . . . No, nothing. Another one."

"It rhymes with 'Barcelona.' "

"Barcelona? What is that?"

Oh, God.

"I'll tell you right now," he said, threateningly, "if you don't make me guess, it'll be so much the worse for you. And for this one *I* swear on *my* child. Now another one. Arizona, my bologna, Barcelona. What kind of stupid clues are those? Those are just dumb clues. No one would be able to guess."

"You're right. It's a very hard name to guess," said Didi. "Want to try to guess my nickname instead?"

"Does anyone call you by the nickname?"

"Sure, lots of people."

"Your husband?"

"Yes."

"Okay, give me the nickname."

"It starts with D, and it rhymes with 'pretty.' It's got only two syllables in it and they're both the same. It's only got four letters."

He was muttering to himself. "Pretty, ditty, deedee, didi—Didi?" he said with hope and surprise.

"Yes!" she exclaimed. "Yes, that's right. See? That's right. Didi." And she breathed again, the tension leaving her body for a moment.

Lyle quickly stopped smiling. "So why didn't you tell me earlier?"

"Because it's my nickname. It's not my name on the birth certificate or my license. Don't you have a nickname?" she asked, grimacing, hoping it looked like a smile to him.

Lyle got a faraway look on his face as he watched the road. "My wife used to call me Lovey. Because I liked Lyle Lovett so much and because she loved me. Lovey."

*Used to?* Why in the past tense? Somewhere in a parking lot in the middle of a hot, perfectly normal Texas afternoon, or was it in the middle of a perfect, posh, pristine mall, sometime in Didi's life, this man had told her something about his wife and baby.

"So what's your full name?" she heard him saying.

"Desdemona," she told him.

"Desde-what?"

"Desdemona," she repeated, slower. "She was Othello's wife."

"There you go again with that damn Othello!" he exclaimed. "Are you Othello's wife?"

"No."

"So what do you keep bringing him up for all the time? And how did you get Didi from Desdemona anyway? Why not Mona, or Desde, or Demona?"

"When I was young I called myself Didimona. I wasn't that good with my s's. So my parents called me Didimona until I started school, and then my kindergarten teacher shortened it to Didi."

"It's a stupid name," he said gruffly, slowing to seventy, much to Didi's disappointment.

"It's an impossible name," she said, turning to the right, staring at the burned grass outside the window.

"Yes, it is," Lyle said. "Barcelona, Arizona, my bologna, pretty Didi. And so much the worse for you."

**R**ich followed the squad car to police headquarters in downtown Dallas. The fifteen-minute ride was the worst of his life. He got through it by willing his mind to go blank. A dull ache flooded his heart. All the while the July sun blazed, and there was no relief outside from the thicket of heat that hung over him. In the back of the station he parked in a lot reserved for police officers.

And emergencies.

Officers Charles and Patterson brought Rich inside through the back door. He had never entered this way. Not that he'd spent much time here. He and Didi had come downtown to report an attempted break-in and also to sign out their stolen car, retrieved nearly whole but without the radio.

Waiting for Rich inside the door was a short, earnest-looking young man with a slight Spanish accent. "Detective Juan Lopez. Please call me Juan," he said as he shook Rich's hand. "I heard what happened. We will do everything we can to help."

**7 6**

Rich was going to complain about Patterson, but then he thought better of it. It wasn't important.

"Come," said Juan. "I'd like you to meet my chief."

"Listen," said Rich. "Not that I wouldn't like to meet all you guys and shoot the breeze, but can we—my wife is—"

"No, I understand," said Juan, his brown eyes softening. "I have a wife too."

"I'm sure you do," said Rich. "We all have wives. My wife happens to be pregnant and missing. So can we just—"

The chief of police came out of his office. "I'm Chief Murphy. John Murphy." He extended his hand, and Rich shook it, wishing for comfort.

"We're going to do everything we can to help. Okay?" said the chief. "Try not to worry."

Rich shrugged him off. "How are you going to find them?" he asked. "How?"

The chief studied him for a moment, then turned to Detective Lopez. "Juan, take the Freshëns Yogurt employee to the photo room. Let's run some photos past this Alex. And you've got an APB out, haven't you?"

Juan said, "No. Not yet. I was waiting for word from the Bureau."

They were all crowded in the narrow hall. Rich wanted to sit down, or fall down. Murphy asked if they had been notified.

"The Bureau?" Rich asked. "You mean the FBI?"

Murphy nodded, an air of resentment on his face and in his voice. "Yeah, something like this, we're gonna do all we can to help. The kidnapper may stay local, you know—especially if he wants money. Technically this is not federal jurisdiction yet. You know? Because your wife is probably still in the state of Texas. But . . . he could be an out-of-towner, from Oklahoma or Louisiana. If the guy is headed out of town, it's hard for us to coordinate that kind of operation. Too many complications. The FBI obviously has more resources," said Murphy, sneering. "Just that, mind you, they only come in on the really big stuff—"

"What do you think, will they consider this really big stuff?" Rich asked.

Murphy shrugged. "Who knows? I sure don't. The other month, we had a child abduction. It was all over the radio. You've heard of our new Child Outreach Program for kidnapped kids?"

Rich fervently shook his head no.

"We have a few select radio stations we notify immediately if a child has been abducted, and they broadcast the information on the missing kids every five minutes. On the case I was telling you about, the feds were nowhere to be seen. It ended up that the girl was from a divorced family and the father took her, but they had no way of knowing that. Listen, that's all by the by. I think you'll have a better chance with them involved, all right?"

"All right," Rich said in a faint voice. All he needed was to be in the middle of a squabble between local law enforcement and the FBI. "Have you called them yet?"

"The radio stations?" asked the chief.

"No, the FBI."

"Yes," said Juan. "I called them as soon as I got word from Charles that there was a situation. One of their field officers should be here soon." Juan was efficient. Rich liked that as much as he could like anything right then.

Murphy said, "Well, we don't have to sit around and do nothing while we wait. Put out the APB on a pregnant woman and a young man, will you? Get the description from Alex. And have Don come back in."

"Don is the police artist," the chief said to Rich. "He's excellent."

Rich felt like an idiot asking, "The APB is going to help?"

"Help? Well, it'll be something."

"It's four-thirty," Rich said. "She's been . . ." He paused. "She's been gone since one," he continued. "Is three hours enough time for them to get near the Mexican border, or into Oklahoma, or Louisiana?"

The chief shook his head. "Not near the border. Oklahoma, Louisiana, yes. But he'll be driving very carefully, I bet. He doesn't want to be stopped for speeding. And if he took her out of state, he's in more trouble than he can find in Texas. Under federal law, it's the death penalty for him if he took her out of state."

"Chief Murphy," Rich said, trying hard to maintain his composure, "to give him the death penalty we have to catch him first."

"Yes. Yes, we do." The chief nodded to Juan, who carefully stepped away from the two of them.

"Look, Rich, I'm not going to bullshit you," Murphy said, averting his eyes.

Rich needed the chief of the Dallas police to look straight at him. He was man enough to take it, and he *was* going to take it, but he needed the chief to level with him. Rich wasn't going to break down in front of a stranger who didn't know his wife and didn't love her.

"Chief Murphy, look at me. Please."

Leveling his gaze on Rich, the chief said sympathetically, almost apologetically, "It doesn't look good, Rich." And then the chief stared interminably at him. It was probably just a few seconds, but the stare was oddly out of place with the apologetic tone. Rich wondered why the chief was giving him what appeared to be a suspicious look. Was he trying to elicit some emotion? Or was it something else?

"Of course it doesn't look good," Rich said loudly, breaking the silence. "Would it look good if your wife had been kidnapped?"

"My wife is dead," said the chief. He waved Rich off. "Don't apologize. I already told you, we'll do everything humanly possible." Murphy paused. "Are you wealthy? Is that why he took her?"

Rich narrowed his eyes. "I have a good job, but Didi is home with the girls, and we just built a house, nothing fancy, so we're house-poor, you know."

"Listen, a couple of things will happen. This guy will call most likely and tell us what he wants. Maybe he'll have your wife call. And maybe someone will spot them somewhere on the road and notify us."

Rich was thoughtful. "If he calls my house, how will we know? I'm here."

"Who's at home?"

"My two kids. The babysitter. My mother should get there soon. But she'll go nuts. She doesn't even know what's going on."

Chief Murphy said, "Now wouldn't be a bad time to tell her."

Rich shook his head. "Can't. She'll go nuts. She won't be able to look after the kids." He added, "And tell her what? We don't know anything."

"I see. Do you want us to send somebody?"

"Where? To my house? Oh, yeah, sure." Rich shook his head.

"The FBI is probably going to send someone regardless. They like to be on the safe side. And if he calls, you'd want someone to answer the phone, wouldn't you?"

"I hear what you're saying," said Rich. "But you have to understand. I have my five-year-old daughter answering the phone. My mother is not going to be able to take care of this. She is very—" He paused. "Emotional."

"Maybe one of our guys then?" said Murphy.

"Maybe," Rich said vaguely. He was not ready to speak to his mother.

Murphy said, "There's a chance the guy is still in Dallas, holed up somewhere. If we have to, we'll put him on the local news."

"Could he be headed for Mexico?"

The chief shook his head. "He'd only head there if—" And then Murphy stopped and stared bleakly at Rich.

"What were you going to say?" Rich said, paling. His knees were giving out on him. "If he what? If he killed her?" He shuddered and crossed his arms. "But she's pregnant. She's going to have a baby. What kind of a person—"

The chief placed his hand on Rich's shoulder and didn't say anything.

Rich thought back to an hour ago when he had called Didi's cell phone and she had picked up. She had been alive an hour ago.

He said, "Just notify the border police, can you do that?" Rich looked away from the chief's face—he didn't want to see his own aching reflected in it.

For a while he couldn't speak. Rich was trying to feel his Didi somewhere in the world. Where was his wife? He felt himself choking. With one fast motion he loosened his tie, and when that wasn't enough, he ripped it off his neck.

When he could speak again, he said, "What I want to know is, if it wasn't for our brand-new car, why would he take my pregnant wife?"

## 4 : 3 0 P. M.

**D**idi felt parched from the inside out. She was so thirsty she felt she could drink blood. The baby was hiccuping. That lucky baby, she thought. He's drinking the amniotic fluid. He's thirsty too, my little guy. We'll be okay, she thought, trying to feel braver.

"Lyle," she said carefully. "Could we stop for a drink? You did promise."

"Yes, Didi," he said. "You don't have to remind me. I said I would and I'm as good as my word."

Silence. Oh, so the kidnapper keeps his promises, thought Didi. That's nice.

"But Didi, Arizona," he said. "Didn't you promise me a kiss?"

Fear enfolding her, Didi wanted to say, but Lyle, you idiot, you didn't get it right. She only said, "Lyle, I can't. I'm a happily married woman. And didn't you say you were married yourself?"

He said, "Didi, I'm counting—this is the third time you've brought up my wife." And then, putting his strong hand on her leg, he added insinuatingly, "You didn't seem to mind when I kissed you in front of those ladies in the parking lot."

"I minded very much, and you know that," she said, shifting away from him. "I'm married."

"I'm sure your husband won't mind," Lyle said.

"You don't know my husband. He's a very jealous man," she said, looking longingly at another rest-stop sign. "Please, can we stop? I need to go to the bathroom, and I'm very thirsty."

"Don't move away from me, Didi," Lyle said to her, his friendly tone disappearing. "I like it when you sit real close and I can talk to you. We have a long way to go, and I don't want to be reaching halfway across the car to touch you. Move closer to me."

Didi didn't move.

He reached out and patted the Belly. She recoiled from him, turning her body toward the door. She thought that nothing could be worse than his touching her pregnant belly.

Groaning throatily, Lyle grabbed her breast very hard, squeezing it, then slapping it roughly. She cried out.

He pushed her away with one hand and laughed. "Look at that," he said, staring at the road, trying to keep the car in one lane. "We had our first fight."

Strangely, after that he ignored her. Didi sat with her arms enveloped around herself, worriedly wanting to feel the baby kick to make sure he or she was all right. She looked out the window and hoped for another rest stop.

Didi tried to beam good Christian thoughts to Lyle but couldn't feel his soul in the car. When she was in church and praying, she felt happy and whole, because she could feel souls surrounding her. In Lyle's car, Didi felt alone.

Why isn't he stopping to call? she wondered. Why isn't he having me call and say he wants a million dollars for me, pay up? Of course, what would her poor husband do with that information? Where could he possibly get that kind of money?

Didi didn't want to think about it.

Lyle had turned up the radio and was humming a country tune, tapping the steering wheel, acting as relaxed and friendly as he had in the mall.

As they neared Waco, Didi watched the fields swim by in a blur. The heat in the car was making her dizzy. She blinked the sweat out of her eyes, and when she looked outside the window again, she thought she saw Amanda and Irene playing on the grass on the shoulder. She whispered their names, *Manda, Reenie,* blinked, and they were gone, nothing but parched grass.

Lyle spoke. "Why did your parents name you Desdemona, Arizona?" She thought he was like a mean kid with good ammunition. A kid in the playground himself constantly taunted now took it out on the wimpy new kid in school. Name-calling, finger-pointing, laughing.

"Why?" he repeated.

Glad he was in better spirits, she answered him. "Because it's my mother's name and my grandmother's name. Just a name passed down through generations. I think my great-grandmother was a Shakespearean scholar, and *Othello* was her favorite play."

He said nothing as he drove.

Trying to sound cheerful, Didi said, "So what's your wife's name?" Calling on his better nature. His married nature.

He was silent so long that she thought he wouldn't answer her, but then he said, "I told you. Melanie."

"Melanie. That's a pretty name."

"My wife is pretty."

"I'm sure she is," said Didi.

"Too pretty," said Lyle. "And she knows it."

Didi blanked at the turn of the conversation, but then Lyle smiled at her and said. "You're not too pretty, Didi."

She said nothing.

"Is your husband pleased you're not too pretty?"

"My husband?" she repeated vacantly. "I'm not sure how to answer that. Are you not pleased that your wife is pretty?"

"Not too pleased," he admitted. "I wish she was less—you know—". He fell quiet and then said, "She dresses up too nice when we go out."

"Oh, yeah? Where do you guys go?"

"Nowhere special," Lyle replied evasively. "We just go for a little drink at night. Sometimes we dance and stuff. Have some buffalo wings."

"That sounds like fun," Didi said. "Didn't you say she just had a baby?"

"When did I say that?" he said brusquely.

Didi tried to recall. "I think at the yogurt place when I first saw you."

"I don't remember saying that," he said, frowning.

The pit in Didi's stomach widened. "Never mind then," she said. "I'm probably mixing you up with someone else."

On the radio, the announcer gave a short news wrap-up and said, "Headline news in fifteen minutes."

# 4 : 4 5   P. M.

**R**ich was sunk into a wooden bench outside Chief Murphy's office when he saw Lopez and Murphy walking quickly toward him accompanied by a black man in a crisp white shirt, khaki dress slacks, and a wide purple-and-orange tie—a funky dresser, Rich immediately thought. Can this guy be serious?

"Rich, I want you to meet Scott Somerville, from the FBI," said Murphy, adding with a sideways glance, "Scott says he will be in charge of this case."

Rich listlessly shook Scott's hand. Scott had an unusually firm handshake. He pumped Rich's hand, and when he let go, Rich's hand buzzed.

Rich noticed that Scott was shorter and much broader than he, but he especially noticed Scott's brown eyes, because they beamed with enthusiasm. "That's right," Scott said, his electric gaze boring into Rich. "I will be in charge of this case." He slapped Rich's shoulder. "I know you're hurting, man. I'm here to get your wife back, okay?"

Rich felt a little better. "You got here all the way from D.C.?"

"Nah," Scott said, furiously chewing on a piece of gum. "The Bureau has field offices all over the U.S. I'm a field officer in Dallas."

"Oh yeah?" Rich said weakly. "Have any experience in kidnapping?"

Scott put a steady hand on Rich's shoulder. "It's my job. Trust me."

Rich said nothing. Scott watched him carefully for a few moments.

He felt all their stares on him. Rich saw Scott staring at him with an inquisitive, serious, slightly suspicious expression. It was the same expression that the chief had earlier leveled on him. Only Juan's gaze was sympathetic. What the hell was going on?

"What?" Rich said. "Why are you guys staring at me as if I'm the sixth guy at a lineup?"

Scott said nothing for a moment, and then asked, "So, tell us again how you knew this guy took your wife."

"What are you talking about? What do you mean?" Rich was so exasperated and raw with emotion that it took him a little while to understand. "Hey—" he stammered in disbelief. "Hey—wait a second, what the hell are you asking me?"

"Just a question," Scott said politely. "I'm just a little vague on the whole thing. Something about a pretzel bag?"

"Oh my God." Rich wanted to pull his hair out. "Don't you— haven't we got better things to do than to question me? What's the matter? Out of leads so soon? Am I not acting enough like the bereaved husband?"

Chief Murphy and Scott continued to stare at Rich. Only Juan lowered his gaze. "Juan? What's going on, man?"

"Just standard procedure," Juan mumbled.

"There's a lot that seems to be standard procedure around here," exclaimed Rich. "Tell me, is it standard to have a young pregnant woman abducted from a shopping mall? Huh?"

No one said anything. Finally Rich said in a slow, flat voice, "I found the pretzel bag that belonged to my wife. I knew it was my wife's because I smelled her hand lotion on the bag."

"If she put it on in the morning, it must have been very faint," noted Scott in a casual voice.

Rich got defensive anyway. "Okay, so? It was faint, yes. You wouldn't have been able to recognize the smell, certainly. And if it smelled of someone else's wife, I wouldn't have thought anything of it. But it smelled of *my* wife. Of all the people in the world, don't you think *I* would know that?"

Scott nodded, exchanging a glance with Chief Murphy. "Sure, of course." He nodded again. "Let's not worry about this anymore," he said to the chief. "I'll take care of it."

"Take care of what?" Rich said, even though Scott was not talking to him.

Suddenly Scott's expression changed. "God help you if you're lying to us. If you're lying to *me.*"

"Oh, for Christ's sake! Look, give me a damn lie detector test if you have to. I'm telling you the God's honest truth. Every minute you're standing here interrogating me, he's one mile farther away from us."

Scott and Chief Murphy stared at each other for a moment, and then Scott nodded slightly. He tilted his head to one side and smiled at Rich. "All right, man," he said in a comforting voice. "The spouse is always under suspicion at first. Standard procedure. Listen, even when you think we're not working, we're working. I'm on the job five minutes and we may already have a small breakthrough."

Rich's eyes brightened. "Breakthrough?" he said.

Scott lifted his hand. "Now, don't get your hopes up."

Blood rushing to his face, Rich said, "God, what, what?"

"Well, this is what we have. At three thirty-five, ten miles south of Dallas on Thirty-five E, a report came in on police radio from a lady about a disturbance in the car next to her. She called nine-one-one on her cell phone."

"What kind of disturbance? What did she say?" Rich's heart pounded in his chest.

"She said that she was driving her car minding her own business, when she noticed that in the car to the left of her a woman was turned to the window while the driver, a man, was hitting her with an object."

"Oh God," said Rich, and thought, *maybe that's not Didi.*

"The lady said," Scott continued, "that the woman looked young and had long brown hair. The woman was saying something through the window, but the lady couldn't make out what it was. She also said the woman was holding her hands up to the window as if in prayer, so she might have been saying something like 'please' or 'help me.' "

"Oh my God," Rich said, his fists helplessly clenched.

"We don't know anything for sure, you understand?" Scott said.

Rich noted that Juan and Chief Murphy had said nothing during the conversation. Scott had a cocksure and intimidating manner that didn't allow for interjection.

"It could have been some couple having a domestic fight," Scott said. "It does happen, you know."

Rich knew it happened. But he had to believe it was his wife and his wife was alive. That was the most important thing. Not knowing what had happened to his wife was the unbearable part. Not knowing if she was all right.

Had Scott said 3:35? What time had Rich called the cell phone? It had been about three-thirty.

The relief flooded out, replaced by weights that dragged him deeper into despair.

He realized that finding out that Didi was alive in a car with a man who was hitting her with an object was not great news, but she was alive. And so long as she was alive, there was hope.

Rich saw Scott watching him intently. He wondered if he passed muster.

Scott put his hand out to comfort Rich. "I know everything you're feeling. Everything," he said earnestly. "We hate this most of all. We hope that he'll contact us, with a ransom note, or a call, with some indication of his intentions, and then we can usually pursue him. We have to hope he'll slip up somewhere. We'll do what we can, everything we can. But right now, we don't even know if we have the right car, much less the right man. You must hang tight, and let us do our job, okay? I promise you one thing—we will catch the bastard."

Rich pulled away from Scott's hand. "You've had many of these kidnapping cases then?"

"Yes," Scott said. "This is what I do."

"How often do you get the kidnapper?"

"Nine out of ten times," Scott said proudly.

Rich nodded weakly. "Maybe we could get on the phone and talk to the lady who saw Didi?"

Scott stopped chewing gum for a moment. "I wasn't bragging. I was telling you, you're in good hands. And I already did talk to the lady. It's the first thing I did when I heard the woman's message. I asked her to turn around and come back to Dallas. She's at the station right now. If you have a picture of your wife, I'd like to show it to her."

Rich didn't allow himself to be even a little bit impressed as he fumbled in his wallet. He took out the wedding picture of Didi, glowing, smiling, in white. Her shiny hair, twinkling eyes, and fresh smile were exactly the same seven years later as the day they married. Rich handed the picture to Scott, who glanced at the photo and said, "She's pretty."

Rich felt light-headed. Yes, she is, he thought. I just want my pretty wife back.

"Come with me," Scott said, as he led Rich down the hallway and opened the door to a room with a table and some chairs. "Have a seat and sit tight. I'll be right back."

Scott left. Rich realized that Juan and Chief Murphy were no longer involved. Rich sat for a few minutes behind the table, but he couldn't stand to be with his thoughts in an empty room. He walked outside and sat on the wooden bench, where he waited.

Wishing he could keep moving, Rich tapped his heels on the tile floor. The worst was sitting there counting off the seconds for something to happen, for some news.

When Scott returned, Rich jumped up. Putting a calm hand on Rich's arm, Scott said, "Take it easy, man."

"Yeah, I'll just do that," Rich said bitterly. "Thanks for the advice." Then, after a moment's pause, he said, "Well, anything?"

Scott, impeccable and proper, said, "Yeah, something." Nodding, Scott said, as if answering his own question, not Rich's, "It's her. The lady recognized her. It's your wife."

Dumbly, Rich nodded himself. "I just knew it. What kind of car were they driving?"

"The lady couldn't really remember," Scott replied. "The man sped off, swerving in and out of lanes, going ninety or more, the lady said. He obviously didn't want her to follow him. She said his car looked like an older-model Ford station wagon. Beige. She didn't have a chance to get the whole license plate. She got the first three letters, though. JZ five."

"Oh," Rich said, disappointed. "Is that helpful?"

"It's better than nothing," Scott replied, as he opened another piece of gum and stuffed it into his mouth. "There are hundreds of plates beginning with JZ five. I already called it in. We're going through them, but it'll take a little time. We'll narrow it down to the few dozen or so that are attached to tan Ford or Mercury wagons, and then we'll start looking at photos. It'll probably take another hour."

"Hour?" Rich exclaimed. "He could be in New Mexico in an hour!"

Shaking his head, Scott said, "I thought you'd be impressed by how fast we work, but there you go. He's not in New Mexico. He's between Dallas and Waco. We notified the Waco police and the state police. The guy *could* be heading down to the border, but it's another four hours. We'll catch him if he stays on I-Thirty-five. It's just a matter of time. Also, the AIC—"

Rich raised his eyebrows. Scott said, "Agent-in-charge. Raul. *Desk* agent in charge," Scott added for emphasis, as if to draw a distinction for Rich between himself, who was hands-on, and Raul, who wasn't. "He's a good guy." Scott lowered his voice. "But a little bossy. Anyway, he called the wire services. Reuters and UPI are now running a description of the car, and we soon hope to have a description of the man. Did Murphy tell you about the Outreach program? We're going to use those stations to get information about your wife on the air. It'll be a big help. Everyone listens to the radio while they drive, in gas stations, at rest stops, everywhere. So we've got the traffic cops looking out for the beige station wagon, and we've got the news alert. He's still in Texas and we'll catch him."

While they were talking, Juan Lopez and Chief Murphy came by to listen to what was going on, and now all three men stood around Rich in a circle as if trying to shield him from pain.

"Is that a good idea?" Rich said uncertainly. "Putting this on the news?"

"Yeah, man, it's standard procedure. We want everyone who can to help us find him. Unless they know, they won't know to help."

When Rich looked unconvinced, Scott said, "You'll have to trust me. That's the hardest thing, I know. But remember, as long as he's driving, he can't harm her."

Tell that to the blood on the pretzel bag, Rich thought, backing away from the men. Tell that to my wife, who's being beaten as she's screaming to passersby. Tell that to Didi.

But nonetheless, Scott was the FBI, and he was here to help Rich. *The FBI.* Rich was in their hands. Looking at Scott's serious face, Rich felt a little comfort. The only odd things about Scott were his feverish gum-chewing and his fruit-salad tie. "Okay, what now?" Rich said.

"Now we wait," Scott said, cracking his gum. "We wait for him to make a move. And he will. Just wait. I won't be wrong about this. The only thing crime breeds, besides jobs for people like me, is more crime. The only move he will make will be another criminal act. You know why? Because that's the path he's chosen. Once he's on that path, there's nowhere else for him to go but deeper into the woods. I don't know what he will do, but he will show himself again in a short while. So we're going to sit tight and wait. I promise you, it won't be long."

**F**inally Lyle got off Interstate 35, near West, Texas. Didi almost felt happy. She said a quick thank-you prayer to God, thinking, okay, well, this is the beginning of the end. We'll go and he'll call Rich, and then—well, and then we'll negotiate. I'll get to hear Rich's voice, let him know I'm okay. Maybe I'll even hear the girls.

And I'll get a drink.

Making a right at the stop sign, Lyle drove a few miles in the direction of Aquilla until he found a gas station. Didi never thought she'd be so glad to see one. Johnny's Auto Repair had a fuel pump out front. There was no pavement, only gravel. There was an old chair and a blaring black and white TV in front of the beaten-down store, but there was no one outside. No one in his right mind would be outside in this weather, thought Didi, sticking her head in front of the vent.

Lyle pulled up to the pump and said, "Now, I want to show you something." Reaching inside his jacket pocket, he pulled out a gun. "Are you familiar with guns?" He stared at her. "I'll take your silence to mean no. Believe me, I didn't want to show you this, but you have a tendency to rant and rave and all. This gun? It's a thirty-eight Super Automatic Colt. It's got a muzzle velocity of thirteen hundred feet per second. That's about half of a Fireball, but pretty powerful, anyway. I want you to know that no matter how nice I've been, I mean business, okay? I don't want to kill you, but I'd much rather kill you than die myself. Do you understand?"

Didi nodded silently.

"If you scream or carry on in any way to make yourself known to Johnny, I'll have to shoot you and shoot poor Johnny, too, who never did anybody any harm. So by your screaming not only are you going to die, but you'll kill an innocent person, too. Do you understand that much?"

Again she nodded.

"All righty then. I'm glad we understand each other. First I'm going to gas up. Did you say you needed a bathroom?"

"Let me go to the bathroom first," Didi said pleadingly. "I'm dying here."

Lyle smiled. "Gosh, I forgot. Pregnant women do have to go a lot, don't they? My wife could barely drink one beer before she was off to the ladies' room." He looked around. "The bathrooms are probably out back. Let me drive you."

As they were pulling around the corner, a heavyset, elderly man walked out of the small convenience store and calmly waved a key on a large wooden ring in front of Didi's window.

"Do you want me to get that?" she asked casually, her hand on the door handle.

"*No!*" he said, slamming the shift into park. "I'll get it."

Nodding, Didi focused straight ahead. Bald, round-faced, kindly-looking Johnny didn't deserve to die because of her.

It made no sense for Lyle to take the key when the man was standing so close to Didi's side of the car. All she would have had to do was roll down her window and stick out her hand. But Lyle went around the front of the car, took the key, and said something to the man. The man nodded, looked at Didi, and smiled. Didi shook her head. They're having a moment on my account, she thought. She tried to listen through the glass. She could barely make out what Lyle was saying.

"I have a riddle for you. See if you can guess."

Johnny stared warily at Lyle's jacket.

Gritting his teeth, Lyle said, "Ready?"

"I'm not much into riddles right now," said Johnny, handing Lyle the restroom key. "Too hot out here."

Lyle didn't extend his hand to take the key. "Listen to me. Tell me if it's easy. My wife over there says it's a piece of cake."

"Okay, shoot," said Johnny.

Didi rolled down her window an inch, straining to hear. Lyle didn't notice.

"You have to guess a female name, okay?" he said. "From an old classic play about a man who loves a woman and another man who wants to, and does, both of them harm. It begins with a D, and it rhymes with—" here Lyle chuckled. " 'Barcelona,' 'Arizona,' 'my bologna.' "

"Desdemona," said Johnny immediately. "Do you want the bathroom or not?"

Taking the key, Lyle looked bleakly at Johnny. "How did you know that?"

"Piece of cake," said Johnny, smiling at Didi.

Didi turned away from Johnny. So hot, so hot. All Didi wanted was a restroom and a drink.

They drove around back. While still in the car, Lyle gave Didi the key, and said, "In exactly sixty seconds I'm coming in to get you."

"Got it," she said. "Can I take my bag?"

He was instantly suspicious. "What for?"

She tried to sound pleasant. "So I can brush my hair and put on some lipstick. I feel yucky."

He eyed her—nervously, she thought. He reached over and grabbed the bag; after rummaging through it, he pulled out the cell phone. Didi's spirits sank, but it was moot. The LCD display on the phone said LOW BATTERY.

He threw the phone in the glove compartment and, handing her the bag, said, "Hurry up."

"Okay," she replied. "Of course I will. Just give me an extra minute to freshen up, okay?"

"Just hurry up, that's all," he said.

Didi placed her fingers around the handle and opened the door. She opened the door!

Opened the door and left his car with her bag.

The outside air stood still and thick and heavy with heat. She had to fight her way through it, *stagger* her way through it, as if the heat were a jungle, full of trees and branches that hit her in the face. It was just as hot as it had been in his car but not as sour. She hoped that airing the car out would help. Her legs moved sluggishly.

The small, dark restroom reeked of old urine and shit. There was dirty water on the floor. Didi didn't want to speculate on the nature of that water. She turned on the light and shut the door. She carefully laid her bag on top of the tank and then squatted above the toilet. Relief.

But just as quickly, terrors overwhelmed her and she felt no better. After flushing the toilet, she glimpsed at herself in the mirror.

It wasn't her own face she saw. The woman in the mirror was drenched and weak and ghastly. Didi turned on the water, and Lyle banged loudly on the door. She heard him say, "Come on." The handle turned. Thank God she had locked it.

"Hold on," she said. "I'm going to the bathroom. Wait a second, okay?"

After hearing him move away from the door, Didi frantically searched through her bag, looking for anything that might help her. A toothpick, a nail file, scissors.

She found a paper clip on the bottom of the bag, a couple of quarters, and Irene's *Hunchback of Notre Dame* board book.

She examined the paper clip and then threw it on the floor in frustration. Stifling her helpless sounds, Didi cursed softly under her breath and ran her hands under the water, then cupped them, filled them, and drank from them. Big gulps, one, two, three, four, five, six. As many handfuls as there had been rings on her phone before she opened it and breathed her husband's name into it. *Rich*, she whispered now. *Dearest Rich, you'll forgive me for standing you up and for shopping so much and for getting caught up in the karma we talked about yesterday. You didn't believe me when I told you I was afraid, but here we are.*

Lyle banged on the door again. "Come on," she heard him say.

"Coming," Didi called out, turning off the water. She reached into her bag with wet hands to pull out a brush. Quickly she ran it through her hair. Nothing could have interested her less than her hair, but she was glad for the extra moment of relative safety. Under normal circumstances, she would have squatted in the woods rather than set one foot inside a place like this, but this afternoon, Johnny's bathroom was a sunny oasis.

After brushing her hair, Didi examined the brush, which was plastic and harmless. She threw it back inside her bag.

She thought, maybe I should put on a little lipsti—

*The lipstick!*

Pulling Elizabeth Arden's New New Rose out of her bag, Didi opened it, and smeared on the dirty mirror, in large letters that got progressively smaller as she started running out of space,

# Help me Please!
## I'm Didi Wood and I've been kidnapped by a man named Lyle.
### He's driving a Tan Ford Taurus Station Wagon
### Please Help.

He banged loudly on the door again.

"I'm coming!" she yelled. She opened the door and turned off the light, resigned.

He stood right outside, smiling. "Everything okay?"

"Yes, fine," she said.

He reached out and touched her hair. "You look pretty."

She wished she could shear her hair off with lawn scissors. "Thanks."

"Wipe off your lipstick and I'll kiss you," he said, leaning close to her.

"I'm not wearing any lipstick," she said faintly, wiping her lips anyway, and beginning to feel a queasy liquid sensation in her mouth.

Outside a stinking bathroom, in the shadows behind a run-down gas station, in the back woods of rural Texas, a smiling, genial young man was asking Desdemona Wood for a kiss.

Didi couldn't hold it in any longer. She retched and vomited the water she had just drunk all over Lyle's pants and shoes.

He jerked away. "What are you doing? Are you crazy?"

"I'm sorry," she gasped, and threw up again in short spasmodic bursts. All she could think of was that poor water and how much she needed it and wanted it. The water was absorbed by the grass, and Didi's stomach was empty again. She wiped her mouth. "I'm sorry. I'm feeling sick."

He grimaced, and his face contorted. "Jeez, that's disgusting," he said. "Let's get out of here, now!"

"Wait!" She put her hand to her mouth. "Can I just go and wash my mouth out?" She wanted another drink of water.

Lyle went to take her arm, but stopped. The look of aversion was plain on his face. Motioning her to walk in front of him, he said, "No, uh-uh. You've wasted enough of my time already. Let's get out of here."

She slowly got back into his car, wishing she could wash away the bitter taste in her mouth—a fine metaphor for her day.

Lyle drove around to the front and parked near a gas pump. He filled the tank, then moved the station wagon to the front of the convenience store, telling her he was going to get her something to drink. As he got out, he tapped the bulge in the front of his jacket, to show her, to warn her, to threaten her. Didi kept her eyes on him as he walked around the car.

As he was walking past the TV, he suddenly stopped. Didi looked at the TV. The news was on, but Didi couldn't make out what the anchorwoman was saying. Lyle, however, stood still, staring at the TV. Then Didi's wedding photo flashed up on the screen. She couldn't believe it and rolled down the window a few more inches. All she could make out before Lyle yanked the cord out of the socket was ". . . armed and dangerous."

Before he went inside, Lyle turned around and cast Didi a cold, determined look.

Didi had no time to get excited about seeing her face on local television. As soon as Lyle disappeared inside the store, she flung open the glove compartment and grabbed her cell phone. Never taking her eyes off the front door, she pressed 911.

Okay, okay, Didi breathed to herself, keeping her eyes on the store. The sun reflected off the glass and she couldn't see inside. Nine— one—one—send. And she waited a few moments. At first it sounded as if it would go through, but then the beep came, the low-battery beep. Shit. She stayed on the line anyway. Beep—beep—beep—then she heard a voice on the phone. She was afraid to put it to her ear. She didn't want Lyle to see her. With the phone still on her lap, she said loudly, almost shouted, "This is Didi Wood. Please help me. I've been kidnapped by a man named Lyle. We're north of Waco, he's driving a tan—"

Didi thought she heard thunder, and then saw Lyle running out of the store. She had just enough time and presence of mind to throw the phone back into the glove compartment.

"What's wrong?" she asked, looking hopefully toward the store, as if she thought any minute now the nice old man named Johnny would come out with the sheriff and her odyssey into karmic chasms would be over.

However, Johnny didn't come. And Lyle drove off, the tires of the car screeching loudly as he made a right to get back onto the road.

"What's wrong?" he said, his foot flooring the gas pedal. "I'll tell you what's wrong, dearie. That Johnny wasn't a nice man."

"No?" Didi said weakly. "He looked nice."

"Well, looks can be very deceiving," Lyle said. "Believe me when I tell you."

She believed him. What was that burnt metallic smell?

"Was the TV on inside?" Didi's voice was very low.

"Yeah," Lyle said rudely. "So?"

"Do—do you want to tell me what happened?"

"Nothing happened," Lyle replied.

Didi closed her eyes and whispered, *God the Father, the Son, and the Holy Spirit, have mercy on Your servant, from all evil, from all sin, from all tribulation, good Lord, deliver him.*

"What are you doing?" he said. "Open your eyes."

"I'm praying for your soul," Didi replied.

He scoffed. "What about your soul, Arizona?"

"My soul is not lost," she said. "You need to be saved before God, and your soul needs to be rescued. It's crying to be rescued. God has to save you, Lyle," she said. "Help me save you. Welcome God back into your—"

"Shut up," he snapped. Then, milder, "You got it all wrong." He chuckled. "Do you know what's really funny?"

Didi couldn't think of anything funny.

"It's not me who needs to be saved, Didi," Lyle said, stepping on the gas.

## 5 : 1 0  P. M.

**R**ich sat idly in the chief's office while Scott was on the phone with what seemed to be half the population of Dallas. He had been juggling the phones as if his job were not as an FBI special agent but as an extremely efficient receptionist at a busy New York City corporate office. Rich thought Scott called nearly every field office in Texas and possibly the United States putting them on SWAT alert and informing them of what was happening. He called the border patrol. He called a local judge to make sure he had a line on a warrant in case they needed one. He called FBI headquarters in Quantico, "just in case," and he called several helicopter stations in Dallas. While on one line, he would pick up the other and talk to both simultaneously, a receiver to each ear. Callers were often put on hold. He sent two agents to Rich's house, as "standard procedure," to sit outside.

Rich bent down and pulled up his trouser leg to see the color of his socks. They were dark brown. Shit, Rich thought, letting go of his pants and sitting back up. Bad luck all around.

He got up, paced, then stood in front of Scott as if he were on an interview.

During a short break between phone calls, Scott insistently tapped on the desk with a pencil and asked Rich, "So, what do you do?"

"I'm national sales manager for a religious publisher based here in Dallas."

Scott looked over Rich's expensive suit.

"Oh, yeah? Are you good at it?"

"Yeah, I'm okay. I can size up a customer in less than a minute."

"Oh," Scott said, almost absentmindedly. "Is that good?"

"Well, I can tell if they're going to buy and I don't waste time on the customers who aren't. I can tell the difference between the buyers and the lookers in a minute."

"Ah, that's great, that's great. Listen, so how much does a sales manager make?"

"Excuse me?"

"I'm trying to establish motive here. You make a lot of money?"

"I don't—what's a lot?" Rich was nonplussed by the question. "You think this is a ransom situation?"

"I don't know. Maybe. Probably. I'm trying to figure that out."

"I don't have that kind of money. No one who knows us would think that—"

Scott raised his hand, asking Rich to keep quiet, and sit down while he answered the phone.

"Okay," Scott said to Rich after hanging up. "We got some action. We got us some nice activity."

"So what's going on?" asked Rich, getting up from the chair in front of Scott's desk.

"We located the car."

"You caught him?" Rich's voice was sick with hope. He couldn't stand it.

Scott shook his head. "No, no, wait, let me finish. Through DMV, we located the car. It belongs to a Lyle Luft, twenty-seven years old, no criminal record. No employment address either. . . . Hmm. His address is listed as Garland, Texas. So he's a local boy. We got a picture and everything. Come around, I'll show you."

Rich, reluctantly, walked around to look at the computer screen. Did he really want to look at the face of the man who had taken his wife? No, he really didn't want to. He looked anyway. The guy looked young, and had longish hair. The expression on his face was somehow vapid and intense at the same time.

"Means nothing, the hair," Scott pointed out. "Alex identified him as having short hair. I'm sure it's been cut several times since the photo was taken."

Scott called on the intercom. "Get Alex in here, quick."

While they were waiting, Scott said, looking at the DMV records, "Now this is interesting, too."

"What?"

"Well, this lists him as the owner of two vehicles. One 1986 Taurus Wagon and one brand-new Honda Accord. White. Where is that car? And if he's going far, why is he driving in a piece of junk instead of a brand-new car? It says here he registered it in June, just a few weeks ago. Where's the car? And where does a man listed as currently unemployed get the money to buy himself a brand-new car?"

"Who cares?"

"Oh, *you* should care," said Scott. "*You* should. It makes no sense, therefore it must be looked at closer. If things make no sense, there's usually a reason."

"Maybe he got a loan."

"Who'd lend money to a jobless man?"

"Maybe he paid cash."

"Ahh! Also interesting. If he's independently wealthy, what's he doing with your wife?"

Rich was tired of thinking. "Maybe he sold the car."

Shaking his head, Scott said, "No, he didn't sell it. The car is still registered to him."

Lopez and Murphy brought in Alex, who looked haggard.

"What's the matter?" Scott said.

Alex rubbed his eyes. "My eyes hurt. Can I stop looking through photos now?"

Scott's expression became slightly contemptuous. "Why don't you take a look at this one."

Alex took one look at the man on the computer screen and said, "That's him."

"Great!" Scott exclaimed.

"So can I stop now?" Alex asked.

Scott said, "Get out of here."

The phone rang.

Before Scott picked it up, he asked Murphy to dispatch men to Lyle Luft's address and get a warrant to search his home, search for and impound the Honda if they found it, and impound Lyle just in case they found him as well.

Scott picked up the receiver and listened intently, nodding a few times, saying yes a few times, and then standing up in the middle of the phone call.

When he hung up, he said to Rich, "Just got a report on a police radio about a homicide thirty miles north and five miles west of Waco, in Aquilla. A gas station owner gunned down behind the cash register. Could be just a coincidence, but a remarkable one, wouldn't you say? How many paths can our Lyle Luft take? I say only one, Rich. What do you say?"

Rich said nothing.

Scott, standing behind the chief's desk, continued, "The man who called the police said he saw a tan station wagon speeding away. The only reason he noticed the car at all is because it was going eighty on a local road. The guy just got scared. Then he pulled into the gas station and found the owner on the floor. Sounds like our man. What do you think?"

Rich, unable to sit, or even concentrate on the individual words, said to Scott in a desperate voice, "Yes, but that's north of Waco. We're here, two hours away. How do we get *there*?"

Scott smiled broadly and walked around the desk to pat Rich on the shoulder. "That you leave to me."

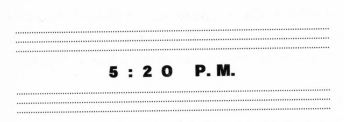

# 5 : 2 0  P. M.

**S**light change of plans," said Lyle. "Nothing major. We need to take care of a couple of things real fast. I'm going to get off the highway. Help me look for a pawnshop, will you?"

"Sure," Didi said, thinking, yeah, when I'm old and gray I'll let you know where there's a pawnshop.

He reached over and patted her belly. This time she sat catatonically, enduring his hand. "I see we've gotten used to me," Lyle said. "That's good. That's really good, pretty Didi. Because I'm kind of starting to like you, too. You look so—so—" He stammered. "So . . . pregnant," he finally said. "Yes, I like you."

*This is new,* Didi thought.

She wanted to say she was heartened by that news. After all, weren't they in high school and wasn't he the boy she wanted to go to the prom with? The boy who called her my bologna and whose shoes she threw up on?

She never imagined that the face of death would be wearing jeans and a jacket on a scorching summer day, coming up to her in the mall saying, Can I help you with your bags?

What time was it? Oh yeah. Tonight we were going to have steak and French fries, Manda's favorite. I promised her she could shuck the corn. Hope Ingrid put the steak back in the fridge. It must have thawed by now.

When was it in her life that she had been happy? When had the future looked so bright she had to wear sunglasses? Wasn't it just this morning that everything was all right except an irrational fear that something was going to happen to her and the baby? Rich had laughed at her.

Yet karma did come to sit on her shoulders, it came to her and said, *I am the black crow that is going to carry you away, but first I'm going to make you suffer and then I will make you cry, and then I will show you the terrors of the world right here in this car, in the woods, in a ravine.*

Lyle was saying something.

"Were you listening?" he asked.

"No, I'm sorry," she said. "I was praying."

"Well, stop that," he snapped. "I need you to help me find a pawn-shop."

"What are you going to pawn?" she asked, trying to sound jovial. Then she actually made a joke. "You won't get much for the car."

Smirking, and pulling up his turned-up nose at her stab at humor, he said, "Maybe we'll have to pawn something else, then, too, pretty Didi," staring at the fingers of her left hand.

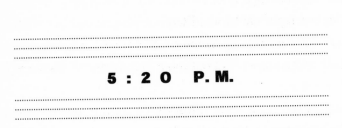

# 5 : 2 0  P. M.

**R**ich paced, sat down, stood up, paced, tapped on every wooden and plastic surface in Murphy's office as Scott called seemingly several dozen more people. Scott's deep, methodical voice grated on him; he tried to tune it out. Murphy brought him a Coke; Rich refused it. Juan tried to talk to him; Rich turned away.

"Maybe we should invest in a cell phone," he muttered, as Scott finally hung up and got ready to leave.

"Got one, man. Let's go to my car and get it, okay? You're impatient, I know, but we have to have help. We can't do this alone. I'm doing everything to see to it that we have all the help we need."

Murphy suggested, "Maybe Rich should stay here."

Scott shook his head while making sure the holster for his gun was properly tightened. Rich's heart skipped a beat. He thought he would just break in two if he had to sit and wait at police headquarters for some news.

"Let's go," said Rich.

"I'm the main case agent. He's coming with me," said Scott to Murphy. "I need him to make a positive ID, I need him to talk to the kidnapper. I need him with me," he said, quieter, "in case he's part of this thing himself."

"Let's go," Rich said loudly.

They went out the back door and walked to Scott's silver Chevy Lumina. "Get in," said Scott.

"We're driving?" exclaimed Rich.

"We're driving to the helicopter," answered Scott.

In the car, Rich said, without looking at Scott, "You know I'm not part of this thing."

"I know that," Scott said. "I just didn't want to discuss it with Murphy another second." He handed Rich the cellular phone and a business card with a phone number scribbled on the back. "Here. Call home and forward your calls to this number. It's headquarters. They'll screen all the calls that come in, and if he calls, they'll trace him and put him through to us."

"Won't that scare him shitless? To know the FBI's on to him?"

"You have any better ideas? You want your mother to talk to him?"

Rich shook his head.

At the charter station, which looked like a tiny airport, Scott parked his car and walked around to the trunk. Rich followed. Scott opened the trunk and Rich saw four black canvas bags of different shapes on the floor. Leaning in, Scott pulled out the dark bags one by one until three were on the ground and the only thing left in the trunk was one long black bag.

"You're leaving that one?"

"Yes. Those are my golf clubs, and I don't intend to play golf today—unless we finish early."

Rich didn't think they'd be finishing early.

"Could you give me a hand with these?" Scott said. "We need to load these on the chopper."

Rich picked up a long, narrow black bag. "What's in this one?" he asked Scott, who slammed the trunk closed, picked up the other two large bags, and started walking briskly to the helicopter. The pilot was already inside. The blades spun into motion.

"Which one? The one you're carrying? Oh, that's the Heckler & Koch MP5."

*Heckler & Koch MP5*, mouthed Rich. He shook the bag gently. Metal rattled inside. "And that would be . . . what?"

Scott turned his head to Rich. "Machine gun. Fires eight hundred rounds a minute. You think that'll be enough for our friend Lyle Luft?"

Rich turned away from Scott. "No," he said.

Then he unzipped the bag and looked inside.

"Scott—"

"Rich, come on, man, let's go."

"Wait, I have a question. Does the Heckler & Koch come with leather grips and little white balls?"

"No. Why?"

"I see," said Rich. "Well, then, I don't think you're going to be shooting anybody with these, unless—"

Scott ripped the bag out of Rich's hands. "Ah, goddammit," he said, turning back to his car. He opened up his trunk again, threw his golf clubs in, and pulled out the other black bag.

"May I make a recommendation?" Rich said.

"No."

"Maybe you can put the golf clubs in, say, a green bag. To avoid confusion in the future."

"Maybe you can get in the helicopter posthaste."

As they were getting in, Scott's colorful tie was blown around his neck by the force of the wind from the blades. Rich's tie was crammed into his pants pocket. When they were in the air, Scott asked if Rich had ever been in a helicopter. Rich said no, never, but he wasn't paying attention.

He was thinking of Didi waddling around the house, barefoot, unable to bend down with her big belly, unable to get up off the couch without his help, so vulnerable.

But for now, Scott's small talk was all Rich had. Small talk and an aching heart, and a Heckler & Koch behind their seats.

"It's a good helicopter," Scott was saying. "I got us a JetRanger. It'll fly at nearly a hundred and seventy-five miles per hour, and its fuel capacity is pretty good too. And do you hear me? We can actually talk inside the cabin. That's what I call a quality chopper."

"Mmmm," said Rich. "Where can we land in this thing?"

Smiling, Scott patted Rich's knee. "Anywhere," he said. "You're with the FBI."

Rich looked through the oversized front glass canopy of the helicopter. The glass gave him a fish-eye view of the sky and the ground. They flew low enough that Rich could make out the cars on the highway. Every car looked like a station wagon, every light-colored car looked tan. He stopped watching the ground after a while and closed his eyes. He wondered what time it was.

Faintly he heard Scott's voice talking to someone, maybe his AIC, maybe his mother. Who knew at this point? It was probably a sheriff somewhere. "Yeah, you gotta remember about this guy, he shot a man at close range four times. He could have shot him once and it would have been enough, but he wanted to set the place on fire. He means business. If your troopers locate him, approach with extreme caution. Repeat, extreme caution. We don't know what other weapons he has, but we have to assume he's well armed."

Scott hung up, and for a few minutes there was no more talk.

"Rich," Scott began, "just want to tell you, man, I know what you're feeling, and I promise you, we'll find him. We'll get him."

It hurt Rich to open his eyes, but he opened them and shifted to look at Scott. Slowly he said, "You mean find *her*, Scott? Don't you? Get *her*."

Scott didn't flinch. Didn't seem to understand Rich either. Didn't seem to or didn't want to, and Rich turned away. Scott said nothing for a while.

"Rich, I know you have no money," Scott began, "but do you have enemies?"

"Enemies?" Rich laughed hollowly. "Lyle Luft is my enemy. But Scott, give me a break. I'm a sales manager for a publisher of religious books. Who's going to be my enemy? God? You think He got mad because I didn't make my projections this quarter?"

Rich wanted to cross himself when he said that. Is God my enemy? All my life He's been my friend, and Didi's too. Has God turned against us?

The Waco police were both more awed by Scott and more resentful of his power than Lopez and Murphy in Dallas. The sheriff kept Scott and Rich waiting in the corridor for ten minutes, although he had been notified of their arrival. When he finally came out of his office, he barely nodded acknowledgment before embarking on a trivial conversation with the dispatcher. Unflappable, Scott chewed gum and talked on his cell phone.

Rich couldn't stand it. Pulling on Scott's sleeve, he widened his eyes at the sheriff standing in the distance and then at Scott.

"Don't worry," Scott whispered. "We get the last laugh, because he'll be giving up his office in a minute."

Rich was glad he was on Scott's side. Looking like an overworked corporate executive, Scott, with his unconcerned confidence, pumped the sheriff's hand and immediately declared his office temporary FBI headquarters. Sitting down behind the sheriff's desk, Scott got on the phone, while Rich and the sheriff stood dumbly in the corner. When Scott hung up, he walked over to the sheriff, shook his hand again, and showed him the door, saying, "Well, that will be all. I'll call you if I need you. Thanks." And closed the door behind him.

"He wasn't exactly nice to you back there," said Rich when they were alone.

"No? I hadn't noticed." Scott shrugged. "Listen, it's the special *double* challenge of being a black FBI agent in Texas. I pay no attention to it." He smiled, going behind the desk and getting comfortable in the chair. "The law is on my side."

"Plus you'll kick their ass."

"Yeah, that too."

The police officers on the scene of Johnny's murder found the scrawled note from Didi on the restroom mirror. The contents of the message were promptly reported to Scott. Meanwhile there were no further signs of Didi and Lyle. Undeterred, Scott called the state trooper headquarters to pass along the description of the car and its license plate number. He faxed photos of Lyle and Didi and reiterated the warning to use extreme caution in approaching Lyle. Scott told Rich that his boss, Raul, had contacted radio stations that had agreed to cooperate and they were now broadcasting reports of the kidnapping every fifteen minutes.

Rich was trying to sort his own emotions. He had been putting off calling home. He knew the girls and his mother would be beside themselves. Overwhelmed by the mass of information coming at him, Rich nonetheless managed a coherent thought. "Scott," he said slowly, coming up to the desk and fidgeting with the ashtray, "what if Lyle hears reports on the radio that the entire state of Texas is searching for him?"

Scott said impatiently, "Yeah, so?"

Rich dropped the ashtray with a bang and moved away. Scott seemed to know what he was doing. Rich certainly didn't want to be stepping on anybody's toes. Yet . . .

"Scott, but won't he get desperate?"

"Desperate? You mean more desperate than kidnapping a pregnant woman and killing a man? I don't think so." The conversation was over as far as Scott was concerned.

Rich felt a bit better for Scott's confidence.

A few minutes later Scott asked to see the dispatcher's records. He found a call at 5:10 P.M. from Didi Wood. When they replayed the tape, they heard a woman's faint voice, pleading for help. While Scott raged against the dispatcher, Rich asked weakly to hear the recording again. And again.

*"This is Didi Wood. Please help me. I've been kidnapped by a man named Lyle. We're north of Waco, he's driving a tan—"*

The sheriff was defensive about the oversight, something about being busy and having too much paperwork, and routines being disrupted. Rich wanted to tell the sheriff to shut up. He saw by Scott's expression that Scott did, too.

Rich wanted to know why Didi had stopped talking so abruptly.

Scott explained that the call had come through right around the time of the man's death. He thought that Didi was probably in the car while Lyle was inside the store. Scott thought that maybe Didi saw something that made her stop talking.

"You think she saw him kill the guy?" Rich asked.

Shrugging, Scott said, "Maybe."

"If she didn't see Lyle kill the man, she might not know how dangerous he is, right?" said Rich. Was that good? Bad?

"Right."

First a glimmer of hope, then nothing.

The only difference was the setting. First Rich sat in a Dallas police station. Now he sat in a Waco police station. After they left the dispatcher's office, Rich sat on the bench. Then he got up and paced the hall. He went to the bathroom, he had a drink, he sat on the bench, he paced the hall.

He went back inside the sheriff's office and said to Scott, "Could I have five minutes? I've been putting it off, but it's time. I have to call home."

Scott left the room. Rich sat behind the sheriff's desk, unforwarded his home phone, and dialed the number, hoping his mother would pick up the phone. No, Amanda got to it first.

"Daddy!" she shrieked. "Did Mommy have the baby?"

In the background, he heard Irene crying, "Mommy, Mommy!" and his own mother yelling, "Manda, give me the phone right this instant!"

The bridge of his nose aching from the tension, Rich said, "Manda, honey, let me talk to Grandma, okay?"

"No," Amanda said. He heard wrestling with the phone, and then screams from Amanda.

"God, these children," his mother said. "So, how is everything? Are you in the hospital?"

"No, Mom, listen, I have to talk to you, something—"

"What?" Barbara Wood said. "What's wrong? Has there been some kind of accident?"

"You could say that, Mom. Didi's been kidnapped." There. He just came out and said it.

"What do you mean?" Rich's mother said. "I don't understand."

"I don't either, Mom, but some man took her from NorthPark."

"What man?" his mother asked shrilly.

"We don't know."

"Oh, my God. Oh, my God. Oh. My. God."

"Mom, please, the girls, please." He heard his mother's calm voice breaking down. "Mom, the girls!" he exclaimed. "Just—please—for them."

It seemed to take his mother minutes to stop crying, and all Rich could do was whisper, "Mom, the girls."

"Oh, God help us, what are we going to do?"

"We're going to find her, Mom. There are two FBI men outside the house in a car, just in case he comes by, or if you need anything."

"What am I possibly going to need from them? What if he calls here?"

"The phone's been forwarded to FBI headquarters, so they can trace his location." Rich heard pained breathing on the other end. "Please try to calm down. I don't want the kids to get scared."

"Scared? Scared? Listen, I've locked myself in the bathroom, the kids can't hear me. But they've got every right to be scared."

"No, it's all going to turn out okay, and I don't want to panic them."

"Panic them? Richard, all Reenie's been saying is when's Mommy coming home? They're hungry."

"So feed them, Mom."

"Reenie doesn't want anyone cooking her dinner but Didi. She threw a fit when I touched that steak."

"So don't feed them the steak. Feed them macaroni and cheese."

"They don't want macaroni and cheese. Manda knows her mom was going to make steak, and that's what she wants."

"Oh, for God's sake!"

Rich kept the phone to his ear. "Mom," he said in a low voice. "I'm asking you please to take care of them, please, as best as you can. Don't tell them anything."

"Richard, what am I going to tell them when they ask where their mommy is?"

"Tell them mommy is trying to have a baby, and Grandma is going to take care of them tonight."

"And what if—"

"Mom!" he exclaimed. "I don't want to hear this from you. Say a prayer if you've got five seconds free. I'll call as soon as I have any news."

When Rich hung up, he thought, well, that was as bad as I thought it was going to be.

## 5 : 3 0   P. M.

Lyle finally found a pawnshop in Valley Mills, near a desolate intersection of Highways 6 and 56. To call the roads highways was generous. One standing stop sign survived. The other had been knocked down. Didi had noticed that after leaving Johnny's, Lyle stayed on the interstate only until the next exit and then took the local roads. Was that in his plans? He seemed to know the roads quite well and never checked a map.

They parked in a small dusty lot in front of a place called Smokey's. Didi tried to stretch her achy body, but her big bag was in the way of her feet. She wanted to kick it out of the way, but there was nowhere to kick it to. Her sandal became tangled up in the strap of the bag, and Didi struggled to break free. It was ferociously hot. With the vents off, Didi had trouble breathing. She thought of again asking if she could roll down the window. She didn't think he'd mind, because there was no one in the parking lot.

Of course there was nothing to drink in the car. Though he had gone inside Johnny's to get some drinks, he had run out empty-handed. What Didi had drunk in Johnny's bathroom was on Lyle's shoes—a small solace. She was sweaty, thirsty, and the baby was tightening in her belly. Her tongue now felt like a fat, immobile slug in her mouth, and her breast hurt where he had grabbed her.

But when Lyle looked at her left hand again and told her to take off her engagement ring, all the thirst and pain vanished.

"No," she said, pulling her left hand away across her body, away from him. Why couldn't she have belonged to another religion, one where they wore the wedding rings on their right hands instead of their left? She had heard the Greeks or somebody did that.

Not that it would have mattered to him. His thin, wiry body rubbing against her belly, he leaned across the bench seat and grabbed her hand.

Holding her left wrist painfully tight, Lyle said to her, "Didi, what are you doing? Don't you know me by now?"

She started crying. "Please don't take my ring. Please."

"Oh, what's the matter, pretty Didi?" he cooed sarcastically. "Don't tell me you'd rather lose your life than your precious little ring."

"Take my ring and let me go," she sobbed. "That's a fair exchange. My ring for me. It's a one-and-a-half-carat stone—a good one. It must be worth six thousand dollars. Take it and let me go."

Still holding her wrist painfully hard, his breath assaulting her face, he said, "Six thousand dollars for your life. Now, now, my bologna. You don't value yourself very highly. Don't you think you're worth more than six grand?"

Trying to pull away from him, she repeated, "Take my ring and let me go."

He said gently, "I'll tell you what. I'll take your ring and keep you with me. How would that be?"

"No," she said. "No."

"But Didi," said Lyle, trying to pry the ring off her numb finger. "I have big plans for you. I can't let you go. That's like asking a lover to leave the love of his life. What kind of lover would I be? Did Othello let Desdemona go?"

Crying, she fought him. She pulled in her fingers toward her wrist and pushed him away with her right hand.

"Goddammit! What's gotten into you?" he yelled. He was in an awkward position. He couldn't get the ring off. They struggled. Pinning her against the seat with his body, he let go of her wrist for a moment and swiped her in the face with his forearm.

"Didi, you have a lot to lose here," he said menacingly, panting. "Stop being stupid. I see that I'm going to have to teach you. Education doesn't come from books, you know. And you have no common sense, you crazy bitch."

"Wait," she said plainly. "Wait."

Squeezing her hands together, Lyle reached over the bench seat into the back. After rooting around briefly, he pulled out a hunter's knife from under the seat.

"See this knife, Didi?"

Before Didi had time to think or speak, Lyle brought the knife down and sliced the fingers on her left hand, opening four of them right across the second knuckle.

Didi cried aloud and tried to pull her hand away, but Lyle was stronger. Blood dripped onto her yellow dress. Holding her bleeding fingers in one hand and the knife in the other, Lyle said, "This is just a warning. Now take off your ring, or I promise you, I will cut your finger off, and then the finger *and* the ring will be mine. Wouldn't you rather just give me the ring?"

Made temporarily breathless by the wound, Didi couldn't speak.

Lyle calmly said, "Take the ring off. Now."

Didi said, "Let go, and I'll take it off."

He let go, still holding the knife against her.

The weight gain during her pregnancy had made the ring a tight fit.

In a few minutes, as the finger swelled from the knife wound, the fit would be even tighter. However, right now, the blood created a slick, slippery surface helping the diamond ring slide off her finger.

Lyle took the ring and then wiped the knife on the hem of Didi's summer dress, picking it up high enough to expose most of Didi's thigh. She wanted to pull the dress down, but didn't dare. In any case, she couldn't move at that moment even if she wanted to.

"Diamonds are forever," Lyle said, smiling and kissing the ring. Then he saw there was blood on it, and he put the ring in his mouth and sucked on it, saying, "Mmmmmm." He bent to her. "Your blood, Didi, it tastes so sweet," he whispered.

She moved her head away in disgust. She heard him mutter, "Do you taste this sweet all over?"

Didi stared away from his face, mere inches away from hers. She wished she had something sharp and ragged in her hands at that moment. *God help me.*

He moved away.

"Lessee if I get six thousand dollars for it," Lyle said cheerfully. "Oh, and while I'm gone, could you clean yourself up?" he asked. "Wrap your hand in your dress and squeeze tightly. The dress is as good as ruined already, and you don't want to bleed to death in my car, do you?"

That is my idea of hell, Didi thought, as he leaned over her to reach inside the glove compartment. He pulled out the cell phone, chortling lightly, and left her in the car with all the windows shut.

Didi quickly rolled down the window to let in some air. She wasn't going to just sit there in hundred-degree weather as the car gained five degrees a minute.

She was alone in the car.

Didi looked around the parking lot, and then on the floor for the knife, but he had taken the knife along with the gun. Taken it with him when he went to sell her ring, the ring that Rich had bought her when they had no money. It had taken them five years to pay off that ring, and it was the only piece of jewelry she owned, because no other jewelry in the world could compare to her emerald-cut diamond. Often her girlfriends would advise Didi to put it in a safe deposit box so it wouldn't get stolen. One day she had mentioned the idea to Rich, who was opposed to it, saying that sure, if someone stole the ring, she wouldn't have it, but if she put it in a safe deposit box, she wouldn't have it either.

"Well, I'd have it," she had argued. "I just wouldn't have it with me."

"Same difference," Rich said. "You can't see it, you can't look at it, you can't show it to anyone. With this ring I thee love," said her husband. "What are you going to do? Every time you feel warmly toward me, you gonna run to the bank?"

That's what he had said, but now she was sitting here with slashed fingers and she didn't have her ring. The small parking lot glistened with heat. It looked as hot as she felt. But it was not an animate object. It could not feel pain. It didn't have another animate object inside itself.

She sat, her fried brain trying to figure Lyle out.

It was clear he didn't want money. He had taken her ring, but as an afterthought, as something malicious, not something essential. He wasn't concerned about money, that Didi was sure about.

Also, he didn't seem to want to kill her.

She hadn't served her purpose. But what would happen, after she had?

What did he want? Did he want to take her home to meet his parents and pretend she was his wife? He already had a wife. Did he want to take her to a bar and make his wife jealous? She leaned back against the seat and breathed heavily. Did he want to have sex with her? She felt bile come up into her throat.

With a pregnant woman?

Was that a fate worse than death? That lascivious way he'd touched her thigh as he cleaned the bloody knife, his lecherous laugh when he asked her for a kiss outside the gas station bathroom, these things cut her and ate at her, they gnawed at her flesh and emptied her heart of compassion for him. She closed her eyes. *That it may please You mercifully to pardon all his sins and make him stop, we beseech You to hear us, good Lord.*

Didi wondered where Lyle was taking her. Where were they going? He could have driven to any deserted place in Dallas, raped her, killed her, driven off. He had mentioned a place before. Why would he need to drive her away from Dallas?

Didi wanted to believe—needed to believe—his plans for her didn't include extreme violence to her and her child. Sitting in his car, keeping her wounded fingers on her lap, Didi Wood needed to believe she would be safe. God wouldn't let her die. She opened her lips and mouthed her prayer as if it were a weapon against him. *Lord, be near me, Your faithful servant Didi, in my time of weakness and pain, sustain me by Your grace, that my strength and courage may not fail.*

That's it, I'm not sitting here anymore. He'll have to shoot me in plain sight.

But she didn't want to be shot.

Didi got out of the car. Holding her bleeding hand gently with the other, she walked as quickly as she could to the road, never turning around to look at the pawnshop. I'm going to stand in the middle of the highway and wave till a car pulls over, she thought.

She took her position in the road.

They were west of West, Texas. They were nowhere and no one was around them. There was unfarmed flatland on Didi's left and a pasture on Didi's right. The pasture was ungrazed, too hot even for cows.

Didi stood.

One minute passed.

No cars came.

*He's going to come and kill me,* thought Didi. Kill me, kill my baby, take my life and my ring, and never be seen again.

Didi could barely get her lips open to pray.

I don't want him to kill me. I have two little girls, God save them, back home, waiting for their mom, oh, God, I hope that Rich remembers that Amanda doesn't like her steak and French fries on the same plate, or there'll be a scandal. . . .

She turned around and slowly, sadly, walked back to the car, looking back at the empty road.

She didn't get in but stood leaning against the car, and soon the door of the pawnshop opened and Lyle walked out with a tall, heavyset man, who nodded silently to her.

Lyle ran to Didi, blocking the man's view of her. "Sit down, honey, sit down, you shouldn't be standing!" And when he got to her, he hissed in her ear, "Do you want him to die, Didi? Do you want me to kill him? Get in the fucking car."

Didi got in the car.

The man walked around the vehicle, wrote something down, and then disappeared inside the shop. Lyle smiled falsely at her, waved, and went back inside himself. A few minutes later, he came out of the pawnshop and headed toward her. His face was dark. Oh, God, Didi thought, what now?

When he got in the car, he sat there for a second not saying anything.

"Everything okay?" Didi asked him.

He said, "No. Everything is not okay. It's not okay at all. Why did you get out?"

"My legs were numb from sitting. I wanted to stretch them a bit. I'm so hot, Lyle. Does Smokey have a drink machine?"

"No," he said. "Do you want to know why everything is not okay?"

Why did she fear whatever it was that wasn't okay had something to do with her? "Because you kidnapped a pregnant woman?" she offered.

He hit the steering wheel, gritting his teeth. "No, that's not it," he said quietly. "Everything is not okay because when I tried to sell your goddamn cell phone, do you know what the guy behind the counter said to me?"

"Uh," Didi said, her breath catching. "That he wasn't going to buy it because you could get them so cheap in the stores?"

"How did you know that? How did you know that?" he said loudly.

"I didn't for sure. Just a hunch."

"Well, you should have told me about your hunch before I went in there looking like a real idiot with that thing."

"Sorry. You didn't ask. I thought you just wanted to make a phone call."

"To call who? Who would I have to call?"

"I don't know," replied Didi. "My husband. Your wife."

"Oh, shut up with the wife shit, all right? Well, the guy pushed some numbers and said, hey, is everything all right, and I said, sure, and he said, because I see here you dialed nine-one-one."

Didi stopped breathing. She moved slightly away from him, toward the partly open door. Thinking quickly, she said, "That was the last call I made. I dialed nine-one-one when I was at the mall. In Warner Brothers."

"Did you indeed?" Lyle said. "Why did you do that?"

"Because I thought you might have been following me and I didn't like it."

"Why would you think I was following you?" he asked.

"Because you went after me into the store. I thought it was strange." She moved a little closer to the door.

"You thought it was strange, did you?" Lyle grimaced. "What, do you think the whole world revolves around you? A thousand people in the mall, and just because two people happen to be in the same store, you think I was following you?"

His words made Didi shudder. *What do you think, the universe revolves around you?* was what her husband Rich had said to her yesterday when they had fought.

"No, I don't think so," she answered, thinking she had been right, right, right. And she was right now. The whole world did revolve around her. Certainly the world in the last few hours. "You just looked suspicious to me."

"Suspicious, did I? Why?" Lyle was kneading the wheel with tense hands, his teeth gnashing against each other.

"Because you were wearing a jacket, that's why," said Didi, moving farther away from him, her dress wrapped around her wounded fingers.

"So what's so suspicious about that?"

"Nothing normally," replied Didi. "Except it's the middle of July and it's a hundred and five degrees outside. No one wears a jacket. It's like seeing someone in a tank top in the middle of winter. It looks out of place. Peculiar." Now she knew why he needed to wear the jacket, of course. Without the jacket, there would be nowhere to stash the gun.

Didi sneaked a peek at Lyle's face. His expression didn't read anger at her anymore. It read anger at himself for slipping up, for not thinking of everything.

"Just a mistake on my part," he said slowly, not looking at Didi.

Didi thought, with other people a mistake, yes, an oversight. With you, Lyle, it's a character flaw.

He broke out of his short reverie. "Okay, get out of the car," he said. Instantly Didi thought maybe he would let her out and drive off himself.

She was obviously suffering from heat exhaustion, because Lyle said only, "We can't travel in this car anymore. It's too dangerous."

Maybe the police are on to him, maybe Rich is looking for me.

"So about this little detour. Don't worry. We're still on schedule. I know this area like the back of my hand. We just have to be a bit more careful. No more getting out to get drinks. Okay, go on now, and I'll take your bags."

Didi got out and then looked back inside, feeling a tiny measure of happiness at seeing her blood all over the seat. She was almost happy he had cut her. Someone—maybe Smokey, maybe prospective buyers—would see the blood.

"I traded my car for a truck," he said, smiling crookedly at her. "Got some cash for your ring. Good thing, too. Otherwise we'd be taking the bus."

What could be better, she thought bitterly, slamming the car door.

As Lyle came around, Didi asked, "Where's the other car?"

"Out back." He looked her over. "Listen, it's too hot for you to walk. Get back in, will you? I'll drive us to the truck."

Didi hoped the truck would at least smell better than the station wagon.

It didn't.

It smelled different, but not better. It smelled of old sweat and sausage. Or old socks and tortilla chips. She didn't want to examine the smell too closely. Lyle now owned an old blue Toyota two-seater pickup, with a little bit of space behind the seats for her shopping bags. The backyard of the pawnshop was densely covered with trees; it looked like an overgrown forest. Trees provided shade, and in the shade it was a bit cooler. Didi lingered near the open door of the Toyota, gulping the hot air. Her thirst went unabated. "Lyle," she said. "You didn't by any chance get anything for us to drink?"

"I did," he said. "At the gas station. But I told you Johnny was not a nice man and I had to leave the drinks with him."

Didi looked around for a water hose. She saw Lyle was doing that too, but probably for a different reason. Most likely he wanted to hose down the bloody station wagon. They were both disappointed.

When they got inside the truck, Didi asked, "Don't you have to switch the plates or something?"

Pursing his lips together, Lyle said, "Tell you what. Try not to worry about my end of this, all right?"

"Fine," said Didi. "Doesn't matter to me." But it did matter to her, quite a bit. If he didn't switch the plates, then how could the police trace them?

They got back on the road. She rolled her window down two inches, for a little fresh air. The truck, unlike the station wagon, did have air-conditioning.

However, it was broken.

Cheap piece of junk, thought Didi. "You didn't trade *way up* with this one, did you? Hope you didn't spend too much."

"No, not too much." Lyle smiled. "I'll be ditching this soon anyway. This is just to get us where we need to get to."

And where's that? Didi wanted to ask him, but she didn't want that nonsensical response coming at her again.

"How much did you pawn my ring for?" she asked Lyle.

"Well, Arizona, nowhere near what you said it was worth. But I didn't pawn it. I sold it. I won't be coming back for it, and I knew that. He gave me a little more for a straight sale. A few thou to keep us honest. So we're flush. We can go anywhere. Where would you like to go?"

"Home," Didi said instantly. "To my husband and kids."

"Oh, that's nice. Wish I could go home, too."

"Why can't you?"

"Oh, you know. Not everybody's home is nice, pretty Didi."

"Your home wasn't nice?" she asked, trying to stir him into a conversation.

"Not particularly," he said, falling silent.

"Is your wife at home now, Lyle?"

Lyle didn't answer her. He seemed to have drifted to a place where she couldn't reach him.

Didi fell silent herself. There was no sound in the truck except for her heavy breathing. Who needs Lamaze, she thought. I'm doing well without the lessons.

Didi had no idea where they were. They were on a two-lane local road. She looked for a route number, then lost interest, perking up when she saw a sign for Route 84. She was somewhere on the Texas map. Didi asked to turn on the radio, and Lyle grunted in reply. Didi saw he was sweating profusely. All his power was in that blue nylon jacket. Without that jacket Samson would be cooler but powerless.

Yeah, jacket or no jacket, he's still stronger than you. So protect the Belly and pray to God to give you some strength real soon, pretty Didi.

They listened to country music.

Didi stopped thinking about her kids and about Rich and about being in a truck with Lyle. She was so thirsty.

All she could think about was ice-cold water. Or warm water. Water out of a revolting bathroom. Water out of the toilet bowl. Water in a dirty pond. Rainwater. Ocean water. She wiped off her sweat and licked her hands again. She knew it would make her feel worse in five minutes but she couldn't help herself—her thirst was the fourth live presence in the Toyota.

At six, the news came on, and the first thing out of the announcer's mouth was, "The FBI has stepped up the search for a man whose name they now know is Lyle Luft and his hostage, thirty-two-year-old Desdemona or Didi Wood—"

Lyle slammed down the power button on the radio and they rode in silence.

Didi tightened all her muscles so as not to show him her excitement—but . . . they knew about him! Lyle Luft. And they knew her—Desdemona. They knew. It's only a matter of time now, she thought. They would find her. The cell phone at the pawnshop, the phone call she'd made to 911. The bloodstained car. She lifted up her throbbing fingers to her mouth and kissed them. They would find them. They *had* to find them before Lyle drove over the border on his way to—she recalled the name.

Mazatlán.

## 6 : 1 1  P. M.

**S**cott received a call from a trooper who had stopped a tan Ford Taurus station wagon with Lyle Luft's license plates in Willow Grove, ten miles northwest of Waco. Only Lyle Luft and Didi weren't in the car; a black couple in their fifties were. They said they had bought the car at Smokey's pawnshop near a small town called Valley Mills, about five miles farther west.

When Rich heard that, he said, "Doesn't sound like Luft is headed to Mexico. Mexico is *south*."

Scott said, "For all we know he went off course to trade cars. Why don't we go and talk to Mr. Smokey?"

They planned to fly, but the chopper wasn't back from refueling, so they drove from Waco in a siren-blaring police car. By 6:33 they were at Smokey's.

Mr. Smokey was closing up. He was a brown-haired burly man of about fifty, and his name wasn't Mr. Smokey, but Charlie Rello. He said he'd thought Smokey's would be a good name for the store.

Charlie told Scott and Rich that around five-thirty a young man had stepped into his shop with several items he wanted to sell. One of them, Charlie said, was his car. Another was a cellular phone, and another was an engagement ring.

"Did you buy the cellular phone?" asked Scott.

"I took it from him. Didn't give him nothing for it."

"Didn't key the numbers into the computer either, to see if it was stolen," Scott said. "As required by law."

"I was gonna do that now," hastened Charlie, flushing.

"Of course you were," Scott said.

"Engagement ring?" Rich asked. "Can I see it?"

"Sure," said Charlie, glad to be changing the subject. "It's a beaut."

It certainly was. Didi's ring was the nicest ring Rich had been able to find. "That's hers," he said weakly, taking out his American Express card.

Charlie laughed. "Was hers. It's mine now, pal."

"Don't you pal him, sir," Scott said. "His wife has been kidnapped by the man who gave you the phone and that ring. I am now going to confiscate both items as exhibits one and two in the U.S. government's case against Lyle Luft."

"You can't confiscate that ring!" Charlie Rello cried plaintively. "Where's your search warrant?"

Scott flipped open his cellular phone. "Do you have a fax machine? I will fax the warrant here in two minutes. I'm warning you, though, with a warrant, I will take a lot more than just that ring. And there will be a nice federal investigation into the legitimacy of your business, I can assure you."

Cursing under his breath, Charlie Rello motioned to Scott to put down his phone. "Come on, man, you can't take that ring. I just paid ten grand for it."

Scott laughed. "Now, I know you didn't buy that ring for ten grand."

"For that ring? Are you kidding me? Look what a beaut it is. He wanted fifteen for it. Said that's what he paid."

"Bullshit. I don't think you ever in your life had a ten-thousand-dollar transaction go through your doors." Scott smirked. "Certainly not out your pocket and into his. Sorry, Charlie, the ring is ours."

Rich intervened. "I will be glad to give you what you paid for it."

"Ten thousand dollars," said Charlie.

Rich took out his checkbook. Scott covered it with his hand.

"The man has offered you something for the ring. You will either give it to him for the pennies you paid for it, or you will give it to him for nothing. What will it be? A search warrant or a sale, Charlie?"

Gritting his teeth, Charlie Rello muttered, "Fifteen hundred." Rich wrote out a check; Charlie reluctantly took it. Rich stretched out his hand for the ring. Scott moved Rich's hand away, shaking his head, no. "Give it here," he said to Charlie.

"Can I have it?" said Rich sharply.

"No," said Scott, asking Charlie for a tissue.

"What?"

"A tissue? A Kleenex?"

Charlie brought out a roll of paper towels from the back. Scott ripped one off and wrapped the ring securely in it. Then he gave it to Rich to hold.

Then Scott gingerly picked up the phone and wrapped it in a paper towel also.

"About the phone," Charlie said nervously. "I didn't really want it. I was just holding it here for him."

"Why were you holding the phone for him?" Scott asked, glaring suspiciously at Charlie. "Did he say he was coming back?"

"No, no, nothing like that. He didn't say," Charlie quickly replied.

He told Scott and Rich that when he tested the phone to see if it worked and pushed the redial button, 911 had come up. He asked the guy if everything was all right, and the young man shrugged and said yes, though they had just seen an accident on the highway and called to report it. That sounded good to Charlie, who now looked embarrassed. He added that the phone's battery had been nearly dead, so he hadn't been able to check out anything else.

"Did the guy say where he was going?" Scott asked.

"He said out west with his wife. He needed a better car, so I sold him the Toyota truck. It really wasn't much better, but it was all I had, and he didn't seem to know the difference."

"You sold his car pretty quickly."

"Yeah, I called a customer right away." Charlie smiled. "They'd been waiting on a station wagon awhile."

Charlie said when he went out to inspect the trade-in, the guy's pregnant wife had been standing near the car. When the guy saw her standing by the door, he ran to her and helped her back in. The young woman watched Charlie very carefully as he went around the station wagon. He had felt a little insulted, Charlie said, because she was acting as if he were going to steal the car with her in it.

"How did she look?" Rich asked as calmly as his breaking voice would allow.

"Pretty good. Long brown hair. You know, like a nice wife. Her dress was dirty, though," he said. "Or I thought it was dirty. It didn't look clean. I thought—a pregnant woman should take care of herself better."

Rich nodded heavily.

"You didn't ask why they wanted to trade the car?" asked Rich.

Scott placed a calming hand on Rich's back and shook his head.

Charlie said, laughing, "What, are you kidding me? If I was to ask every person who comes in here why they want to sell this or that, I'd have been out of business ten years ago." He laughed again. "And this guy actually looked better than most of my customers. He had a cute wife. I don't ask questions."

Scott said, "Okay, thanks. So that's everything?"

Rich noticed that Charlie cast Scott a furtive look, but said, yes, that's everything.

"What else?" said Rich.

"That's all."

"That's all," said Scott, pulling Rich's arm.

"No, there's something else," Rich insisted. "What else?"

"There's nothing else," said Charlie quickly, and this time Scott noticed it too, because he came back to the counter and said to Charlie, "I don't have a lot of time. He's close, and we have to find him. What else?"

"Nothing that's gonna help you find him," said Charlie.

"Tell us anyway," said Scott.

"I had to wipe down the inside of his station wagon before I sold it."

"Why?"

Charlie became lost for words.

"Why?" said Scott, much louder.

Charlie jumped. "Don't yell, man," he said quietly, leaning over to Scott. "I just don't want to upset him, you know?" He pointed at Rich.

"Upset me?" repeated Rich. "You're too late. I'm already there."

Charlie said, "The passenger seat of the car had blood on it. Not a lot of blood, but blood, smeared, like, all over the seat."

Rich wanted to break something.

"Also, he was supposed to switch the plates. He told me he was going to do it. But he didn't, the jerk. If it's helpful I can give you the plate number of the truck."

Scott took the number, and they left the shop. In the car Scott immediately called in an APB on a blue 1984 Toyota pickup. "Armed and dangerous," he repeated. "Approach with extreme caution."

Rich asked Scott, "What did you need the phone for? It's just a cell phone."

"Oh, I know. It's all evidence against him. Fingerprints. Skin particles. If we should go to trial and all."

Rich thought about it. "What do you need the damn phone for as evidence? You'll have my wife to say she was abducted by him."

Scott didn't reply and didn't look at Rich, who felt increasingly uneasy about Scott.

On the way back to Waco, when Scott wasn't looking, Rich opened up the paper towel and fingered Didi's ring. He brought it to his mouth and kissed it—the band, the diamond, and the inside where her skin had touched it.

# 6 : 3 0   P. M.

**A**re you hungry?" Lyle asked Didi.

"No," she replied in a whisper. "I'm thirsty." She tried to keep her eyes closed, not wanting to look out of the window. The prairie swimming by her eyes was making her dizzy. She remembered that Irene had to be given Dramamine whenever the family went on long trips. She thought, if I die, I hope Rich buries me close to where we live so that Reenie won't get nauseated every time they go to visit me. Otherwise, she'd associate throwing up with coming to see me and then ask not to go. It made Didi unspeakably sad to think that her precious baby girl wouldn't come to the cemetery to visit her. Comfort, comfort, she prayed. Please, Lord, let me think of something.

There was little to comfort her. At home it would have been dinnertime, and Didi wondered if the girls had had their dinner, whether Amanda had let Rich make her the steak, whether they were giving Rich any trouble or were playing nicely. Tonight was big bath night.

What was Rich going to do without Didi? He'd probably have to give them a fast bath, but then their hair wouldn't get washed—

Rich, what is he thinking now? What *could* he be thinking?

And now what? What's he doing now? He must be going crazy. He probably hasn't eaten since lunch.

Didi remembered lunch. Oh, no. There was no food at lunch. Unless he just went in and ordered himself a sandwich while waiting. But he wouldn't do that.

Poor Richie. Hungry, all alone with the girls. My parents are in Europe, his mother can't be much help. What's he thinking?

Didi prayed for Rich, prayed for Manda and Reenie, prayed for God to give them a little bit of comfort.

The sun was in front of them, so they couldn't be going south toward Mexico anymore. They were traveling west. What was west of Waco? Didi couldn't think. El Paso? Big Bend? A long way away. New Mexico? Arizona? California? Where are we going? she said again, but to herself, thinking about her babies, her hand on the Belly.

Closing her eyes, seeing Rich on the road, seeing Rich mow the lawn and afterward run through the sprinkler with naked Amanda. Mandabanda, he was screaming, and she was screaming back, Daddy-baddy. It wasn't Rich Didi had been thinking of, and it wasn't Amanda. It was the sprinkler. Didi had put on her bathing suit and joined them and the sprinkler wet her skin in the sun and it felt so—so—wet.

She licked her lips.

No solace in prayer. No solace in thought. A month ago, in June, Leslie, her oldest friend, had given birth by cesarean section, and when they were sewing her up, they must have nicked her colon, because she got a massive infection and nearly died. She was still in the hospital for the July Fourth weekend and couldn't come to Rich and Didi's bash. Didi had sent Leslie flowers and homemade chocolate-covered strawberries, and had prayed for her, hoping she would soon see her baby son, who was at home without his mother.

And then just yesterday—really yesterday? Yes, yesterday—Didi had called another girlfriend, Joan, who had been expecting a baby around the same time as Didi, and found out from Joan's husband that the baby had been stillborn.

Didi couldn't imagine anything worse. Joan was forty-three and pregnant for the first time. When Didi hung up, she cried for an hour. Even her girls couldn't cheer her up.

It was about Joan and Leslie that Didi had had her fight with Rich. It wasn't their fault. It was Didi's fault. Well, actually, it was Rich's fault for not being more sympathetic about her fears, because Didi had been right.

It was nobody's fault, but Didi had been right.

She opened her eyes, blinked, tried to concentrate on the road. She fixed her gaze straight ahead. The sun was in her eyes, and all she saw was white spots. She closed her eyes again and licked her lips. The lips stayed dry. The white spots wouldn't go away. She felt the Belly tightening, hurting. She tried to forget about where she was. She tried to think of Florida and her parents' winter home in St. Pete. She thought of the Gulf of Mexico and her own swimming pool. Water. She thought of Disney World, but again, the water parks. She thought of vacations they had had. The Hamptons—water. Canada—many lakes in Quebec. Hawaii—such a beautiful blue Pacific. Cancún—such a beautiful blue Atlantic. St. Croix—the dazzling Caribbean. The white spots in her eyes turned to blue water. She dived into them, headfirst, and didn't come up for air, dived and felt the water on her face. Water, water, water.

*Yesterday, when Rich came home he had been upset because there was no dinner. But Didi was so miserable about her friend she couldn't cook. They had Oodles of Noodles and Kraft macaroni and cheese, and Cokes. The girls loved it. Rich grumbled. After they put the kids to bed, the fight started.*

*Didi told him about Joan, and Rich said he felt badly for her. But he was not getting it, wasn't getting the strident tone in Didi's voice.*

*"Rich," Didi said, pacing around their bedroom, her hands on her heart. "Listen to how scared I am."*

*"Scared of what?"*

*"That something horrible is going to happen to me."*

*"Why would something horrible happen to you, Didi?"*

*"I mean, something either to me or the baby."*

*He got mad then. "Why would something happen to the baby? I don't even like you saying that out loud."*

*Didi tried to explain. "Leslie is still in the hospital. She hasn't seen her son, and she is so sick that it's taking her forever to get better. I mean, how often do you think these things happen? A raging infection the doctors can't cure?"*

*"It happens, Didi, it happens," Rich said impatiently. "But what does it have to do with you?"*

*"Wait, listen. And now this thing with Joan. Have you ever heard of anything more awful?"*

*"No," Rich said. "I haven't."*

*"That's right. It's the worst thing in the world. I mean, just imagine if something awful like that happened to us."*

*"I don't want you talking like that, Didi," Rich shouted.*

*"No, but listen, omigod, this is exactly what I mean," she said tearfully. "Do you remember last year, when I had all those car accidents? I plowed into a Nissan's rear end, not a mile from our house? It was fate. I stop at that light a thousand times a year, but that one time I couldn't stop. I mean, just fate. And then the next day, I'm driving the rental car through the parking lot of the supermarket and bam, I get too close to the illegally parked truck and swipe its bumper right off. I mean, yes, he was parked in a fire lane facing the wrong way, and yes, it was night and hard to see and the road was narrow, but we rent a car all the time when we go to Florida and that never happens."*

*Rolling his eyes, Rich said, "That's what I love about you, Didi—you chalk off your auto—how shall I say?—mishaps to fate."*

*She narrowed her eyes at him. "As opposed to what?"*

*"Nothing, nothing," he said quickly. "What are you getting at?"*

*"Richie, you know how bad things come in threes."*

*"Who told you that?"*

*"Everybody knows that. All sorts of things come in threes. Like death around Christmastime. Have you noticed that it's always not one celebrity but three that die right around Christmastime? Remember how a few years ago Jill Ireland died, and then Sammy Davis, Jr., and then Jim Henson? That's the kind of thing I meant."*

*"Didi, this is crazy. What the hell are you talking about?"*

*He went into the bathroom. She followed him. He said, "Look, this is silly. I don't want to talk about this anymore. Besides, with the car, it was only two bad things."*

*"Wrong!" she exclaimed. "I was so paranoid, I was looking for that third thing, and do you remember what happened?"*

*"No," he said tiredly, putting toothpaste on his brush and running it under the water. "What happened?"*

*"I pulled away from our house, and when I made a right at the light, my door swung open, and I almost fell out."*

*He brushed his teeth, and she stood behind him listening to him gargle and rinse. Then he turned the water off and dried his face. "Didi, Didi, Didi. Where are you going with this?"*

*"Maybe I'm the third link in a chain of bad things that are going to happen in the universe at this time, and I'm next. Something bad is going to happen to me or the baby."*

*"Oh my God." Rich laughed. "Didi, so what are you saying, that something terrible is going to happen to the baby because you crashed the family car last year? Our insurance went up three times, isn't that punishment enough?"*

*"Be serious—"*

"*I am serious,*" Rich interrupted her. "*Listen to me,*" he said, taking her by the shoulders and kissing her nose. "*Listen. It makes me mad just to hear you talk like this. So your friends had some bad experiences. I'm sorry for that. But why do you think the cosmic universe is going to finish off with you? Maybe Leslie was the second link in the chain and Joan the third. I mean, what do you think, the universe revolves around you?*"

"*Yes,*" she said. "*My universe does. They're my friends and something terrible happened to them and now something terrible is going to happen to me.*"

"*Yes, but this baby is mine, too. So how are your friends connected to me? Why does their bad karma have to all of a sudden end in a third anything with me? Can't you see it's silly? It has nothing to do with you. Your life and mine, it goes on. Their bad thing didn't happen to you, Didi. It happened to them. It really doesn't affect us.*"

"*That's not true,*" she said.

"*Of course you feel bad—*"

"*I feel terrible—*"

"*Of course you do. But this is not karma, this is not a circle of horror. Their cosmic karma has nothing to do with ours. I've been a decent man, and God is not going to end the circle of badness with me.*"

Didi said, "*It's just the way the universe moves. In threes.*"

"*Oh, for God's sake!*" he exclaimed, walking away from her into the bedroom. She followed him, her belly heaving. "*Didi, listen, nothing bad is going to happen to you or the baby. Trust me on this. Besides, I know two guys at work who just had babies and their babies are fine and healthy and their wives are too. So I think I'm third in that chain of good things.*"

Didi didn't say anything for a while. Then she said, "*Just like you to think the universe revolves around you.*"

*She felt better.*

Didi thought of the water that had run between Rich's fingers as he washed his face and gargled. That sweet softened purified water. If only she could have some water now, she would feel better about everything.

Not only did bad things happen in threes, Didi thought, but they actually gathered momentum. With the cars it was different. The karmic momentum was strongest with the first crash, lost some power with the bumper swipe, and was nearly extinguished with the freely swinging car door. Here, the karma made Leslie very sick, killed Joan's baby, and was still swirling in fury around her, darkening her universe.

Didi opened her eyes and gasped. She saw a police car, parked on her side of the road.

Oh, God! Please, please, please. She peeked at the speedometer. Damn. They were moving slow and steady at sixty on a two-lane highway. She wouldn't dare turn around. She counted. Twenty seconds passed. *That it may please You, we beseech You to hear us, good Lord,* prayed Didi.

She glanced at Lyle, who was lost in country music. He wasn't looking in the rearview mirror.

And then Didi heard the wail of a police siren.

Lyle was not slowing down. When Didi looked over at him, he was still staring straight at the road. She wanted him to stop for the cop.

"Lyle?" she said gently. "Lyle?"

He came out of it then. His head shuddered slightly, and he blinked. "What is it?"

"The police, Lyle," Didi said. "They're behind you."

He stared at her for a moment with a mixture of fear and anger.

"What did you do?" he cried.

Hoping sweet relief wasn't showing on her face, she said, "Nothing, Lyle. I was sitting here, thinking. Just like you."

"You weren't thinking, you were praying," he spat. "And I wasn't thinking, my bologna. I was driving." The menacing expression left his face and he looked less anxious. Slowing the car down, Lyle said, "Let's see what the nice police officer wants." Didi saw him stick his hand in his pocket, pull out his gun, and release the safety lever. He gently put the gun between his legs and covered it with his thighs. Then he pulled over, put the gearshift into park, and waited.

Didi waited too. The sun blazed into her eyes. They were parked on the side of an empty road near a burnt-out fallow field. Didi's heart was pounding. She started to pant and placed her hands on her belly.

"Stop panting," he said, without looking at her.

"Sorry," she said, and closed her mouth. "Can't breathe."

"I don't give a shit," he said. "Don't breathe, for all I care. Just stop panting."

Didi tried. She held her breath. A few moments later she released it in a mad exhalation.

The patrol car was behind them, and without turning around, Didi knew from being stopped for speeding that the cop was calling in the license plate number on his radio, to see who owned the truck. Her heart sank a little lower in her chest when she remembered that the Taurus plates were still on the Taurus. These plates were registered to Smokey. Didi didn't want to think about it. Yes, Lyle should have followed the law. He shouldn't have broken it.

They sat and waited. Finally Lyle rolled down the window. Didi sucked her breath in and then let it out again in a great whoosh. She felt as if she had been running and couldn't get her breath back. Baby, baby, baby, she thought.

The police officer came up to the truck.

"Hello, officer," Lyle said politely. "What seems to be the problem? Was I going too fast?"

The officer peered into the truck, not looking at Lyle at all, staring right at Didi. "Is everything all right, ma'am?" he asked in a concerned voice. "Your hand is bleeding."

She panted twice before she answered. "Oh, this, it's nothing. I accidentally cut myself. I'm fine, thanks."

The officer looked over at Lyle. "May I see your license and registration, sir?" He was a very young patrolman. Didi noticed he looked as if he had barely started shaving. She saw a wedding band on his left hand as he leaned toward the window.

"Sure, of course," said Lyle.

Didi looked intensely at the officer. She wanted to mouth "Help me" to him, but then thought that if things didn't go right, and the cop asked her to repeat herself in front of Lyle, all would be lost, and the young man would lose his life and she hers too. She sat and stared.

Lyle was fumbling with his license, stuck in his back pants pocket. "Here it is," he said finally, laughing lightly. "Knew I had it somewhere."

"And the registration and proof of insurance, sir," the police officer said patiently.

"Ah, yes, the registration. Well, you know, I just bought this truck, and haven't had a chance to get it registered yet."

"Is this vehicle insured?" said the police officer.

"Yes, yes, it is."

Didi knew that driving without insurance was a big no-no in Texas. But oddly, the officer couldn't have known anything about the vehicle when he pulled Lyle over. He didn't know it wasn't insured. "It's insured through my previous vehicle for thirty days, isn't that right?" Lyle said, grimacing. Didi didn't see his face, but she saw his hand on his thigh.

Lyle turned to Didi, his gaze boring into her. "Darling, could you look in the glove compartment for the insurance card, please?"

Didi leaned over.

The policeman waited.

She opened the latch and looked in. There was nothing in there.

"Nothing here," she said.

"Oh," he said. "Must be in one of my pockets. Let me take another look."

The policeman waited.

"Can't seem to find it, officer," Lyle said easily, shrugging his shoulders. "Thought it was right in my back pocket."

"Could you have left it in your other car, honey?" said Didi. "The one we traded for this one?"

Lyle slowly turned and looked at her. She gazed back at him innocently, panting and holding on to the Belly.

"I think that's what I probably did," he said to the officer. "I guess you'll just have to write me up. Sorry about that."

The officer moved away from the door and said, "Could you please step out of the vehicle, sir?"

Didi saw the back of Lyle's head and his hand on his lap. "Why?" he said sharply. "I mean, is everything all right, officer?"

"Everything is fine, sir. Could you please step out of the vehicle?"

"Step out of the vehicle," Lyle repeated. "Yes, yes, sure. Of course." He placed his left hand on the door handle and Didi heard it click open. "Right away, officer."

And with his right hand, he raised his gun to the open window and shot the policeman in the face.

It seemed to Didi that the policeman flew back several feet before he landed heavily on the highway.

She screamed. She saw his legs convulsing, and she couldn't help herself. She screamed again.

Lyle, without even turning to her, said, "Shut up!" and hit her in the face with the butt of his gun. Her brow split open.

Didi didn't faint; she felt as if she were standing under a red waterfall. Then she couldn't see; she thought she was going blind. She forgot about the police officer.

She heard Lyle shout, "Shut up!" She didn't think she was saying anything, but she closed her blood-filled mouth.

Didi spit the blood out onto her dress. She wiped her face. No use. The blood was pouring out of her brow.

Didi felt Lyle stick something into her face. "Here, wipe yourself with this," Didi heard Lyle say. "Get yourself together. I'm going to need your help."

Didi knew her help was needed. The cop was lying on the road. One passing car, and he'd be cut in two. The driver would turn around and call 911, and the cops would be all over them in five minutes. Lyle needed a head start. He couldn't leave the cop on the road, Didi knew that. This wasn't in his plans, and it would slow him down.

Whatever Didi could do to slow him down, she would do.

As she wiped herself with the rag he'd given her, she was thinking despondently, *there's nowhere to go from here. He shot a cop. He kidnapped me and shot a cop, there is nowhere for him to go, no one will let him go with a warning anymore. No one will let him go now to save me. They'll want his blood here in Texas and they won't rest till they have it.*

Belatedly Didi realized the rag had been used by the Toyota's past owner to wipe oil off the dipstick. She squinted with her one good eye to see if there was a clean portion of the cloth. There wasn't. It smelled foul. Pressing the towel against her brow, she wished she were lying unconscious.

Then Didi felt her baby move. Amazed and heartened, she tried to pull herself together.

"What can I do?" she said.

Pulling the keys out of the ignition, he said, "Clean yourself up. We'll be going in a little while."

"Okay," she said.

"You and your whining. Now look what you've done to yourself."

"I'm sorry," Didi said automatically, realizing not only didn't she mean it, but as she was saying *I'm sorry,* she was thinking *fuck you.* Didi was a religious person, and yet here she was, cursing at a sinner. Fuck you, she repeated to herself, and oddly felt better.

Lyle got out of the truck, quickly walked to the police officer, and dragged him by his feet down the embankment in front of the Toyota. A car whizzed by as soon as he was finished. Then Lyle left the officer and walked to the patrol car. Through the rearview mirror Didi watched him as he turned off the police lights. For a second, she was filled with insane hope that maybe he would drive off and leave her here, God, please—

Lyle ran back to the dead officer and began dragging the body into the field. Didi watched him, wondering if he had left the keys in the police car and if she could run fast enough to drive away before he came back.

She thought, what do I have to lose, and then the baby kicked again and she placed her hand on the Belly and sat still in the car.

If Lyle could shoot a police officer, he could shoot me. It's the death penalty for killing a police officer once they catch him. *If* they catch him.

The police officer had been detrimental to Lyle's plan, and that's why he had died. But Didi was instrumental to Lyle's plan, she began to realize. That would explain his resistance to killing and abandoning her.

She held no illusions. She knew he could always kill her, disappear into Big Bend for two months, and then get himself another woman at another mall.

She sat and waited, watching Lyle drag the man's body farther into the field of high grass. He must have found a drainage pit, because Didi couldn't see the police officer anymore, just Lyle.

She said a prayer for the officer's soul. *Almighty God, look on this Your servant, and comfort him with the promise of life everlasting, Amen.* But Didi said it as rote, as she sometimes said prayers while thinking of other things. And that's how she felt now. She was praying for him, but thinking of other things.

He needs a minister to ease him into eternity, and all he's got is me. And I'm no good.

As the day wore on and became evening, and she faced the prospect of darkness with Lyle, Didi felt less concerned for other people. Less concerned for her two baby girls. Less concerned for her husband. He was not trying to keep a baby alive, himself alive. He was not thirsty.

I was at the NorthPark Mall on the wrong day at the wrong time. That was the reason the officer was dead, and probably Johnny too. Because she had gone to the NorthPark Mall. Who will be next? she thought. What innocent person will die next because of me?

Lyle returned wearing the dead man's uniform. Didi felt briefly but sharply sick. He took clothes off a dead man's back, she thought with revulsion.

"Okay, get your bags out of the truck and let's go." The clothes were too wide for Lyle and too long, but he had cuffed the pants and adjusted the holster. The uniform was covered with dust and dirt from the road and dry grass from the field. When Lyle turned to the window, Didi noticed that the back of the dark blue shirt was moist with blood. Some of it had smeared off on Lyle's neck. He took *bloody* clothes off a dead man's back. Didi wondered if Lyle had gone mad.

She said, "We're changing cars again?"

"Yes, we're changing cars again," he said. "We need to be safe."

**149**

Didi slowly got out of the truck. "I can't get my stuff," she said to him. "I can't reach it. Forget it. Leave it."

"Oh, no, no, pretty Didi," said Lyle, pushing her out of the way. She stumbled on the embankment and fell sideways. The rag fell out of her hands. She quietly groaned and pressed her hand to her eye. The gash oozed more blood.

While Lyle pulled out the bags, Didi struggled to her feet. When he turned to look at her, he smiled and said, "It's a good thing you're not a hemophiliac."

Yeah, it's a good thing for you I'm not Schwarzenegger, she thought as she trailed behind him to the police car. Because you'd be dead, motherfucker.

She couldn't see out of her right eye. She felt caked, sticky blood all over her face.

They got into the car. Didi was glad she had followed her instincts and hadn't run when Lyle was "burying" the police officer. Lyle pulled the keys out of his pocket. Didi knew he was too smart to leave keys lying around.

Though he was dumb enough to try to sell the cell phone. Dumb enough to wear a jacket in July. Dumb enough to wear an ill-fitting uniform with blood on it. Who'd ever mistake him for a cop?

In the middle of the dashboard was the police radio. Didi stared at it longingly, and he must have seen her, because before she could speak, he grabbed the radio and ripped it out, leaving the wires dangling. Then he threw it in the back seat.

"Nice job," he said to her. "Thanks for reminding me."

They pulled out onto the highway and quietly and steadily gained speed on US 84. Empty US 84 must have seemed too busy to Lyle, because soon they got off and drove north on a country road. The road was quiet and the fields were flat. Opening her mouth, Didi breathed the air in the car. Belatedly she noticed the air was cool. There was air-conditioning. No matter—she was burning up. She wiped a little condensation off one of the vents and put the fingers into her mouth. Was that better? With her heart numb, she prayed for the dead police officer, lying in the field, shot in the face while his wife maybe cooked chili at home and waited for him. *Depart, O Christian soul, out of this world, and may your rest be this day in peace, and your dwelling place in the Paradise of God. Amen.*

Lyle hit ninety miles an hour.

# 7 : 0 0  P. M.

**A**t the Waco police station, Rich and Scott sat across from each other at the sheriff's desk. Scott asked Rich if he wanted something to eat, but Rich wasn't hungry.

The radio had another Didi bulletin on the local station. Scott immediately got on the phone with Raul, and they spent a few minutes congratulating each other on the success and good positioning of the bulletins. "Keep the pressure on," Scott said, before hanging up.

"Scott," Rich said when the FBI man had finished talking with the agent-in-charge, "isn't it a bit premature to pat ourselves on the back? I mean, we haven't found them."

"I know. But we will. I told you. I have a great record in this."

"In what, Scott?"

"In this. In catching the perp. The perpetrator," Scott added, as Rich stared at him in confusion.

Rich felt the warm sting of anger rushing through him. "We haven't caught him, Scott."

There was a knock on the door. Scott went to answer it, and as he passed Rich, he patted him and said, "Don't worry. Leave it to me. I'll take care of everything." Rich moved away from Scott's hand, and watched silently as Scott brought in a sandwich from Arby's.

Rich needed to call home and talk to his girls again. It was getting late, but he had no news. Lyle Luft hadn't called. He had nothing to tell his mother. What could he say? All he'd learned since his last phone call was that Lyle Luft was a murderer as well as a kidnapper. Was that going to comfort his mother? Was that going to comfort his girls? Poor Manda. She probably had had to eat a sandwich, the only thing her grandmother could make with some success. Hope Mom helped her with her homework. Ah, heck, thought Rich. She can stay home tomorrow. If this doesn't warrant being absent from school, what does?

Then Rich wondered what they were going to do at home. Sit, wait for the phone to ring while I don't call, while I have nothing to tell them? I'm probably going to have to come home without Didi, and then I'm going to have to tell my daughters something.

What am I going to tell them? What *can* I tell them? What will they understand? What won't make them crazy?

What won't make *me* crazy?

All Rich wanted was to hear Didi's voice tell him she was all right and the baby was all right. Then he could call home and not lie to his girls. He could say that Mommy was all right. He'd have other problems, of course, like where to get the ransom money. But he'd get it. He'd go to the owner of his company and ask him to put up the money and then drastically reduce his salary until the debt was paid.

The bastard wasn't calling. He had kidnapped Didi, killed a man, sold his car and Didi's ring, and then disappeared, and was on the road somewhere, running away from Rich, while Rich sat restfully in a chair. Rich wasn't doing much chasing. The only thing that connected Rich Wood to Lyle Luft and to his wife was the nervous-sounding bulletins, coming every fifteen minutes, alerting the state of Texas that Rich's wife was missing and that the man who had abducted her was armed and dangerous.

Something besides the obvious was bothering Rich, something closer to anger instead of pain, and the anger wasn't at his wife or her kidnapper. It was at someone else, and as Rich sat there and watched Scott wolf down a roast beef sandwich, that something bothered him until he couldn't keep quiet any longer.

He stood up. "Scott, I want you to call Raul and tell him to ask the stations to stop broadcasting reports of Didi's kidnapping," he said at last.

His mouth full, Scott said, "Why?"

"Because it's going to lead to no good," said Rich.

"Trust me." Scott smiled and continued to chew. "This is the way we do things. And we're going to catch the bastard."

"See," Rich said, coming to the table, "I think that that's my problem with you, Scott. Not that you're not a professional. But what the *hell* are you talking about?" Rich felt as if he had a fever. His whole body was shivering. "Scott, I don't give a shit if you catch the bastard. Trust *me* when I tell you this. I couldn't care less about anything else in the whole world. The only thing I care about is that I get my wife and baby back alive. And I think your pursuing the 'bastard,' as you call him, doesn't account for that. I think, and I may be wrong, but I think that you personally don't give a shit whether you get my wife back to me, all you care about is whether or not you catch the bastard. So I'm telling you, I want you to call Raul right now and tell him to stop with the stupid bulletins. Luft could panic and harm her. It's the only thing you should care about, Scott. Not eating your fucking sandwich, though I'm sure you're hungry, and not catching the 'bastard,' though that would be nice for you. But getting a pregnant woman out alive. Do you understand what I'm saying to you?"

Scott temporarily stopped eating, and then resumed again. "I see you're upset. We'll talk again when you've calmed down—"

"No," said Rich, raising his voice. "We'll talk now."

"Rich, I don't want to talk to you when you're like this—"

"Like what?" Rich screamed. "Like what? Crazed, you mean? Insane? Livid? Scared shitless? Like what, Scott? Tell me how you would like me to be. Like you?"

Scott stood up. "The Outreach program and the radio stations are our friends, not our enemies, okay? Lyle Luft is our enemy. I know it's him you're angry at—"

"You're wrong! Right now I'm angry at you! Don't you get what I'm telling you? Don't you see that if he hears the police reports coming at him, he's going to panic? He's going to feel there's no way out."

"No," said Scott. "He's going to turn off the radio. Then he's going to get scared, and that's okay. They usually get scared. Then they make a mistake. He's got to get gas on the way. He'll go inside the store, your wife will need to use the bathroom, he'll get hungry. All we need is one phone call from a passerby, and we're on him."

Rich began to speak, but Scott cut him off. "Look, look, like I said, I know you're upset, man, and I appreciate that—"

"Get the hell away from me, you appreciate that!"

"Wait a minute! You need to understand that we have a way of working, a standard procedure, and that's what we're going to do here."

"Oh, this is standard procedure for you, is it?" Rich exploded. "Well, you know what? Not for me. And tell me, if this is just standard procedure for you, how come he hasn't called, huh? How come the kidnapper hasn't called and told us what he wants? Is that standard too?"

"It's a little deviant," Scott admitted. "But this is what we do for a kidnapping. And we're usually successful."

"Usually successful, huh? You told me how many kidnappers you catch, but you didn't tell me how many hostages you get out alive."

Scott was momentarily silent. Then he said, "What do you mean?"

"What do I mean?" Rich said. "Which part didn't you understand? You told me you catch nine out of ten kidnappers. How many hostages do you get back alive, going by your standard procedure?"

Scott replied, "I don't know the answer to that question. There are many different types of kidnappings."

Suspicious, alarmed, and frightened, Rich walked around the desk where Scott stood and said quickly, "Scott, stop bullshitting me, man. Tell me how many."

"I don't know. For something like this—"

"How many?" Rich yelled.

"Oh, for fuck's sake! Twenty percent, all right?" He let out a deep pained breath.

Horrified, Rich said, "Twenty percent? You lose—twenty percent?"

"No," Scott said, looking down at his half-eaten sandwich. He picked it up and threw it in the trash. "We get back twenty percent."

Rich staggered back. "You—you lose *eighty* percent?" he whispered.

Scott said nothing.

Rich began to shake. Clenching his fists, he struck out, hitting Scott on the side of the face. "You bastard!" he screamed. "*You* are the bastard, not him! How could you not have told me this?"

Scott reeled from the punch but didn't fall. He went for Rich, grabbed him by the shoulders, and pushed him hard away. "What the hell are you doing?" But his expression read what Rich felt: shame, guilt, fear. Scott was helpless and he knew it.

"Scott!" Rich cried. "Scott, you're telling me that if you follow procedure, four out of five victims *die*? Oh my God! I want you to call Raul right now, right now! And stop those reports. Do you hear me? Do you understand me? Because if anything you've done results in the death of my wife, I'll kill you myself."

Rubbing his jaw, Scott pushed past Rich to walk to the door, but stopped and said huskily, "No hard feelings. I know you're torn up inside."

"You don't know," said Rich fiercely, shoving Scott away. "You have no idea. And it's all right because I have hard feelings for the both of us."

When Scott was near the door, he turned to Rich and said, "I'm going to go talk to our favorite sheriff. I think it's too late to call off the radio reports. They've been broadcasting it for over two hours. All the radio and TV stations know. They already have the news. They're going to keep broadcasting until Lyle Luft is apprehended."

Rich was silent, trying to get his breath back.

"And if you felt this strongly about it, why didn't you say something before?" Scott asked. "Why didn't you tell us at four-thirty when there was something we could still do about it?"

"Scott, let me ask you," Rich said, his voice trembling. "How many kidnapping cases is this for you? Is this your first?"

"No," Scott said indignantly. "I've had thirteen other kidnapping cases in my career."

"You can't win this one, Scott," Rich said. "So don't let your pride ruffle your feathers. Well, this is *my* first kidnapping case ever. I hope it'll be my last. This is not a job for me, this is not a day at work. That's why I didn't think of it at four-thirty," Rich said, slamming the desk with his first. He realized he hadn't unclenched them since he punched Scott and now fought to regain control of his hands. The fists clenched involuntarily.

"All right, man," Scott said quietly.

Rich said loudly, "I didn't think of it, but *you* should have thought of it. You are supposed to be great at this."

"I am good at this."

"I think you have your goals messed up. My goals are clear. If I get out of this halfway sane, I'll read up every book ever published on kidnapping so I can do better next time."

"There will be no next time, Rich," Scott said. "This only happens once in a lifetime."

**157**

Rich went on, "I'm sure in one of your stupid FBI books it says somewhere that the most important thing is to try to get the hostage out alive. I mean, you must have had some training in Quantico other than climbing trees, or whatever the fuck else you guys do. I don't know how you're going to do that by threatening the kidnapper. He's going to feel trapped, he's going to feel caged. And when he feels he's come to a dead end, he is going to kill my wife and my baby and then kill himself."

Tears were rolling down Rich's cheeks, but he didn't care. "And then you're going to go home and go to sleep."

Scott sat in front of Rich on the edge of the desk and spoke without looking at him. "I'm sorry. We're rated on our apprehension record. Just like the DAs are judged by their conviction records. Sometimes I can lose sight of my main objective—"

"How can you?" Rich said weakly. "When you know the odds?"

"If anything I've done results in harm to your wife, I'll quit my job." Scott extended his hand. Rich felt Scott's emotional handshake.

"Don't quit," said Rich. "Get her back."

Scott left the room. When he came back, he sat down, saying nothing. They waited.

At seven-thirty, the phone rang. Scott listened for a couple of seconds and then dropped the phone and jumped up. "Come on, let's go," he said urgently. "They found Smokey's truck."

The helicopter was screaming white noise from its rotor. Rich wanted to get in, but Scott told him to wait.

In the parking lot, he took off his shirt and tie and stood barechested while he rummaged around in his bag. The tie was scooped up in the tornado of rotor wind and blown away.

Rich barely saved Scott's shirt. Scott screamed something. Rich didn't hear and leaned closer.

Scott pulled a black shirt out of his bag and put that on. Rich noted that Scott was powerfully built; it was probably a good thing that Rich hadn't angered him with his punch. Rich felt better about Scott, because he knew Scott understood. They were in it together now.

Passing a black vest to Rich, Scott yelled, "Here, put that on."

"What is it?" Rich said.

"It's a safety vest! Put it on!"

"What about you?"

"I have another one!" Scott pulled out a bigger black vest, this one with a groin protector.

Rich yelled, "Hey—"

"Hey, beggars can't be choosers! Put on what I give you and don't put your groin in the line of fire!"

Scott pulled off his dress slacks and put on a pair of black pants. He put the safety vest over the shirt and pants. Over the vest he put another piece of equipment—a black mesh load-bearing vest.

In a minute, they were in the air.

Rich asked about the vest. "What's in here?"

"What isn't in here is more the question. Lessee, I've got bandannas for my head, two pairs of handcuffs, a steel baton, extra clips for the Colt and the Glock and the H&K, a light mount for the H&K, and a couple of hand grenades."

"Ahh," said Rich. "No actual gun, though."

"That's where you're wrong." Scott reached behind his seat and retrieved a weapon from one of the black bags. Rich thought it looked light and unimpressive, but it was a 10mm Glock 17. Scott said it was one of the most powerful automatic pistols available, standard issue for the FBI.

"What's the seventeen stand for?" Rich asked.

"Seventeen percent plastic."

"It's a plastic gun?" Rich said incredulously. "Are the bullets plastic, too?"

"Don't worry," said Scott. "All the parts that matter are metal."

God, it was hot. He noticed that Scott was sweating profusely. Scott pulled out a black bandanna and wiped his forehead with it before tying it over his hair.

"It's all right," Scott said. "It's air-conditioned in here. If I can't handle a little heat, I don't deserve to be in the FBI."

"So, do you think they're in the truck?" Rich asked. He was afraid of the answer.

"No. The report said an empty truck. I think he switched cars again."

"What cars? Where would he get another car?"

"I don't know. Someone ran out of gas, or had a flat tire. He could have pulled someone over, killed them for their car. We'll see when we get there. I just better have some support."

Rich felt sick from the tension. They had found the truck. They hadn't said his wife was in it. Was that good? Or was it very bad?

"So tell me," he said to Scott, speaking hoarsely. His voice felt weak after yelling under the helicopter. "Tell me why you had to change your pants too? Why couldn't you just put the safety vest and the other one on over your regular clothes?"

"Couple of reasons," said Scott. "One—if I get shot, I don't want you to get light-headed seeing me bleed to death in my starched white shirt."

Rich was going to tell him not to worry, but decided it sounded too flip. "And another reason," Scott continued, "is that this material, called BDU, is fire-repellent."

"Are we expecting a fire?" Rich said.

"You know what my motto is?" Scott said. "It's the Boy Scout motto. 'Be prepared.' " He paused. "In any case, this is our uniform for all contingencies, not just Lyle Luft."

Rich was thinking. He wanted to listen to Scott, he wanted Scott to keep talking. Something about being armed, ready, dressed, nearly comforted Rich.

"Sorry about earlier," Rich said.

"It's all right," Scott replied. "I'm pretty good-natured. Otherwise, you'd have a serious rap sheet for your behavior. What was it?—threatening to kill a federal officer, assault with intent to do grievous bodily harm—"

"Not grievous," said Rich lightly.

"I'd better not give you a gun. You're a little trigger-happy today."

"About the gun," Rich said. "If this Glock you have is standard-issue, why didn't you carry it in Dallas? How come it was in your bag in the trunk of the car?"

Scott shrugged. "I prefer the more traditional approach to firearms. I say if you shoot well, you don't have to shoot so frequently. So I carry a Colt forty-five."

"Ahh. Is that the gun you guys carried till this ten-millimeter Glock came along?"

"No, just till the nine-millimeter Glock came along. That was a good gun. But the Bureau says it doesn't do enough damage."

Rich found that ironic. "What? The holes aren't big enough?"

"Exactly right," deadpanned Scott.


In a few minutes they were east of Goldthwaite on US 84, near Center City, not a city, really, just a burp on the map. Scott had asked the local police to close off the road a mile west and a mile east of the Toyota truck. The helicopter landed on the highway next to a patrol car with two officers in it.

"Jesus! Where are my men?" Scott was yelling from the chopper door. "I called fifteen minutes ago. Where are they?"

One of the police officers shrugged. "They're probably on their way. In the meantime, we'll help."

Scott motioned for the pilot to kill the engine.

When he could talk normally, Scott looked the police officer over and asked, "Are you wearing a vest?"

The officer shook his head.

"Is your partner wearing a vest?"

Again no.

"So what are you going to do?" Scott yelled. "Stop the bullets with your chest? Rich, give me your vest."

Handing it to one of the officers, Scott said, "You can fight about who gets it later. Now I want you to come with me." The officers seemed to have barely heard him.

Rich found himself unable to get out of the helicopter. "Come on!" Scott yelled. Rich shook his head and withdrew from Scott's hand. He waited in the helicopter. He didn't want to look inside the truck that was parked at an angle off the road. He was too afraid of what he might find in there. He turned away and faced the other direction.

Scott came back.

"Come on!" he yelled again. "They're not there."

Rich got out and ran toward the truck.

"Stop!" Scott said. "There's blood on the road."

The policemen looked closer. "Not blood," one of them said. Rich saw stains that a number of cars had passed through near the white line of the shoulder. "Not blood, sir. Just a stain."

"Just a stain?" Scott asked. "No, not a stain. Blood." The two officers looked closer. One of them shook his head.

Scott said, "See, let me explain. We have a dangerous criminal on the road. He has already killed an old man in cold blood. The truck he was driving is right here." He pointed. "When I see something that looks like blood in these circumstances, I let my good sense tell me it's blood. After all, this is not a spill in the middle of my kitchen."

In the meantime, Rich went over to the truck.

Scott looked along the road. "Not only is it blood," he said, "but look, there's a whole trail of it disappearing into the field. Why don't you two go—no, wait," he said, staring off into the distance.

Rich looked up from the windows of the truck. "What is it?"

"Better not go there," Scott said. "There aren't enough of us. God, where are my men? What if he's in the fields with your wife?"

Rich paled. "That's not my wife's blood on the road," he said.

"How do you know?" asked Scott.

Rich had no answer, but he said no. *No.* His Didi hadn't died in Center City in the field, on a road. She wasn't roadkill, she hadn't been dragged into the field. Not his wife.

"Let's go," Rich said. "Let's go right now. I'm not waiting another minute. He could be there with her."

Shaking his head, Scott said, "Hold on, hold on. I'm going to radio in for help. I don't care if I get sent a whole bunch of incompetents. We need help. His truck is here but he's not. Where is he? He's probably running with her into those woods at the end over there. That's where he is. That's where I'd go—to the woods. Away from this open space."

Rich felt his legs buckling, but he straightened out and said, "I'm not waiting. Now, are you coming with me?"

Scott held him back by grabbing his shoulder. "It'll be all right, Rich. Please. Let me do my job," he said gently. "Stay here."

"No," Rich said, twisting out from Scott's arm. He jumped down the embankment and ran along the trail of blood.

Scott ran after him, calling the police officers to come. "Wait!" Scott yelled after Rich. "Wait, goddammit! What are you, crazy?"

Rich didn't answer. He wasn't listening anymore. He heard Scott running after him. The two policemen followed. The four raced by the side of the trampled grass.

Rich followed the path through the grass, and then suddenly he stopped and groaned. He thought he felt shock, but it wasn't shock. It was relief. The half-naked body lying faceup in a ditch wasn't Didi. Rich asked God for forgiveness, but the feeling of relief did not leave him. Half of the man's head had been blasted by a gunshot wound, and glassy eyes stared blankly up at the cloudless summer sky. He was dead.

Coming up behind Rich, Scott looked down at the ground and said, "Bastard. Oh, goddamn bastard."

The other officers followed. One of them looked down at the dead policeman and cried out, "That's Ernie. God, that's Ernie."

The four stared vacantly into the ditch. Scott placed his hand on the patrolman's back. "I'm sorry, man. Let's go back and call EMS. He's dead, though. Wife?"

"Yes, Jesus, I went to their wedding a year ago. Ernie and Eileen were expecting a baby in a few months. What am I going to tell her?"

The policemen remained by the body of their fellow officer. Rich and Scott slowly walked back to the road.

"Why was he naked?" Rich asked quietly.

"Because the bastard took his clothes."

"You don't think he's around here?"

"Nah. Ernie's patrol car is gone. Luft switched cars again."

When they reached the highway, Scott went to the patrolmen's car to call headquarters. Meantime Rich opened the door of the Toyota. He was stunned by his weakness. He had to hold on to the truck. He had just felt a moment of relief and the hot air almost cooled him in his fear, but now as he opened the door and saw the inside of the truck, nausea overwhelmed him.

*The truck smelled of Didi.*

It smelled of other things too. It smelled of sweat and vomit and something even more acrid. It was filthy and oily. But through it all, Rich Wood smelled his wife. Her perfumed lotion smell redeemed the foulness in the Toyota.

There was blood on the passenger seat and the passenger door, and on the door handle. Rich touched it; the blood was not yet dry. It soiled his fingers. Recoiling, Rich stepped away from the car and saw the rag on the grass. He picked it up. It was still moist with blood. Is this my wife's? he thought. He pressed it to his face, rubbed his own face in it, this oily bloody rag, a rag with her life on it. "Didi," he whispered, trying not to scream, "where are you, where?"

The field was empty and burnt. The grass was short, the sagebrush silver-green and flowerless. Nothing moved in the heat and the sun except Rich's hands pressing the rag to his face and to his chest.

Scott came to the truck. "What is this?" he said, looking at the cloth and then at Rich's face. "What are you doing?"

Rich didn't answer him. "Where's my wife?" he whispered. "What am I going to tell my children if she dies, if he kills her? What?"

Gently, Scott pulled at Rich's arm. "Come on, man, we've got to go. We'll talk in the air."

Rich followed slowly. "Where are we going?"

"I don't know," said Scott. "West of here."

The pilot asked where to; Scott in turn asked him what the next big city west of here was.

The pilot told him it was either San Angelo or Abilene. Both were more than a hundred miles away.

"Okay," Scott said. "We're going to San Angelo."

Aloft, Scott said, "This is what happened. The cop must have pulled them over, and Luft shot him and dragged his body into the fields, changed into his uniform. Took his patrol car. He's now disguised and better armed."

Rich said nothing, still feeling thick guilt about feeling comfort at a man's death. He was anxious. What about the blood on the rag? Could it have been the dead cop's? But how could that be? Luft had probably shot him when he was standing near the driver's window, and Rich had found the rag on Didi's side of the car. The rag was Didi's. Still clutching it, Rich thought, that's an awful lot of blood. Did he shoot her? Is she having the baby? Both thoughts were terrible. He could find no comfort.

Scott was on the phone, barking orders, yelling at the Waco cops for not sending the SWAT team when he needed them. He was now calling the field office in Abilene—for there was none in San Angelo—and ordering as many SWAT men as possible to remain on standby. He also called Raul and asked him to send Dallas men to Abilene. Then he called San Angelo police headquarters. And Waco again, requisitioning all the available helicopters in the area to fly over every major road from Center City to El Paso looking for the missing patrol car.

Rich asked how the SWAT team were getting to San Angelo. Were they flying?

"Flying? No, only the President flies. They have their equipment in the trunk of their cars. Like I did. They're driving."

"Oh my God, driving!" Rich exclaimed. "Why don't they just take a bike or jog? They're never going to get there in time."

"Rich, they'll be in San Angelo in an hour."

Rich waited until Scott was finished, and then said, "Don't you guys have a jet or something?"

"Yeah, in Quantico. The hostage rescue team is there, and they're ready to help us instantly. But frankly ... if we can't do it with the three hundred or so SWAT guys we have here in Texas, then I just don't know. To apprehend one man ... I mean, really."

They flew in relative silence under the numbing din of the helicopter.

After ten minutes in the air, Rich said, "What are we going to do, Scott?"

Scott said nothing.

Rich's head fell back against the seat.

"We are so ignorant," he said. "We know nothing. If we knew more about him, we would know more about what he's planning, where he's going. It's getting dark soon. We'll never find them in the dark." He knew he sounded desperate. "If this man has a plan, he will have a whole night to execute it. If he has no plan, he will have nine hours of night to drive. Six hundred miles. He'll be in Arizona in that police car."

"No," Scott said. "Not in that police car. It's a patrol car. He won't get out of Texas in it. And if he does, he'll be easier to spot than a palm tree in Canada."

Rich fell silent. Scott opened his mouth to speak and then stopped. "What?" Rich said. "What is it?"

Scott was quiet.

"You don't think he's planning to leave the state?"

Slowly, Scott shook his head. "I don't think he's planning to leave the state in that car."

"Is that good or bad?" Rich turned to Scott and studied his face. He didn't like what he saw and turned away.

Scott didn't answer, and Rich didn't press further.

After another noisy ten minutes, Rich said, "We have to find out more about him. What do we know about this man? That he lived in Garland and at the time of the kidnapping was unemployed? That's not a hell of a lot. Where is he from? Has he been to prison—"

"We don't think so. He has no criminal record. There are no fingerprints in our archives. He has never filed his taxes."

"Never?" That was unbelievable to Rich.

"The IRS had no information on him. He was a transient worker, I think. Working for cash. Never filed a return."

"Maybe," said Rich, "he mistook my wife for someone else. Someone rich."

"Could be," said Scott tentatively. "But we know he's not acting like a man out for ransom. He's not in hiding. He's on the road as if he's on a mission. Think about it. If he wanted money, he could have stopped at any motel after he shot the gas station attendant. Called us from a pay phone, or from your cell phone. He wouldn't have tried to sell the phone. He would have used it to demand money."

"So if it's not money, what is it?" Rich asked. "We can try to give him anything he wants." His voice shattered against the noise of the helicopter.

Scott stared straight into the crimson sun. "I think," he said thoughtfully, "he already has what he wants."

**D**idi and Lyle rode silently in the police car. Didi's brow throbbed. She felt her face swelling. Pretty soon my eye will close up, she thought. The pain blurred her vision. The bleeding had stopped, but that hardly made her feel better. Earlier, when the gash had been pouring blood, it hadn't hurt. Now the blood clotted, and it felt as if a hundred needles were sending sharp electric currents into her eyebrow. She couldn't keep her eye open. Placing the palm of her right hand above the eye, she tried to relieve the pressure, but it was no use.

The shadows grew longer. The sun burned deeper crimson. After driving north, Lyle made a U-turn and headed south until he reached Highway 84 again. He made a right and stayed on it until the road seemingly ended in a T, but Lyle didn't go left or right but straight across onto a barely paved, unmarked farm road. Open, flat fields, deserted road. Didi had no idea where they were. She couldn't place where they were in the state of Texas. The ground was dirt, not sand, so they couldn't have been very far west. They were somewhere on the

Great Plains. The colors of Texas were sepia as the sun beat on the still countryside. Didi opened her mouth to catch some air, hoping for a water molecule to drift in and settle on her tongue.

They were still heading west. Once the sun was down, Didi knew she would have an even harder time figuring out her whereabouts. She didn't see any road signs.

The baby kicked.

I'm going to hell, she thought.

I was going to hell in a beat-up Ford station wagon. That was bad.

Then I was going to hell in a beat-up Toyota truck, and that was bad.

Now I'm speeding straight to hell in a brand-spanking-new police car. It doesn't really matter. Except this car has AC.

It's been a lifetime since I drank. That will be my hell—having a parched mouth for eternity. She touched her lips with the tips of the fingers of her right hand. Her mouth was swollen. Dried blood streaked her cracked lips. The corners and crevices were now raw wounds. She licked them, but she had no saliva left. She tried to swallow but swallowed nothing. If only she could ease the aching in her throat, the thirst aching, the fear aching, the end of life aching. Nothing.

At home it would have been almost time to start getting the girls ready for bed. She couldn't stop thinking of sitting in Reenie's big cream chair, reading her books, and at the end of every book, putting a cup of milk to her mouth and saying, "Milk?" and Irene saying, "No milk. No way. Not me."

Now Didi was saying, yes milk, yes way, yes me.

She glanced over at Lyle. He wasn't spacing out, his eyes weren't glazed over. He had a determined look on his face. Both hands gripped the wheel. In a loosely fitting police uniform, he had never looked more sinister.

I wonder what his hell will be. What for him represents horror? What represents pain?

What does he want from me? What can I give him? Maybe if I knew—then I'd be dead. And my baby dead, too.

Her left hand rubbed the tight belly. There were too many other pains all over her body for Didi to pay attention to minor cramping. But she noticed it now, and thought, my poor belly. It needs some water and a cool shower just like the rest of me.

"Where are we going, Lyle?"

"Let's not talk anymore," he said. "The talking part is over for now. I have to get to where we're going. I have to concentrate."

"Lyle," Didi said carefully. "We haven't eaten. Couldn't we stop for something?"

He laughed then. "You've got to be joking, missy," he said.

"Maybe a drink for me, Lyle? I haven't had anything all afternoon, and I'm so thirsty."

"You should have thought about that when you were playing all cutesy with the cop back there. 'Oh, officer,'" he said, mimicking Didi's high voice, " 'I just cut myself, it's nothing,' and 'oh, honey, maybe the insurance is in the car we traded.' Well, thanks to you, he's dead, and you're not getting your water."

She turned forward to face the road.

"We can't stop anywhere," Lyle said. "We could've before. But look at you. Look what you've made me do." He glanced at her face. "We can't stop. It's okay. We'll be there soon."

Didi fell quiet, shifting uncomfortably in her seat. "There? Wherever 'there' is, do you think there'll be a drink for me there?"

"I didn't think of a drink," he said gruffly. "I didn't think our trip would take so long. Things haven't gone as smooth as I hoped."

"Anything," she whispered. "A sip of anything."

"White lightning?" He smiled.

"Even that," she said.

"Come on," he said. "Be strong." He reached over and patted her belly. She didn't move a muscle. "You've got to be strong for the baby."

"You're right. Then help me. Get me some water. I'll feel so much better then."

"I have no water here, and we can't stop," he said sternly. "You'll just have to find strength from elsewhere."

"I have nowhere else."

"You're carrying a life. Seek strength from that."

Didi felt her uterus tighten in a way that was not just distracting or unpleasant, but alarming. She thought, what is this? And waited with gripped tense hands, waited out the seconds that it took the Belly to finish the contraction. It began quietly, just another Braxton Hicks, gripping the belly, except . . . at the crest of the wave, what gripped the belly wasn't a Braxton Hicks. It wasn't a tummy ache or gas but a cold talon of steel that wrung out her insides as though they were a wet towel, and then when it was done, it threw the insides on the floor in a heap, and waited.

"Is everything okay?" Lyle asked.

What a strange question, thought Didi, trying to get her breath back. Is everything okay in this perverse universe you've created for us, in the universe where a nice young cop is dead and I'm heading straight to hell? "Yeah," she said, gritting her teeth not to let a moan of pain escape. "Everything is fine."

And then she said, "My face is hurting."

"Well, whose fault is that, pretty Didi?" Lyle said.

"Mine, Lyle," said Didi. "Doesn't make it hurt any less."

He drove.

"So tell me about your wife."

Lyle paused. "Nothing to tell."

"Come on, something. Are we going to see her?"

"Maybe."

She lowered her head, then tried again. "What about your baby—"

"Okay, enough now, my bologna. We're through with talking for now."

She fell silent but couldn't bear sitting and waiting to see if she was going to get another contraction.

Didi spoke. "Lyle, do you want to know about me? I am the middle daughter of two teachers in an Episcopalian private school."

"And I'm the only son of a housewife and a railroad worker," said Lyle.

Didi continued, "My mother and father have been married for thirty-seven years."

"And mine have been married for nearly thirty." He paused. "Not happily."

"My father retired two years ago."

"My father is still working."

"What about you, Lyle?" she asked. "Do you have a job?"

Pursing his lips, he said, "I'm in between jobs right now."

"What were you doing before?"

"This and that. What were you doing before?"

Didi felt her spine tingle at his *before*.

She went on as if she didn't understand him. "Before I married Rich, I was his assistant. That's how I met him. I was twenty-two."

Lyle didn't respond.

Didi rubbed the Belly with a steady circular motion.

"How did you meet your wife?"

"I don't want to talk no more," he said grumpily. "Put on some music if you want to."

"I don't want music," she said, wishing the police radio weren't lying disemboweled in the back. He shouldn't have done it. Just as he shouldn't have tried to sell her cell phone.

Wherever they were going, they should have taken the bus, she whispered to herself, and then heard him say, "Bus would have been out of the question." Didi looked at him, startled. He smiled. "I can hear your soft thoughts, Didi."

"Can you hear my hard thoughts, Lyle?"

"You don't have any. I feel that. You're a good person. You tried to save me with your prayers. That was brave of you. I feel connected to you. I can feel your exhaustion, your pregnant belly, your thirst. I know what you think. I can feel what you feel."

Shaking her head slightly so as not to hurt it, Didi said, "I don't think so, Lyle. If you could feel what I feel, you wouldn't be doing this. We're here because you can't feel what I feel."

"Oh?" He laughed softly, his features rounding out with his smile. He almost looked like a normal human being to Didi. "Oh?" he repeated. "And what should I feel for? Shopping?"

"God," said Didi.

"Shopping," repeated Lyle.

"If you hate shopping so much, Lyle, then what were you doing at NorthPark?"

"Looking for you."

Didi's mind blanked. "No, really."

"Really." He glanced over at her. "Surprised, huh?"

"But you didn't know me," Didi said incredulously.

"I had a feeling about you. For you," said Lyle. "I had a feeling from when I first saw you—that you were going to mean something to my life."

Funny, she thought, trying to quiet her heart by tapping on her chest. I had the same feeling about you at the Freshëns stand. I didn't know why but I wanted to get as far away from you as possible. I called myself paranoid and went on. That's me, the paranoid, pregnant Didi.

She was staring at him.

Lyle's gaze dimmed. "Should have followed your feeling, Desdemona," he said to her.

"I tried, Lyle," she said. "God knows I tried."

They were silent. The countryside was flat, burnt, sad, thirsty.

Didi spoke. "Lyle, is it too late to ask you again to let me go? I swear, swear on my life—"

He interrupted. "Worth about six thousand dollars, right?"

"I swear on my children's lives—"

"Don't do that, don't swear on your children. It's sacrilegious."

Didi couldn't believe her ears. "Lyle, it's not sacrilegious. Your kidnapping me is sacrilegious. You must know that, don't you, that you're acting against God?"

"So?" he snapped. "I don't care about Him."

Shaking her head, Didi said, "Lyle, you have the potential to be good, to be very good. Cows are not much good or bad, or dogs or dolphins. No, just us, humans. An average man can be only so good and only so bad. A better man can be better, and worse. A man of genius the best yet, but the worst too."

"Well, I'm no genius, Didi."

"No," Didi said. "But you can be good, Lyle. Very good. Great, maybe. You have that ability inside yourself."

"And how do you know this?"

She chose her words carefully. "Because," she said, "I've seen you be very bad."

He didn't reply at first but then said, "I haven't been very bad, Desdemona. I've been expedient."

She shook her head. "No, Lyle. Without a doubt, you let evil enter your heart. You're a Christian man, I know you are. We can help each other—"

"Oh, I know it."

"You can still be saved, Lyle."

He laughed. "You're kidding me, right? You think any cop is gonna let me go now?"

She stared at him, amazed. "The cops? No, saved before God, Lyle. Before God."

**175**

He shook his lowered head. "You're not getting under my skin, Didi. You're not. I don't want be saved by Him. I hate Him. Plus He doesn't exist."

"That's a contradiction in terms," said Didi softly. "You cannot hate that which doesn't exist."

"Didi, as I told you before, you should worry less about saving me . . ." Lyle nearly smiled. ". . . and worry more about saving yourself."

"The two are synonymous," said Didi.

Shaking his head at her, Lyle said, "Forget it, Didi. I'm trying to build a new life here, and you're bothering me with bullshit."

She looked at him in wonderment. Her body stopped hurting for an instant, as her thoughts stood still trying to make sense of him. The mind couldn't do it, and the body began aching again. "Lyle, what are you talking about? You've kidnapped a woman, killed a police officer, probably killed that old man, Johnny. You're in Texas, Lyle. What do you think the punishment is for killing a police officer in Texas? What kind of life are you thinking of? Are you thinking of life on death row?"

"That's not much of a life," said Lyle, and Didi felt her low spirits sink beneath the earth.

"Is this—your first kidnapping?" she asked.

And he laughed. "Yes, Barcelona. This is my first kidnapping. Is this *your* first kidnapping?"

The Belly began to squeeze tight. Omigod, she gasped, closing her only open eye and holding her belly. Oh my God. *Hear my voice when I cry to You.*

Didi knew she didn't have much time.

........................................................................................
........................................................................................
........................................................................................

# 7 : 4 5   P. M.

........................................................................................
........................................................................................
........................................................................................

**W**hen they arrived in San Angelo, Scott said it was good that all the cities they were checking out were near each other, because otherwise the helicopter would be out of fuel. As it was, they had gone about as far as they could. "Choppers don't have very good range," he said.

Would it take them to El Paso? Rich wondered. To New Mexico? To Arizona? To Mexico? Would they follow Lyle Luft all the way to Mexico in their fuel-guzzling noisy bubble with skis for landing gear?

The San Angelo police precinct was tiny and ill-equipped, but the officers were friendlier than those in Waco. They tried to accommodate Scott in every way. The sheriff himself went out and brought Rich and Scott something to eat from his favorite Mexican place. Scott ate again.

Rich didn't touch his food.

Scott said, "I don't think he's leaving Texas, Rich." He paused to point toward the enchiladas. "Have something to eat. I feel he's close. There isn't a hell of a lot of Texas left."

"There's plenty left, like another three hundred miles to El Paso."

"Only a hundred and fifty miles to El Paso," said Scott. "The chopper makes you lose your sense of distance."

Rich knew it wasn't just the chopper that was making him lose all sense.

"Why do you think he's not leaving Texas?"

"Eat and I'll tell you."

"I can't," Rich said. "Do you think he's feeding my wife?"

"Probably. He doesn't want her to die. Rich, you're no good to your wife starving and thirsty."

"I'm no good to my wife anyway," Rich said. "What am I doing to help my wife?" He looked at Scott. "What are *you* doing to help my wife?"

Scott stopped eating. "What would you like me to do?"

"He's in a police car. Put out a bulletin saying you won't go after him if he releases her."

"Another bulletin? You think he'll buy it? He shot a cop. He knows we won't mean it. It's the oldest trick in the book."

"Only if you're really old. He's not a professional criminal. He's nuts. Maybe he's scared for his life. And a man who's threatened isn't going to be acting rationally."

"He hasn't been acting rationally from the get-go."

"No, that's not true," said Rich. "He's been acting according to his own logic. However skewed we might think it is, it's rational to him."

"That's the definition of crazy, Rich. When you're doing fucked-up things and thinking you're completely sane."

"Tell him that." Rich paused. "If he lets Didi go, tell him you won't pursue him. Tell him you have no jurisdiction over him if he goes into another state—"

"But that's a lie. That's when our jurisdiction begins."

"Who cares?" Rich snapped. "It's going to get dark soon. He's going to get away. We don't have a lot of time. Either we find him, or we—"

"He's not leaving the state," Scott said. "He's staying right here. There aren't too many cities around here. I'm sure that right now we're farther west than he is. Remember he's driving cautiously. And he's not leaving. He could live in El Paso. He could be from here. He could be from Abilene. No, our man Lyle is heading back home."

"Why do you think he's not heading out of state?"

His mouth full, Scott said, "Because his Social Security number is a Texas number."

"So? Mine is from Illinois. What does that prove?"

"That if you kidnapped someone without thought of ransom, that's where you'd be heading."

"Illinois is a big place."

"Yeah, it is." Scott continued to eat his rice and beans. "First place I'd look for you would be in Chicago. Then I'd try everywhere else. You'll forgive me, man, for being hungry, but I work better on a full stomach. Anyway, usually we're able to get a whole bunch of information about someone through our database. We have access to every record imaginable. The credit records usually tell us a lot."

"What does his tell you?"

"His is nonexistent. The only thing he's got in his name is the Honda. He paid cash for it, though, since there are no liens on the title. We still haven't figured out where he got the cash."

Rich shook his head. "How can that be? How can a twenty-seven-year-old man not have any credit records?"

"By not having any credit," Scott said. "I know, I know. It's rare." He smiled. "Imagine a world where we had no credit history."

"There is no such place," Rich said, his strained expression relaxing. Then he thought of something. "Ah . . . Scott, Scott. Wait. If you look up my credit file, there'll be a load of information on me. . . ."

"Yeah?"

"But I bet not so much on my wife. Bet you my wife will have little or no information on her. Most of our credit cards are in my name."

"What are you saying?"

"Maybe his credit was all in his wife's name."

"We spoke to his landlord in Garland. He was single."

"Yes, in Garland," Rich said excitedly. "But he's not headed to Garland, is he? He's headed somewhere west of Waco. Maybe wherever he's going he has a wife."

Scott pushed his food away and got up. "Maybe. But all we have is his last name. Luft. And it may not even be her last name. We don't have a first name for her, if *she* even exists. No date of birth. No Social Security number. What kind of records are we supposed to get?"

"You've got your crime directory, don't you? That famous FBI database?"

"You mean the NCIC, the National Crime Information Center," said Scott. "If the guy or his wife had stolen weapons, ever committed any kind of crime for which they needed to be fingerprinted, ever stolen a car, then yes. But Rich," Scott said, "Lyle Luft was not in the NCIC."

"Maybe his wife is."

"We don't know that he has a wife!" Scott sounded exasperated.

"Please check. I'm telling you. People have credit reports."

"Not if they live hand to mouth or never had a credit card or never borrowed money."

"Do you know any such people?"

"No," said Scott. "But there's obviously one, and he's the one who's got Didi."

Rich mumbled, "Shit."

Scott put his arm around him. "Let's go to the phones again. I'm going to call the Bureau in Abilene and El Paso and see if they have anything on a Lyle Luft—"

"Any Luft. We're looking for a phantom wife."

"Your wife is not a phantom, Rich," Scott said.

"Not mine," Rich said, shaking his head. "His."

Rich had avoided calling home since they were in Dallas. Now it was eight o'clock and he had to call his mother. With a heavy heart, he dialed the number.

"Mom?"

"Oh, God! Have you found her?"

"Mom, please don't sound so panicked in front of the kids! For God's sake!"

"They're in the bath. I put them in the bath together. Those two are a pair."

Didi's parents usually looked after Manda and Reenie. Rich's mom was too proper to get her hands dirty with the girls.

"They certainly are. Are they okay?"

"They're fine. Have you found her?"

"Not yet, Mom."

"Oh my God. What does he want? Money?"

"We don't know. We don't think so."

"Richard? Are the police helping you with this? Where are you calling from?"

"Yes, Mom," Rich said tiredly. "The police are doing all they can. Don't worry—"

"How can I not worry? What are you saying?"

"No, I know. Just please—hang tight. Don't forget, Reenie likes warm milk."

"Richard, where are you? You have to come home. Reenie told me she's not going to bed until her mommy reads her a book. She wants to read the big Peter Pan book. She's got it all picked out."

Scott had come back, and Rich lowered his voice and tried to sound as casual as possible, belying his anxiety and his great, ugly anger.

"Mom, you'll have to read her that book. I can't come home. I'm in San Angelo."

"Where is that?"

"Far."

"Is Didi there?"

"We don't know." Rich was exhausted. He couldn't blame his mother, but he was exhausted just the same. "Listen, just tell the girls that everything is going to be okay, and that we will be home soon."

"You will be?"

"I don't know."

"Richard, you have to call me more often. I haven't heard from you for hours, and I was just frantic."

"Yeah. Mom, there was nothing to tell you. There still isn't."

"So you should have called earlier then."

"Okay, yeah, look, I need to get off the phone. Kiss the kids for me. Tell them Daddy loves them."

"Reenie was hysterical for her mother," his mother said sharply and hung up.

For a few seconds, Rich couldn't look up at Scott. Then he placed the phone on the hook.

"It's tough, man," said Scott, sitting down behind the desk. "It's tough talking to family."

"No. It's tough talking to my mother," said Rich.

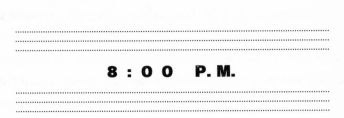

# 8 : 0 0   P. M.

**D**idi remembered when her two girls were born. Amanda had arrived five years ago, and the labor with her was harder. Didi didn't recall much of it except that it was painful as she drifted in and out of consciousness. Then the doctor said, a beautiful baby girl, and Rich cried, and Didi tried to cry but she was still drifting, and then she slept for what felt like weeks, and then she went home, and slept some more, and then all of a sudden Amanda was a month old and Didi was conscious again.

Irene's arrival three years ago was similar, except she was two weeks late and the birth had to be induced. The contractions got bad fast. Then Didi was given an epidural and stopped feeling. Someone shouted push, push, and then someone pressed down hard on her belly to get the baby out, and then the head was out and the nurse said, look, Didi look, at the head, there it is, touch the head, look at it, one more push and the baby is out. But Didi couldn't look or touch. When the baby was out, Rich cried, and Didi may have cried that time, too—and regretted she hadn't touched her baby's head. But the regrets came later. She couldn't have looked down for anything. She couldn't open her eyes.

When people asked her how her labors had been, she'd say she didn't remember. Or she'd say she was knocked out for most of it. How did your labor start, do you remember? Yes, Didi would reply. I was marinating a chicken with Amanda and watching a Queen concert on TV with Irene.

But what was she going to say about Adam or Evelyn? How did your labor start, Didi? Oh, I was sitting in a stolen police car next to a complete stranger. I couldn't see out of my right eye. I hadn't had a drink in eight hours. If only she could write that down somewhere. When she was younger and unmarried and childless, she used to write in her diary. About friends and adolescent longings and real and imagined slights. But then her easy life took hold of her, and she didn't have time to write.

She would have liked to have a piece of paper to write down her thoughts for today.

It would be a short diary entry. Dear diary, please let my baby get out of this alive. All I want is my baby's life.

Didi stared out the window with her one good eye, while Lyle continued down the narrow country road at seventy miles an hour. Didi felt every bump.

Where were they headed?

Her belly contracted again in a vise of pain. She tried not to breathe, nor pant, nor move a muscle. She closed her eyes and clasped her hands together for better control. Trying to remember a prayer for labor, she failed, and remembered only *I cry in the daytime, but You do not answer; by night as well, but I find no rest.*

This wasn't karma, thought Didi with palpable bitterness. This wasn't punishment. This wasn't cosmic revenge. This was—this was God forgetting about Didi's forty-three-year-old friend and letting her baby die. This was God slicing up Leslie's colon during a C-section. This was God on another highway, looking after someone else. Well, He can't be everywhere at once. And Rich couldn't be everywhere. Maybe there were children in Bosnia or Africa who needed Him more than Didi did. Otherwise, how could God let her go into labor now in the car with Lyle?

At that moment, Didi believed in Rich more than she believed in God, because she knew that Rich was searching for her. God, who could find her in a jiffy, was looking the other way.

Is this my punishment for shopping, for loving shopping? Well, you know what, Didi thought angrily, if I get out of this, then I'm going to shop more than ever, shop with a vengeance—but from catalogs.

Didi started to pray again, but she had another contraction and stopped. God wasn't on this farm road, He wasn't on his way to—

"Eden," said Lyle. "Fifteen miles." And he drove faster.

Eden? thought Didi. What did that mean? Soon she saw a green sign that said, EDEN, 11 MILES. And she thought, we're going to Eden?

"What's Eden?" she asked.

"Eden is where Mel lives," Lyle said.

"Oh," said Didi. "So we are going to visit your wife?"

"Yes," he said brusquely.

Keeping one hand on her pulsating eyebrow and one hand on the Belly, Didi fretted. Why would he want to bring me to visit his wife? Are they kinky or something? Didi had heard about people like that. A husband and wife would kidnap teenage girls, lure them into their house, have violent, abusive sex with them, and then kill them and cut them up into pieces. She had read about something like that not long ago. But it had happened in England, and Didi had thought, yeah, that kind of crazy thing happens in England, it's a foreign country.

It doesn't happen in God's country. In Texas. We're God-fearing people.

Her heavy heart was pounding hard inside her empty, thirsty chest.

A flame of sun singed the horizon to a crisp. They were still heading west to Eden.

Didi thought back to the last few hours with Lyle in his car. Could she have escaped? Could she have run? Run where? Onto the road, to get hit by an oncoming car, to get shot by him?

She put her hands on her belly. Her cut-up hands, brown with dried blood, and her brow weren't hurting anymore. Only her belly. And her heart.

Didi wasn't scared. She was sad.

Heartbroken to be abandoned by God in the thick of her life with a life inside her. She couldn't fathom dying, being nothing, but she could fathom being alone, and she thought, well, if I'm abandoned now, when I'm still living, who is going to watch over me when I die, and when my baby dies? Who's going to take care of Richie, of my little girls? If there is no God, then where do we go? Where are we headed?

And Lyle said, "After Eden—Mazatlán."

Didi felt such emptiness, such desolate melancholy inside her.

She must have been making wretched sounds, because Lyle looked over at her. "What's the matter?" he said.

She wiped her face, but it was no use.

"What have I ever done to you?" she whispered. "I've never done anything to you, I've never hurt you. I've never hurt anyone."

"That's funny, pretty Didi, because until today, neither had I," Lyle said, unmoved.

"Well, you've made up for it today, haven't you?" she said. "What's left for you to do?"

"Still plenty left," Lyle said.

Didi wished she hadn't asked.

He laughed.

Didi thought that if he didn't have the blood of two people on his hands and her and her baby's life in his hands, he'd almost have a nice laugh. He would almost seem like a nice man. Clean, quiet, well-behaved.

But he wasn't. And when Lyle laughed, Didi trembled.

"I know you're afraid for your life, Lyle, I know you are," she said. "Believe me, you still have the chance to undo what you've started here. Think about it. The police, my husband, they don't want you, Lyle. They just want me. Make a deal with them. Tell them you'll give them me, and they will let you go."

Lyle broke into a hearty laugh. "Desdemona, my optimistic girl, then what will I get in return?"

"Your earthly life," she stated flatly. She didn't want to mention his eternal soul.

"But I could have just as easily not taken you for a ride with me, if all I wanted was for the police to let me go."

"Things have gone wrong, Lyle. You didn't expect it—"

"Everything is still going to be just hunky-dory."

"No, they'll find you."

He appeared amused. "I'm starting to really enjoy your innocence. You're so naive, my bologna," he said, tapping the wheel lightheartedly with his fingers. "First of all, they'll never find us. You'll see. Second, you think your life is so important that the cops would forsake me to have you back? You're not the President of the United States, you know. You're only some pregnant woman who's not important to anybody but your husband, and you don't even know if you're important to him. Imagine that, Didi, imagine that he went home and is fuming now because you're still shopping away somewhere, blowing his hard-earned money on Estée Lauder. He's home watching reruns on TV, thinking, wait till she comes home." Lyle howled.

Didi didn't reply. Not because what he was saying made any sense, but because it was all she could do not to moan aloud with her contraction. Thirty, forty, fifty seconds passed, and her contraction passed, too. How many minutes had it been since the last one? Fifteen? Ten?

Less?

Didi wouldn't think about it. "Lyle, what are you talking about? If it wasn't for my husband, then why would I be on the news? On the radio? Why would anyone be looking for me at all, if it wasn't for him?"

Her Richard wouldn't abandon her. No. Rich wouldn't turn his back on his wife and watch reruns. The knowledge made her stronger.

"Lyle, they don't care about you, don't you see that? They care about me. They'd let you go to have me back."

Didi could barely make out his features in the twilight of the day, but she saw him stop tapping cheerfully on the wheel. "No," he said firmly. "They would certainly *say* they'd let me go to have you back. But we both know they wouldn't mean a word of it. As soon as you were in their hands, all bets would be off. No."

She knew he wasn't going to let her go. She wasn't going to ask him again. "Can you tell me, then, what your plans are?" she said. "For us?"

"You'll know soon enough."

They passed a sign that read PFLUGER PARK. It meant nothing to Didi, but she noted the oddity of the name.

"Be patient, Didi. Be patient. We're almost there." And then he added, "You shouldn't be in such a hurry."

Suddenly Didi was in the middle of another contraction, but still his words appalled her. "I'm not—in . . . a hurry," Didi breathed out.

Didi needed to get to a hospital in a hurry. She needed her Rich in a hurry. She needed to get away from Lyle in a hurry. But she wasn't in a hurry to get anywhere with Lyle.

They passed by a sign that read WELCOME TO EDEN. POP. 1597.

They continued straight ahead on the road at reduced speed, and then he made a right. Didi watched the road more carefully now. She wanted to remember the street address, but it didn't look as though

Lyle was going to a residential area. There were no houses nearby. Maybe Lyle and Mel were farmers.

Then they passed a sign that read EDEN CEMETERY, NEXT LEFT.

Didi thought nothing of it until they'd made the left.

Her fear was interrupted by another contraction. Then, quickly, fear gripped her insides again. It wasn't over in thirty seconds or even a minute. Fear came to stay.

"Oh, God, what are we doing here?" Didi said weakly.

"We're here to visit my wife," Lyle said. He stopped the car, left it running, and unclipped a pair of handcuffs from his policeman's belt.

"Your wife is dead?" Didi gasped. For some reason, this single, mystifying turn made her day seem surreal.

"Put your hands in them," he said.

Back to reality.

"Lyle, I'm harmless," Didi pleaded, not moving, not budging toward the metal cuffs that seemed to her to be the end of her life. "I'll walk with you. Where am I going to go? It's not like I'm going to run."

Somberly, Lyle reached over and grabbed her hands. "Don't get smart with me, Barcelona," he said, roughly clasping the steel rings around her wrists. Didi groaned. She was caught now. Caught with her hands chained.

As soon as Lyle turned to get out, Didi yanked her hands until the metal bands of the handcuffs dug painfully into her wrists. She didn't care. If she could have pulled her way out of the cuffs by dislocating her thumbs, she would have.

# 8 : 0 5 P. M.

Collapsed in a chair, Rich watched Scott move about the room, cell phone to his ear. After a while, Rich asked, "How many names does the NCIC contain?"

"Forty million," Scott replied.

"How many fingerprints on file do you guys have?"

"In the neighborhood of a hundred and seventy-three million."

Rich gaped. "You're telling me that out of forty million names and a hundred and seventy-three million prints, you can't locate a Luft?"

"We can locate a Luft all right," Scott said. "But no Lyle Luft. And no—"

Rich got up. "Scott, let me ask you—have you tried the phone book?"

"What? And sit down. You're making me nervous."

Rich didn't listen. "The phone book—have you tried it?"

"To find a . . . ?"

"A Luft. Hey, why not? You said you've tried everything else."

Scott shook his head, but called in the sheriff and asked for the phone book. In San Angelo there was no Lyle Luft, but there were two other Lufts. After five minutes of calls, Scott learned that no one had a relative named Lyle.

Rich must have looked dejected, because Scott said, "Don't look so sad, Rich. It wasn't a bad idea. You know, laypeople can have them too."

"What, good ideas?"

"Exactly right," said Scott, sitting at the edge of the desk.

Pacing, Rich waved Scott off and then stopped. "Wait. Did you get a search warrant for his room?"

Scott put a gentle hand on Rich's shoulder. The two men stared at each other for a moment, one softly, the other helplessly. Rich backed away.

"Rich, man. We did that three hours ago. We were still in Dallas. Remember, Lopez and Chief Murphy sent men there to see what they could find?"

"What did they find?" Rich said impatiently.

"Nothing. Nothing at all. He was renting a room from a woman in a two-story house. She said he was quiet as a clam, never had any guests, paid her fifty bucks a week in cash, had no lease, and was always on time with the rent. There was no kitchen in the apartment, just a fridge. The place was furnished, and nearly empty when the police checked it out. He had a couple of magazines. There was a second set of keys to his cars, an old beat-up suitcase with some clothes in it. A few towels."

"How did you find all this out?"

"What do you think I do when I'm on the phone? Talk to my mother?"

Rich was thoughtful. "Did they find the Honda?"

Scott shook his head.

Trying to shrug off the pressure in his head, Rich said, "So what do you think? Lyle will be where the Honda is?"

Scott nodded. "That's exactly what I think."

Rich still couldn't understand it all. "What kind of a man lives with absolutely no personal belongings?"

"The kind of man who's running from something, or to something, or has lost his reason to live," Scott said. "The kind of man who lived his entire life without a credit card, without filing a tax return—" Scott paused. "Hey, I just thought of something. I'm going to call Social Security on the West Coast. I'll find out if Lyle has ever paid his Social Security tax. Maybe there'll be a list of his employers."

Rich shrugged. "The IRS has no returns for him. Why would the SSA? Maybe he worked off the books all his life. Maybe he never worked at all. Listen, call. We have nothing to lose."

"It's all we have now," said Scott. "Otherwise, you think TRW or other credit-reporting bureaus are going to give us a list of all the women named Luft in the United States?"

"Only the ones in Texas," Rich said morosely, knowing it was a long shot, probably nearly futile.

Scott spent the next ten minutes on the phone, talking to one of the helicopters that was zigzagging across west Texas skies, trying to locate patrol car number 538. He also talked to the Social Security office and to TRW. He had connections. He could talk to the best, most competent people in every area, and he had the entire Texas branch of the FBI at his disposal.

The only problem was that Lyle Luft and Didi were in a police vehicle that had disappeared off the face of the earth, and the FBI had no idea of Luft's destination or even of his motives. After all these hours of searching, Rich didn't feel much closer to finding Didi. He felt he was in the middle of nowhere, and the sun was going down. Rich glanced at his watch. 8:15.

• • •

Scott threw the phone down and bolted up. "We got something."

Rich exclaimed, "You found the car?"

Shaking his head, Scott said, "No, but we're leaving. Come." He drank the rest of his Coke and threw the can in a wastebasket.

"Where are we going?"

"Abilene."

They ran out to the parking lot in the back of the station, where the helicopter was waiting, its blades bursting the air into tiny particles of dust.

"What's in Abilene?"

"Get in and I'll tell you."

When they were in the air, Rich said, "We have our best conversations cooped up in here, en route to nowhere."

Scott replied, "They're not that good, our conversations, Rich."

Rich agreed. "What's in Abilene?"

"Lyle Luft's past is in Abilene. There's a good chance Lyle's there too."

"How do you know?"

"Because the Social Security office told me that a Lyle Luft paid his Social Security tax out of eight different places in Abilene, Texas, from 1964 until now."

"1964?" Rich tried to do the math and failed. "Was our Lyle even born in 1964?"

"No. I think it's the dad."

Rich got excited; his hands became agitated. "Does Lyle Luft Senior have an address in Abilene?"

"Sure does. That's where we're going."

Rich thought. "The white pages could have told us all that."

Scott smiled ruefully. "You're right, Rich. But how long would it have taken us to look for a Lyle Luft through all the telephone records in Texas?"

Rich said, "About five minutes. To plow through the Texas area codes looking for a Lyle Luft."

He didn't mean it as a rebuke. It was coming back to the same thing—he was an amateur, he wasn't supposed to have any of the answers. And they were the FBI. They were supposed to find his wife. And then Rich remembered they were only supposed to catch Lyle. The wife was incidental. He briefly felt hostile toward Scott again, but Scott was his only ally.

"Scott? Tell me," Rich asked after staring out the glass of the helicopter. "How long you been doing this?"

"Twelve years," said Scott. "I joined right out of law school. The only job I ever had."

"Do you have a wife? Kids?"

"Got an ex-wife. One son." Scott was quiet. "They live in Oklahoma. I see my son once a month and during vacations sometimes. If I'm not working."

"The FBI is your life," Rich said.

Scott nodded. "The FBI is my life."

"Then how come you don't have any answers for me?"

"What answers do you want, Rich?"

"Tell me this is all going to turn out all right."

Scott was quiet. At last he said, "It will all turn out all right."

"You're lying." Rich fell back into his seat. His shoulder was pressed into Scott's. He couldn't look at him.

Dear God, Rich prayed. I promise I will never take Didi for granted again. I will never have her say to me, you don't touch my pregnant belly enough. If you get her out of this, I will never take my hands off her belly. I'll keep my hands on her and I'll caress her, and I'll feel my baby kick. I will kiss her breasts and kiss her belly, and press my ear against the navel to hear the baby, and she'll never have to ask me to do any of it. I think I have been a good husband, but she has been even a better wife to me, and I will never take her for granted again if only—

Rich turned east, away from Scott; he didn't want Scott to see his eyes.

Time was running out for Didi. The sun hovered above darkness.

"Scott," Rich said again, in a voice thick with heartbreak. "Tell me why a man would kidnap my wife."

Scott was silent.

"You must know all the types. We know he didn't kidnap her for money, right?"

"Right," said Scott. "Though he did hock her diamond ring."

"Yeah," Rich said. "But that would be too pathetic. He didn't kidnap my wife for fifteen hundred bucks."

"I agree." Scott paused. "That would be pathetic."

"We pretty well know he's not an international terrorist, and he didn't kidnap her to get Libyans out of Turkish jails, right?"

"Yes, we can eliminate that."

"We know he is not her ex-husband or an old boyfriend, so he didn't kidnap her because she was Didi."

"Yes, we can assume he is a total stranger."

"Well, what else is there?"

"About a dozen kidnappings a year are done by women wanting newborn infants. They dress as nurses, go into hospitals, take babies."

Rich felt keenly uncomfortable. "Yes. Well. We're not in a hospital, are we? What else is left?"

"Not much."

"What, though?"

Scott was quiet. "Come on, Rich," he said, staring into the clouds. "Nothing left, except he's a psycho and wants your wife for some crazy reason."

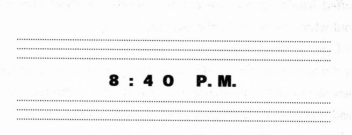

# 8 : 4 0  P. M.

**D**idi got out of the car as Lyle instructed her. Dusk had fallen, but she could clearly see a path and gravestones. Beyond them was a small forest. He had turned the car off but left the lights on, and they shone onto a gravelly walkway.

"Your wife is dead?" Didi breathed out. She was having another contraction and struggled to stand still on her buckling legs.

"You're so smart, pretty Didi. So smart," Lyle said, taking her arm. Reaching under her handcuffs, he rubbed her belly, and she involuntarily shuddered. Funny that she could stand still during labor pains, yet when Lyle touched her, she jumped. He repulsed her, and she sensed that he knew it.

Despite her cringing, he didn't release her arm. He pushed her forward through the grass and tombstones. The car lights shone at her back. He was walking too quickly, and she stumbled as he forced her onward.

They came to a small graveside. Lyle moved her out of the way of the car lights, and Didi read the inscription: MELANIE LUFT, WIFE OF LYLE, MOTHER OF LYLE, 1971–1998.

Right next to her plot was a smaller tombstone, a tiny one. It read, LYLE LUFT III, SON OF MELANIE AND LYLE, MAY 14, 1998–MAY 17, 1998.

Didi sucked in her breath. She wanted to double over. Clasping her handcuffed hands tighter, she numbly mouthed a short prayer for a little soul whose body lay in the ground.

Poor Lyle, thought Didi.

They did not speak. Didi suffered another pain that she bore silently, and then she kept her one good eye closed along with the bad one. Her head was bowed, and she heard Lyle sobbing next to her.

Lyle has grief. And he's not bearing his silently.

Or alone.

"I should tell you what happened."

"It's all right, Lyle," Didi whispered. "You don't have to say any-thing." Tears rolled down her face. The salt made her cheeks sting.

"No, I want to. Mel and I were expecting our first child this July," Lyle said. "But back in May something went wrong. I told her and told her not to smoke while she was pregnant, but she was so sure of herself. I told her to drink more milk, but she said, who needs dairy products? They're bad for you, spinach is much better, blah, blah. And she went into labor three months early. No one could figure out why." He sniffed loudly.

Didi wanted to wipe his face.

"After an emergency C-section, the baby hung on, but something went wrong with Mel. They couldn't stop the bleeding. She was just bleeding to death from the inside out, and all those great fucking doc-tors," he sniveled, "they could do nothing to help. Nothing. Imagine that. All those years in med school and nothing." He paused.

Her own heartache abating for a moment, Didi said, without looking at him, "I'm very sorry, Lyle—"

"She died."

That was too bad for Melanie, thought Didi.

And too bad for me.

Too bad for me that a woman I don't know died hundreds of miles away from me. She died, and somehow I am here staring at her grave.

"She bled to death," Lyle continued. "When they autopsied her, they discovered she had something called, I don't know what, postpartum hemophilia, or some shit. Apparently happened to only three people in the entire United States." He wailed.

Four, thought Didi. To *me*, too. *I* didn't smoke. *I* drank milk. And now it's happening to *me*, too.

Didi didn't have the courage to ask about the baby. She didn't have to.

His voice slipping into choking spasms of stuttering emotion, Lyle said, "The baby . . . he couldn't—couldn't . . . couldn't m—m—m—make it on his own."

"I'm really sorry, Lyle," was all Didi could whisper.

"He was t—t—too small . . . they said he was too little to survive . . . barely a pound. Eleven inches long. My little boy . . . not even a foot long."

"I'm sorry, Lyle," Didi repeated hoarsely.

He turned to her, his face a crushed contortion of pain. "I held him in my hands. I held my dead son in my hands before they took him away."

Softly, Didi said, "Most merciful God, whose wisdom is beyond our understanding, deal graciously with Lyle in his grief, surround him with Your love that he may not be overwhelmed by his loss—"

"Too late," interrupted Lyle.

Didi stopped praying.

"We buried him here," Lyle told her. "Then I moved to Dallas. I didn't know nobody in Dallas. I just wanted to disappear. To die."

Didi stood with a bowed head, wondering why he hadn't. She'd be home right now reading books with her kids, not standing here with him in a cemetery in Eden, Texas.

"But it's just not me," continued Lyle. "I'm not the suicidal type."

"No?" Didi said wistfully.

They stood side by side, both shackled: Didi by her metal restraints, Lyle by his grief.

Didi yanked on her handcuffs, and one hand almost went through. *Many young bulls encircle me; they open wide their jaws at me, like a ravening and a roaring lion. Packs of dogs close me in, circle around me; they pierce my hands and my feet; I can count all my bones.*

When didn't *almost* count? she thought. In land mines and pregnancies. Well, it didn't count here either. But she would get her hand out. She would get her hand out if it meant tearing the outer layer of skin right off. She would get her hand out.

And then?

Then she would run.

Okay.

She would run. Run back to the police car with no police radio, and then? Maybe then she could roll down the window and shout, "Come on, Lyle, let's go!"

Or maybe she could hit him over the head with her handcuffs.

But she didn't want to hurt him. He was already so broken.

I just want to break free. That's all I want. I want to get myself to a hospital—at the very least to a police station where a cop can deliver my baby. I have to get us out of the cemetery.

It was hard for Didi to stand, because her legs were folding under her in another contraction.

Yeah, run.

Do contractions stop for a running pregnant woman? Does the baby say, oh, wait, I'm not coming yet? My mother is running, and I can't possibly be coming now when she is running in a cemetery at night.

Didi thought, maybe Lyle could deliver her baby.

She wondered if she told him she was in labor, if he'd—maybe he'd take pity on her. Buoyed by her hope in human nature, Didi said cautiously, after the pain passed, "Lyle, I'm very sorry for your loss. Really. I'm very, very sorry. I feel awful for you." She meant it.

Then Lyle said, "Have I told you about Mazatlán, Didi? Mel and I drove there. We were headed for Acapulco and the car broke down."

Do I *need* to hear this? thought Didi.

"I want you to hear me out, Didi," he said. "It's important. Mel and I thought we had bad luck. But it wasn't bad luck. Because one day in Mazatlán made us forget the rest of our plans to go down to Acapulco, then cut across to Yucatán, see the pyramids. We didn't care about seeing anything anymore after spending a day in Mazatlán." His back was to Didi. He sank down to this knees. "We sat on a bench and ate fresh fish. We bought fruit from the stands and at night we had coffee and chicken mole and sopapillas."

Didi slowly backed away. Lyle seemed to be in a trance. If he continued talking, she could back up all the way to the car.

And then what? How would she get it started? Spit on the spark plugs and rub them between her hands? Or should she just cast a spell? If Didi could cast spells, it certainly wouldn't be to start some silly old car.

"The car got fixed the next day," Lyle continued, "but we never left. I don't think we even went to get the car from the shop until we were ready to leave for Texas." Lyle was talking to the gravestone, not to Didi, who took another couple of steps back. "I remember watching an old man make a straw hat. Out of straw."

Lyle laughed lightly and turned to Didi, who froze, looking at him with wide eyes. "Where are you going, Didi?"

"Nowhere, Lyle."

"No. That's right. Nowhere." He was facing her but not coming any closer. "You seem to be farther away from me than a few minutes ago. Or is that just my imagination?"

Didi took a couple of steps forward.

"What's the matter? You don't like my story?"

"I like it very much," she said. "Tell me, was it pretty, this Mazatlán?"

"Pretty? We were on our honeymoon. I thought my wife was pretty. I thought the sun was pretty and the ocean. I guess Mazatlán was pretty, too. And it's great for kids. It's got nice beaches. The water is warm. We saw lots of kids playing."

"It sounds nice," she said.

"Wouldn't you like to go see it?" he asked

She didn't know how to answer.

Yes?

No?

Among all the thoughts in her head, Mazatlán was negligible.

She didn't dare move, even though he turned his back to her to face Melanie's gravestone.

"I remember the first day I met Mel. She was at a bar in Abilene with some other guy. I thought she was hot, you know, so hot. She went home with me that night," Lyle said proudly. "The guy and I had a fight. Mel didn't want him anymore without his front teeth." He paused.

Didi hoped he wouldn't turn around to see her mortified face.

"Do you remember the first day you met your husband?" he asked.

"Ahh—yes" she stammered.

Didi thought, if I could have any day back I would have back the day I met my husband. He was my new boss, and he took me out to lunch. We were gone the whole afternoon and I knew then I would never go out with anyone else after that day. That's what I'd like to have back. The beginning of my life with him.

"The sand is cool at Mazatlán," Lyle said to the gravestone. "Right, Mel? So that the kiddies don't burn their feet. They run around barefoot. We were so happy at Mazatlán."

Didi waited.

*Oh my God.*

It had just occurred to her that perhaps this *was* what he wanted—to take her to Mazatlán with him. The thought pummeled her guts. Oh, Lord, help me. He'd take me with him forcibly? What is he thinking?

"All I want to do is be in Mazatlán forever," said Lyle mournfully. "Have it be forever sunset, and warm. I want to walk the streets in our T-shirts."

*Our* T-shirts? thought Didi.

"And shorts," Lyle continued. "Not own a car, but eat tortillas and drink margaritas outside, get drunk on tequila, and just walk and walk, and feel Mazatlán under our feet. I'm stuck there. I want it back."

I want my life back, thought Didi. The one I had before I met you.

"Things are different now," he said.

Didi nodded, but he didn't turn around.

"They'll never be the same," Lyle said.

She agreed.

"Death can do that to you," Lyle said. "Crash through your life and spill your guts on the floor."

Didi said quietly, "Bend down, pick up those guts, put them back inside, stitch yourself up, and keep going."

"Easy for you to say, pretty Didi. You've lived a charmed life."

He's crazy, isn't he? That's what's wrong, and I can't right that. Anything can happen.

And it already had. In the middle of a perfectly nice day, she was abducted. Hours later, upon hearing about Mazatlán, she was *just* realizing he was crazy? Maybe I'm not too swift, Didi thought.

Lyle shook his head. "I'm not crazy, Didi. Even if I do sound it. I'm only crazy with grief."

"Of course, Lyle," she said hastily. "I didn't say anything."

"You think you have to say something for me to know what you're thinking?" He turned to her when he said this, and in the dying light, she could have sworn he was reaching for his gun. She felt as if glass had exploded in her chest. She swayed.

But he didn't reach for his gun. He didn't kill her.

"She was a good wife, Didi," said Lyle, clutching his hands to his heart. "A better wife than you." She stared back at him incredulously. "That's right. A better wife. She was worth ten of you," he said cruelly. "She never would have carried heavy bags."

"Bags—" Didi repeated dully.

"We never had any money," Lyle went on, "but she didn't complain. Not once. She wished we had a little more, but she didn't complain. And she certainly didn't go to the mall and spend the money we needed to eat on makeup or underwear or some shit—" He stopped abruptly, as if thinking of something.

Didi mumbled, "That's because she was busy spending all her money on booze and cigarettes."

"What did you say?"

"Nothing, nothing," Didi said quickly. "I said, she must have been busy getting ready for the baby and everything."

He eyed her suspiciously. "You're too far away. Come closer to me." She reluctantly stepped closer.

"What did you buy at Victoria's Secret, Didi?"

Didi could no longer remember the morning's events and remained silent. She needed to sit down. She needed to get back in the car.

"What did you get?" he asked again.

"I don't know, Lyle," she said. "Something for the hospital."

"The hospital?" he repeated, as if not comprehending.

"To have my baby," she said weakly. Was this a good time to tell him she was going to have her baby very soon? Was this another good time to ask him to let her go? Oh, Lyle, please let me go, please, I won't tell, I'll be good, I swear, I promise. Let me go, 'cause I'm having a baby.

Would compassion suddenly be born in Lyle's small heart? He didn't care enough about her pregnancy to give her a drink all day. He didn't care that she spewed blood out of her face, but all of a sudden he was going to feel really bad she was having a baby?

Didi's faith in human nature dimmed.

Suddenly Lyle smiled at her.

With a warm and open expression on his face, as if he were welcoming her to his house for Christmas, Lyle said evenly, "You won't be going to the hospital, my pretty Barcelona, honeymooning bologna, pregnant Desdemona. No hospital for you."

Didi staggered back and fell.

He didn't even reach out to catch her.

She fell on the earth, and he watched her with a papery smile on his face. As she looked up at him standing in the lights of the cop car, Didi thought, is this it? Is this where my life ends?

She screamed.

Didi was on her knees, her belly hurting, her arms at her breasts, and she was looking at him and screaming. He came up to her and dragged her to her feet, and she was still screaming. He started to shake her, and she suffered a contraction. It was almost convenient. It allowed her to writhe in his arms and scream into his face.

With a single slap he silenced her, as if he had pressed a mute button on her. Pop! Shut up. No sound, but the crickets and her breaths.

Finally he released her, and she sank back down to the ground.

Kneeling in front of her, Lyle said. "Scream all you want. They're all dead here." And he laughed.

She reeled from the violence of his laugh.

He looked intensely into her face. "You scream and scream, you flail at me, you hit me, you cry to God, and no one comes." He clambered to his feet and spun around in a demented dance around his wife's grave. Didi thought it looked as if he was dancing *on* his wife's and son's graves.

"You are good your entire life," he railed, his body twitching in constant motion. "You're honest, you don't steal, you hurt no one, and then one fine day, when you are praying for help, when you—for all the good you ever did in your life—want help, just once in your fucking life, real help, because you're in trouble, no one helps you at all. And do you know why? Do you know why no one helps you, pretty Didi?"

"No," Didi said, her voice barely audible even to herself. "Why?"

"Because no one gives a shit! No one cares. Because sometimes bad things happen to good people and no one cares to make that wrong right."

Crouching on her knees, Didi felt vulnerable on the ground, two feet tall to his eleven. At least she was off her legs. She became dizzy with another pain that squeezed so hard even the terror inside her heart subsided for a minute. She was grateful for that, but the minute was soon over.

When she wasn't watching, dusk had turned to dark.

Didi leaned to the ground. With blood caking one eye and the other throbbing, she could barely see, but she searched for a rock or a stick, anything.

There was nothing, just dirt and some pebbles. She scooped up a handful of dust.

When Lyle came up to her, Didi tried to get up. A little at a time, the dust sifted through her fingers and fell.

"Why are you on the ground, Didi?" he said quietly. "Are you praying for my wife?"

She tried to get up. "No, Lyle," she said. "No more. I'm praying for me now."

He crouched down in front of her. "No one can hear you, Didi," he said, almost tenderly, she thought. "Don't feel so bad. No one heard me either. No one heard my wife. No one heard my baby."

They were facing each other, she on her knees, unable to get up without his help. He crouched a few feet in front of her, looking into her face. She lifted her eyes off the ground, still clutching what was left of the dirt and stared into his face. His eyes were clear and sad. His mouth was slightly open and his breathing was shallow.

It was a steaming night. The lights from the car made it seem hotter.

Didi threw the dirt at him underhand, hampered by the handcuffs. Lyle spit out the dirt she had flung at him.

He crawled to Didi on his knees, leaned over, grabbed her face, and kissed her very hard on the mouth. She leaned away from him as far as she could—she would have fallen backward if he had let go of her—but couldn't move her face away.

At last Lyle pulled slightly away from Didi, remaining inches from her face. Looking up at the starlit, moonlit sky, he whispered, "Where's God, Didi? Here we are, in the open field, in the open cemetery. Scream, shout for Him. Where is He? If He's not here among the dead, then where is He?"

"I don't need God to help me, Lyle. I need you to help me. I need you to lift me up off my knees and put me in the car and drive to the nearest highway, and leave me on the side of the road—"

"Dead or alive, Didi?" Lyle interrupted with a smile.

"Alive, Lyle, alive! I need you to consider me one of the living. I need you to see me as a human being and stop hurting me." He didn't interrupt, so she continued. Her voice rose with intensity, until she was groaning, moaning, clutching her hands to the Belly. Didi was having pain she didn't want Lyle to see. "I never did one thing to you, Lyle, not one thing. I didn't turn away from you when you needed me, I didn't hurt your wife, I didn't hurt your baby—"

"You were hurting yours, though," he said, "by carrying all those damn bags."

"I wasn't hurting the baby!" she yelled, hurting herself.

Then the contraction was over. She spoke softer. "I wasn't hurting the baby. No more than if I were walking or jogging. I wasn't carrying bricks, I was carrying toys for my kids. I was fine, Lyle, and my baby was fine." She paused. "We were fine until you came along."

"You weren't fine, Didi," Lyle said. "You thought you were fine, and one second you were, but the next you weren't, and that's the thing about life and fate. They're unpredictable things, aren't they?"

"Lyle, they're not the unpredictable things. You are. If you hadn't come into my life, I would have had a good day."

"But I did come into your life," he said. "I came into your life and you came into mine with your big belly." He paused as he tried to get control of his breaking voice. "Death came into my life. I didn't invite it in, I didn't ask for it to come. My wife always tried to make Sunday service—"

*What, when she wasn't hung over from the night before?* thought Didi.

"She would give her last piece of bread to a homeless bum in Abilene. She never begrudged me anything, yet death came into her life and into mine." He was crying openly now.

Despite herself—maybe because of herself—Didi again felt something for Lyle. Something rose in her throat, a bubble, and burst into an echo of sympathy.

He collapsed in front of her. She raised herself from a crouching position to kneeling. This man was weeping in front of her, broken down, broken-hearted, grieving. He seemed so alone, so non-threatening, so lost.

Reaching down, she gently touched his head with her manacled hands. "It's all right, Lyle," she whispered. "You'll be all right." Then, on her knees, she backed away from him. He is a soul before God. He's a soul in darkness.

"Lyle," Didi said softly. "You don't think I know how you feel?"

He looked up at her. "No, I don't think you do, pretty Didi. You've never lost anything in your life."

"But that's not true, Lyle," she said, lying. She really never *had* lost anything in her life that was as dear to her as a spouse and a child.

He shook his head. "It's true, Didi. I could tell just by the look of you. You were just so happy waddling into the mall, shifting around, gazing at the stores without a care in the world, smiling at the pretzel man, talking to the cashiers. You were so happy. And your husband too. He's happy, isn't he?"

"Not now," said Didi.

And Lyle said, "Never again."

If Didi hadn't been gritting her teeth through another contraction, she would have railed at his words. How could she have touched him when he was down?

"If you . . ." Didi fought to get the words out. "If you ask . . . God . . . for forgiveness, you will have eternal life."

The pain was great. Didi started to cry. It seemed to take longer than sixty seconds for it to pass.

"It's God who should be asking my forgiveness," Lyle said coldly, getting up.

"Help me off the ground, please," Didi said. "My legs are falling asleep."

He didn't offer her a hand. "Help yourself."

She reached out her hand to him. My belly is too big, she wanted to say. I have thirty pounds of life pulling me to the ground. I need your hand. And then she thought, I'm asking the devil for help. If he extends his hand, I've invited him in, and once in, there is no driving him out, me with my vanished strength. I have no will to drive the devil out. Didi's hand lowered.

She struggled to her feet. At last she was up. Much better. She stared at Lyle. He looked much too strong for a pregnant Didi.

A pregnant Didi in labor. She had another contraction while she watched him walk over to his wife's grave. He lay down and kissed the stone. "Good-bye, Mel. I won't be back. You'll understand. It's all going to work out, though. I have a good feeling about it."

In a few moments, Lyle got up and said, "Let's go, Didi. Back to the car."

She walked slowly, pretending to study the ground. "Could you open the door for me?" she asked.

He opened the door and shoved her inside.

If I don't have a drink now, I will die. *I am poured out like water, my mouth is dried out like a clay pot, my tongue sticks to the roof of my mouth, and you have laid me in the dust of the grave.*

As if that's the most of my problems.

Didi flung her head back and closed her eyes.

She heard Lyle start the car, felt it pull away.

And then he said to her, "Have you ever had an abortion, Didi?"

"What?" she quietly asked, and all of a sudden—

That was enough for her.

Didi raised her hands, flung herself at him, and hit him as hard as she could over the head with the metal edges of her handcuffs.

Didi thought she broke skin. He yelped in a way that satisfied her. She stayed long enough to hit him again, harder.

He thrust his right arm at her to stop her, but she hit his arm away, grabbed the door handle, opened the car, and threw herself out on her side.

Her ribs exploded. The car had been going slowly, but the ground was hard. Didi realized that only intellectually. She immediately picked herself up, got onto her feet, and began running away from the car. She heard Lyle scream, *"Didi!"* She didn't turn around. She ran into the darkness and gravestones and the trees. Unable to see, she collided with a stone that cut her across the knees. In pain, she went around the stone and kept running, her hands out in front to protect her against a branch or a tree. She couldn't hear Lyle behind her, couldn't hear his footsteps, couldn't even hear her own.

In the moonlight she saw the shape of a tree, then of a number of trees. She ran toward them. She knew she was running slowly. With the tension in her belly, her feet were barely moving. Come on, come on, she whispered to herself. She dropped to the ground and crawled until she found a small ditch behind a tree. She fell into it, rolled to one side, and tried not to breathe.

# 9 : 0 0   P. M.

The helicopter landed at the intersection of a suburban street, a block away from the Lufts' house in Abilene. Three black vans waited. The back doors to the vans were open and the "special agents," as Scott called them, sat with their feet hanging over the edge, waiting for instructions. They were dressed like Scott, though few were wearing black bandannas. Farther down the block, Rich saw at least ten cop cars, no sirens, but lights flashing.

Scott popped out of the helicopter, his H&K in hand, walked over to the men in the van, and said, "Did you guys bring the map of the neighborhood I asked for?"

One of the men brought out the map from inside the van. Scott studied it briefly. "We probably won't need gas masks, but bring the light mounts for the rifles, because we don't know how long before this guy shows up. Hell, bring the smoke, too. If he's in the house, we'll smoke him out."

"And then we'll kill him," Rich whispered.

"Shhhh," Scott said, and then added, "Here, don't forget the vest, will you? Make sure it's zipped all the way up on the side. I know you're hot, but zip it up right, okay?"

Rich shook his head. This could not be his life. He could not be standing in the middle of a quiet, tree-lined street zipping up his safety vest.

"Can I have a gun too?" asked Rich.

"Shh," said Scott, glancing at the men sitting in the black van. "I can't give you a gun. It's against protocol."

"Fuck protocol."

"If I gave you a gun and anyone found out, my ass would be grass."

"So the answer to my question would be no? I can handle a gun. My father and I hunted when I was little," Rich said.

"Ah, blood sports," said Scott. "That's good. This is almost the same. Thankfully, you won't be the one doing the hunting."

"Too bad," said Rich, looking behind Scott at the SWAT men. "Do we really need them?" he asked.

"Yes, we really do. We're not Butch and Sundance, for God's sake. We can't go in alone. What would we do without them? Talk sense into him?"

"What do you guys have in there, anyway?"

"I don't know. Usual stuff. Tear gas, rifles, bombs."

"Oh."

"What were you expecting? We don't have, like, a howitzer in there."

"Why not?" Rich asked, staring into Scott's sweating face. "I mean, why can't we go to the Luft house by ourselves? We're just going for information. You don't think Lyle Luft brought my wife to meet his parents, do you?"

Scott glanced at Rich and then away.

Rich was too numb for fear. "What?" he said tiredly. "You think he already killed her and came over to his mom's house for a little Monday-night steak? I don't think so."

"You're right, of course," said Scott, prodding Rich along down the street, and then motioning the men to come with them. "All right," he said to them, walking backward as he spoke. "Listen to me, and listen carefully. We may have a man inside who is holding a pregnant hostage and is trigger-happy—armed with at least two powerful guns. Use all possible caution and common sense when approaching. I want at least one man for each window and door in the house. The Abilene cops know to close off the area, right? I don't want our friend Lyle driving off in his Honda with this man's wife while we're adjusting our crotch straps. Now, then, come with me, and then disperse. I want to walk up to the house alone. But I need two men to cover me. Rich, you stay here."

Shaking his head, Rich said, "Absolutely not."

Scott looked surprised. The SWAT guys shifted uncomfortably from foot to foot.

"My wife could be in there," Rich said firmly, not allowing any argument. "I'm coming in too."

Scott sighed deeply. "And two more men to cover Rich. Got it?"

"We can never be too careful," Scott said to Rich as they started walking. Scott had given his H&K to another SWAT team member to carry. The bandanna was not much good at keeping sweat off Scott's face.

"I don't know how you can walk with all that shit strapped on you," said Rich.

"I'll admit I'm a little warm," Scott said. "And I'd rather be wearing my suit and tie when I come to knock on people's doors. It always seems more civil—"

"What? To blow their brains out in a suit and tie seems more civil?"

"Exactly right."

"I see."

The SWAT men with their high-powered rifles spread out between the houses. Some ran ahead of Rich and Scott, disappearing into the trees. Some trailed behind them. Four men flanked them.

Before they turned the corner to Washington Street, Scott said to his group, "Do you think we could be more conspicuous?"

The men stared.

"Okey-dokey, I meant *less* conspicuous," explained Scott. "Listen, just stay close, but don't crowd me, okay? If he's in here, we don't want him opening fire."

Rich looked around him as the SWAT men took their positions. Rich felt better that they were here for him. He opened up his shirt a button and kept walking. His undershirt was damp with sweat, and his short hair was wet at the roots. Then he looked over at Scott and was ashamed at himself for being hot. "Man, that stuff on you is heavy, isn't it?" he said.

"All in all it weighs thirty-seven pounds. That's with the light mount. But hey, I don't have my machine gun, so really it's only twenty-seven pounds."

Pulling out his Glock 17, Scott made sure it was loaded, felt in his load-bearing vest for more clips, and then said, "Cover me if I get into trouble, man."

"Are you talking to me?" asked Rich.

"No," Scott said, nodding in the direction of an armed officer.

"Oh," said Rich, walking fast beside him. "Because I could sell you a really nice counter display that holds twelve inspirational titles. That's about all I can do."

This was an old, well-kept neighborhood. The small houses were mostly one-story, surrounded by mature trees. It was late, and there were only a few people on their porches, sitting in their lawn chairs looking out onto the street with passively alarmed faces. The rest had gone back inside; Rich could see them through the open windows, watching TV in their living rooms.

*Husbands and wives watching TV in their living rooms.*

All Rich could do was keep walking.

Scott was unsmiling and focused.

"We're not going to fuck it up, are we, Scott?"

Without slowing down, Scott put a heavy hand on Rich's back. "Let's go and talk to mister and missus."

The Luft house was a small brown bungalow with a long porch. Scott didn't like the length of the porch, and Rich knew why. If Lyle was in the house, he could easily point a gun out of one of the front windows and shoot Scott dead as he stood at the door.

"Your men will cover you, right?" Rich asked.

Scott nodded. "After he shoots me from the far end of this porch, my soldiers will cover me up and take me away before I'm cold."

He asked if they were ready before he mounted the porch. Turning around, he made sure his men were in their places. "Let's go."

He pounded hard on the door with the butt of his Glock.

Rich said, "No time for niceties."

"None," said Scott.

The door was opened by a thin, bald man.

"You must have the wrong house," he said immediately. "I seen you guys outside. You're making a mistake."

"FBI," said Scott. "May we come in?"

"Not without a warrant—"

Scott burst the door wide open and pummeled through past Mr. Luft. "Leave that for the movies, Mr. Luft, and for celebrity defendants. We're investigating a felony kidnapping. We think the kidnapper may be in your house. We don't need a warrant to find him. We have exigent circumstances. However, since you asked so nicely, I'll tell you that we do have a warrant for your son's arrest. Now, where is he?"

"I don't know what you're talking about," said Mr. Luft. "You get out of my house—"

But he was stopped as three of Scott's men kicked down his back door and pushed into the living room, a gray-haired woman in front of them. "Doris?" said Mr. Luft.

"What do they want, Lyle?" Doris said shrilly.

"We want your son, Mrs. Luft," said Scott. "Lyle Luft. We want him."

"Well, he's not here!" she said defensively. "What's he done?"

"Kidnapped this man's wife," Scott said. Rich watched speechlessly. In a matter of ten seconds, ten SWAT men stormed through the house, flooding every room with their rifles and their black uniforms. The small living area was dwarfed by their presence. Rich heard their footsteps and shouts. They ransacked the whole house in half a minute. "He's not here," said one of the men as he came out of the hall bathroom.

"Well, of course he's not here," barked Mr. Luft. "Doris told you he wasn't."

"Lyle," she wailed. "What are they talking about? Lylie didn't kidnap anybody."

"You know that?" Scott said.

"I know my son," she said. "He wouldn't hurt a fly."

"No?" Scott said. "He would kill two human beings, though, in cold blood and kidnap a pregnant woman."

Rich noted that Doris's expressionless face had clicked on. Murder and kidnapping didn't impress Doris Luft. But when Scott said "pregnant woman," her look suddenly changed.

Scott said impatiently, "Your son is wanted for first-degree murder and kidnapping. If you know where he is and don't tell us, you'll be arrested and tried. You could get ten years if you're lucky. If you're unlucky, you'll be convicted of conspiracy to commit a felony, and for that you'll get twenty-five. Now, where is your son?"

Rich, placing a calming hand on Scott's back, stepped forward to Mrs. Luft and said, "Is everything all right, Mrs. Luft? You looked a little—stricken just now when Agent Somerville said—"

"Pregnant? Did you say pregnant?" Doris said in a squeaky voice.

"Shut up, woman," said Mr. Luft. "For God's sake, stop your whining."

Turning back to Scott, he said, "We're telling you he's not here."

"That much we know," Scott said. "Where is he?"

"We don't know. We haven't heard from him for three weeks, and that's the truth."

"But, Lyle, remember I said to you how strange it was that he hadn't called?" Doris turned to Rich. "It was his birthday a few days ago, and we couldn't get in touch with him."

"Shut up, Doris!" said Mr. Luft. "God, woman."

Rich and Scott exchanged glances. "Okay," Scott said. "Let's have it. Where is he?"

"We don't know. He lives in Dallas now."

"Yes, we know," said Scott. "Have you heard from him today?"

"No," said Lyle.

"Have you seen him today?" Scott persisted.

"No, again," said Mr. Luft.

Scott came up to him, "Don't get smart with me, sir," he said. "I won't put up with it."

Lyle Luft backed off. "Would that be all, officers?" he said. "Sorry we couldn't help you."

Rich and Scott looked over at Doris, who was crying quietly in the corner. Rich asked, "What's the matter? Why are you crying?"

Lyle Luft said, "Oh, she just gets hysterical for no reason. Doris, what did I tell you?"

Doris tried but couldn't stop sobbing. "Hope my boy is okay," she cried.

Scott shook his head, and Rich looked down. *Mothers,* thought Rich.

Rich said, "Mrs. Luft, is your son married? Is his wife pregnant?"

Doris stammered. "My son is—my son was—"

"Doris!" said Mr. Luft.

"Mr. Luft!" said Scott. "Quiet."

Narrowing his eyes, first at Rich and then at Mrs. Luft, Scott asked, "Now, you say your son was married?"

"Yes, yes," Doris cried. "Such a tragedy, such an awful tragedy, oh dear God, oh God, keep my boy, oh, just awful—"

"What happened?" Scott said. "She leave him?"

"No, she died," said Mrs. Luft. "Her baby was born too early and she hemorrhaged or something. She was in a real bad way." Doris kneaded her fingers and didn't look up at Rich or Scott. "They had a baby boy, and after Melanie died, all of Lyle's hopes were for that baby. I think if he had lived, Lyle would be okay."

"He didn't make it?" Rich asked, ashen-faced.

Doris shook her head. "He was just too tiny. God took him to a place where his soul didn't need lungs to breathe." She sniffled.

Rich bowed his head. He didn't want to be looking at Doris any longer.

She said, "Lyle was a very nice boy before this all happened—"

"Oh, Doris, don't be so naive!" said Mr. Luft. "He wasn't a nice boy. Stop covering for him the way you always do."

"I'm not coverin' for him," she said firmly. "He was my son and he was a nice boy—"

"Yeah? Then how come he never had a real job? How come about that? And how come he kept coming home all the time with black eyes, with broken teeth, with police on his back? How come our cars would get smashed and our windows broken? He brought nothing but trouble to our house ever since he was little."

Shaking her head, Doris whispered to Rich, "That's not true. He had no criminal record. He was a confused boy, that's all. Didn't know what he wanted. But Mel set him straight, and the baby, he just wanted that baby so bad."

Mr. Luft turned away from his wife with a fed-up expression. "Is he still just confused, Doris? Kidnapping, murder? Is it still all just confusion?"

She continued in a whisper, "The baby and the Mel thing just broke him up. He would have been okay if not for that baby dying."

"Aw, come on, Doris!" Mr. Luft yelled. "That baby dying just made him more of what he always was—a bum, a loser."

Raising her voice, Doris said, weeping, "He's your son! How could you say that? He's your son."

"He's my *only* son," said Mr. Luft quietly, collapsing into a chair. "He's my *only* child."

Rich thought of the million people in Dallas and Lyle Luft finding *his* wife. He couldn't speak. Everyone was silent.

Finally Scott said, "I'm very sorry, Mrs. Luft. Where do the girl's parents live? We'd like to talk to them."

"Oh, Bernie and Maureen Bleck. They don't live here," Doris said. "They're all the way in Eden. That's where Melanie was from."

"Eden, Eden," said Scott. "Doesn't ring a bell."

"Very small town, south of here—"

Rich was pulling him by his sleeve out the door. "Thank you!" Scott called out to her.

"Let's go," Rich said when they were out the door. "I bet you that's where he parked his Honda. Eden."

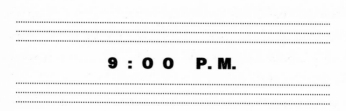

# 9 : 0 0   P. M.

In Eden cemetery, Didi lay silently on her side in great weakness. She wanted water.

She thought, this is the only place I could possibly hide, so this is the only place he would come to look for me.

She thought about her own mortality. Before today, Didi's thoughts about her own death had never progressed beyond the theoretical. Did that poor police officer have any idea when he left for work in the morning it would be the last day of his life? No more than I. When I kissed Rich on the lips this morning as he left for work, I said, don't forget to file those medical forms and please go to Tom Thumb and buy some bananas. In between the kisses, I got a couple of nags in, too. Had I thought this might be my last day, I would have left more explicit instructions. I would have written down a recipe for meat loaf somewhere.

He's coming for me, isn't he? Any minute now, he's going to be here. Didi closed her eyes and opened them again. She thought she saw the moon above the trees, and then quickly closed her eyes again. If she could see the moon, she could see him. She didn't want to see him. Maybe if she closed her eyes he would go away and she would wake up and be back home.

She wanted to cry but there was no water left in her body other than the protective water around the baby. She was surprised she hadn't broken her water when she fell out of Lyle's car.

She clutched her hurting belly, moving her thin wrists up and down in the handcuffs. If only she could place her hands in soapy water. That's all it would take. A little soapy liquid, a little twisting of the thumbs, and the cuffs would come right off.

Of course, if she found some water, getting the cuffs off would not be the first thing she would do. She licked her caked lips with her dry tongue.

Lyle's coming for her filled Didi with a desperate anger and a desperate fear. *I was a pretty good daughter to my mom and dad; I was a decent sister to my two sisters. I graduated school, learned how to type, got a job at a small publishing company, and met Rich. I'm a good wife to him, and I'm a good mother. What I want to know is, when, in the middle of my life, did I fall from grace?*

Didi smelled something familiar. It made her think of her teenage years, some remnant of adolescence. She couldn't quite put her finger on it, and didn't want to, but yet . . .

She knew what it was: she smelled an old fire.

Oddly, it mattered, smelling old ashes. Why would there be a fire here?

Her addled brain couldn't focus. She heard faint footsteps, a voice. With her heart slamming into her chest, she focused on the fire. What? What? Closing her eyes, thinking about the fire.

Kids—that's what it was. It nearly amused her, the morbidity of kids coming to a cemetery to light a fire to prove they weren't afraid of the darkest dark, to prove they weren't afraid of ghosts. Teenagers came here and lit a fire.

*Teenagers came here and lit a fire.* The thought pumped through her head like electric current. Omigod. Yes. Of course. It was exactly what she needed.

Didi weighed the consequences. If she got up, Lyle could easily see her moving. Here in the ditch she was as good as dead. It was a no-brainer.

On all fours, she pushed off the ground and heaved herself up with tremendous effort. She may have groaned. She thought she felt another contraction and fought it because she had to keep moving. Gritting her teeth, she walked a few feet and then realized she couldn't smell the fire when she was standing. She fell to her knees and crawled, her face to the earth. She smelled the fire again, but slowed to a stop. Tears of frustration clouded her eyes. Goddammit, help me just a little, just a little.

And then she heard him. "Desdemonaaaa, where are you, my lovely?"

She stifled a despairing cry. Keeping her hands in front of her, she used her elbows to help propel her forward. She moved, smelling the ground for the fire.

"Desdemonaaaa, my Sharonaaaa, my bolognaaaa, where are you?"

Her elbows were getting scraped to raw flesh, but she didn't care. Her face against the ground, she slowly moved in the dark. She could barely hear him through her heart's pounding, but she heard him. He wasn't getting any closer, just more persistent. *If only I could find that fire, I know I'll find what I'm looking for—*

"Desdemonaaaa, come out come out wherever you are. . . ."

And then, "I'm gonna find you, my Desdemonaaaa, I'm gonna find you. I'm gonna find you." The laugh echoed through the gravestones.

The fear made Didi's belly feel hollow. The loathsome, vast emptiness shattered against her ribs, shattered her from the inside. Outwardly Didi barely moved. Her own slowness revolted her. She only wished she were limber and thin, running instead of crawling away with her belly dragging on the ground. Still, she smelled the fire close by.

She threw herself down on the ground and frantically searched for a beer bottle. She heard Lyle's shattering laugh. Before she could get up or turn around, she felt him fall on top of her.


"Didi! I'm surprised at you. Why would you run away from me?" Lyle said.

She was breathing hard into the ground. He was lying on top of her and wouldn't let her turn over. It was too much for her belly, Lyle squeezing her baby into the earth. She tried to raise herself to lift his weight off her and failed.

"You're hurting me," Didi whispered. "Get off." She had wanted to shout it, but he had knocked the breath out of her.

Lyle didn't move. "Get off, huh? Get off? I don't think I should be getting off you. You're not to be trusted, Didi. At any moment, you lash out against me when I least expect it."

"Get off me," she said again, louder. "You're hurting the baby."

He didn't hear her or he ignored her, because he continued to grind against her. "Tell me why you hit me, why, why, *why*?" he asked.

Not letting her answer, he pressed her face into the ground and said, "You're still trying to get away. You're just so damn stubborn. Don't you realize it's impossible? Don't you realize this is your fate?" He spoke into her knotted hair. "Jesus Christ died for our sins, Didi. Are you willing to die?"

Her mouth pressed against the dirt, she said, "Get off me, goddammit." *And Christ didn't have a baby inside Him when He died,* Didi wanted to shout. "God will curse you, Lyle. He'll curse you. Now be a man and get off me."

He nuzzled in her neck, moving his pelvis slightly off her back. She breathed easier.

"You sound upset. I'm sorry," he said sarcastically. "I didn't mean to upset you with what I said. Let's start fresh, okay? You're not going to be running away from me, are you? Or do you want me to put you in leg irons? There are some in the trunk. I didn't know if I should bring them with me. They're kind of heavy. Certainly would be hard to run away with them on."

She stopped paying attention to him. Something was cutting her on the side of her cheek. It could have been a stick, or coal, or wood.

It could have been a piece of glass.

Didi felt it gnawing at her cheek as Lyle lay on top of her and whispered—almost lovingly—into her hair.

"Desdemona," he whispered. "Desdemona . . . I don't want to hurt you. But I don't want you to fight me either. Now what will it be? Will it be the hard way for you? It doesn't have to be, you know. It can all be so easy. And painless. Tell me how you want it to be."

In the middle of another contraction, Didi said nothing as she scratched at the ground. When the pain was over, she whispered, "I want it to be easy."

Her handcuffed hands were in front of her. She pulled them down to her face and tightly grabbed a broken bottle neck.

Thank God, thank God.

When she opened her mouth to speak, dirt had got in. She didn't care; she found what she came looking for. Oh, but to wipe the dirt away from my lips. To wipe all of this away. Were her eyes closed? She couldn't tell. She blinked. Nothing. Darkness. I have to stay sharp, she thought. I have to stay conscious. I can't lose focus.

But she *was* losing focus. She was catching only the end of his sentences. Or the beginnings. And then drifting out. In and out.

In and

out.


Suddenly Lyle got off her.

She turned over on her side, panting, clutching her belly, clutching, too, the broken neck of the beer bottle. The—

Another contraction.

That was fast. That was so fast.

Oh, God.

She clenched her fingers around the bottle neck and moaned. He said nothing. He must have thought she was panting, getting her breath back.

When it was over, Didi said, "I want a drink. I want my husband." A drink first, she thought. Then my husband.

She could swear Lyle was smiling at her in the dark. He extended his hand, but she didn't want to give him her hands lest he feel the bottle. She raised her elbow instead, and he took it to help her up. "Come on now, go easy on me," Lyle said. "I can't have you beating at me and trying to escape every two seconds. It makes me tense. Now, then," he said, fumbling with her dress in the dark, adjusting it, straightening it out. "You okay? I almost forgot I was lying on the baby."

"I'm fine, Lyle," she said, moving away from him.

She saw the whites of his teeth. "I know you, Desdemona. I know what you're thinking. We're not done yet, me and you. We haven't had a chance to sit and talk. You were making your way to this fire? Did you want to light a fire, Didi? Would that make you happy?"

Make me happy? thought Didi. Lighting a fire here with you, in a cemetery, in the woods, while I'm in labor?

"Yeah, sure," she said.

"Then come," he said. "But I don't want to stay here. We're not safe here. Too exposed," he said cryptically. "We'll go to the place where I proposed to my wife. Where she first told me she was pregnant."

She didn't want to go anywhere. "What's wrong with here?"

"Cemeteries creep me out," he said. "I don't want to overstay my welcome. What if God decides we're so close to Him that there's no reason for leaving?"

Didi swayed a little, almost fell. There was pressure and aching between her legs, overwhelming all other throbbing in her body. "I thought you said there was no God, Lyle?"

"I didn't say there was no God," he said, and his voice sounded harsh in the darkness. "I said there was a God, but He wasn't looking my way." Pausing, he added, "Wasn't looking your way either."

"You're lucky, Lyle," said Didi menacingly, "that He isn't looking my way."

Lyle brought his face close. She saw him in the moonlight. His eyes feverish, his mouth ajar, he said right into her lips, "Not even God can help you now, Desdemona."

Where were the keys to her handcuffs? Who knows? she thought. Who cares?

Lyle was here. The keys would do her no good.

*Not even God can help you now.* It rang in Didi's ears. She wasn't so far from God now, standing here amid His angels and sinners, standing next to Lyle under the Texas sky.

She didn't want to stand any longer. The day had been too long, she had been too long without water, without hope. She wanted to lie down. Her girls, her husband, her young life, they all felt behind her now. She rocked from side to side in front of Lyle, holding the broken bottle between her hands.

This is as bad as things get, she thought.

Is this what dying is? Didi wondered, swaying, weakening. Every labored breath I take, I think this is my last, and death is standing in front of me, looking at me with his shiny eyes, wondering how best to take my life from me. How best to take my heart from me.

"Where are we going, Lyle?" Didi said wearily. "Because I'm very tired. I need to sit down."

"Yeah, this isn't NorthPark, is it, Didi?"

"No, it isn't, not by a long shot." She stepped away from him, tightening the grip on the bottle.

He led her out of the forest. Squeezing her arm, he added, "Maybe in Pfluger Park you can show me the nice things you bought at Victoria's Secret."

She obediently went with him. Not that she had much choice. Maybe there were people in Pfluger Park. Maybe teenagers were there.

He kept his hand on her all the way to the car. It was dark even under moonlight, and there were many gravestones Didi would have tripped over if it hadn't been for his helping her. He walked slightly in front of her, finding the way, holding her solicitously.

Losing herself for a moment, longing for help, she leaned into Lyle. *Save me,* Didi prayed, *my life from the power of the dog.*

She was so grateful to sit down in the car that she threw her head back on the headrest and soon felt herself drifting off. She lost track of him for a short moment but was brought back to life by another violent pain in her belly.

The car kicked up a flurry of stones, speeding in the night toward Pfluger Park.

They were in the air again, and Rich couldn't sit still. All he wanted to do was pace. Scott, too, was jittery. He took off his load-bearing vest, and frantically spoke on the phone to a member of the San Angelo police force and the sheriff at Eden, asking for reinforcements to come to the home of the Blecks on Wyona Avenue in Eden. He had already instructed the SWAT men from Abilene to drive to the tiny town.

When he got off the phone, he said nervously, shoving a stick of gum in his mouth, "Rich, we got him, man, we got him."

"We got nothing," said Rich.

"No, you were right, man. That's where he's going. Eden."

"Going? Yes. Staying? He isn't going over to shoot the breeze with the in-laws."

"No, but our Lyle is obsessed with ending up in Eden. Think about it. He wasn't going to change his course for anything. He's on the run, he knows we're on to him, he knows he doesn't have much time. So what does he do? Nothing. Changes cars. But continues on. Why? Because there's something in Eden he wants."

*Yes,* Rich thought, *to kill my wife,* but couldn't say the words out loud.

"It's dark now," he said. "Where will we find them?"

"Let's talk to the Blecks first," said Scott. "They'll tell us."

Rich tried to see in the dark. Wasn't it dangerous to fly a helicopter at night? What if something hit them? He didn't care. Let something hit them. Where was his Didi?

Rich said, "Why don't we call ahead this time?"

"Are you kidding me?"

"Well, yes," said Rich, shrugging.

"You may have something."

Perplexed, Rich watched as Scott got the Blecks' number from information. "The phone's ringing. What do you want me to say, Rich?"

Rich grabbed the phone away from Scott. "What, are you crazy? Yeah, and why don't you tell them how many federal agents are going to be at the scene, while you're at it."

Scott grabbed the phone back. "Why do you think you're the only smart one around here?" He listened into the phone. "Ah, shit. It's an answering machine."

Shaking his head with disbelief, Rich said, "Hey, leave a message."

"Hello?" said Scott. "Mr. and Mrs. Bleck, this is Scott Somerville with Federal Express. We have a package here for you. We'd like to know when is the best time to deliver it to you. You can reach us at . . ."

After Scott hung up, Rich stared at him for a few moments. "Does that *ever* work?"

Scott smiled, dialing another number. "We'll find out, won't we?"

"What if he's there?"

Scott stopped smiling. "We'll find out, won't we?"

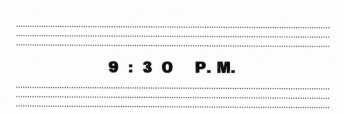

# 9 : 3 0   P. M.

**D**idi noticed a twitch at the corner of Lyle's lower lip as he drove out of the cemetery. She hadn't seen it before, but it was pronounced enough that she noticed it in the darkened interior of the car.

He spoke to her soothingly. "Don't worry, Didi. Don't worry. Everything will be all right. I think you'll be pleased with the way it will turn out."

Didi barely listened to him. Okay, she thought, anytime the good Lord wants to make His plan clear to me, He can. I open the car door on I-75. I scream to Rich. I call 911. I jump out of Lyle's car. I hit Lyle in the head—and nothing. It's almost as if—

As if—

She couldn't think it. Couldn't think the words.

*As if I'm meant to die.*

How close do I have to get? I'm in the car, and he is next to me. Is that close enough? She looked over at Lyle. She remembered praying for his soul earlier in the day, an eternity ago. Gradually, she had stopped wanting to pray for him and had started to pray for herself. Now, after a day with Lyle, she didn't want to pray for him, she didn't want to pray for herself.

She wanted to kill him.

Clutching the beer bottle neck between her manacled hands, she was consumed with the notion of killing him. Come here, Lyle. Come closer to me. Come closer so I can kill you. How many chances will you give me? And if I have only one chance, will I take it? She moaned under the weight of her helplessness.

I talk the talk, but can I walk the walk? At the cemetery, when he was splayed in front of me sobbing, I took pity on him, and for what? She squeezed the sharp glass tighter. Case in point—when I finally did hit him, he barely flinched.

Am I a person who can kill another human being? Has my life led me to be a person who can kill another human being? She shuddered.

No.

Too late to think about it. She had another contraction. She couldn't keep track of time. Since they'd returned to the car, she'd had three contractions. How many minutes had it been?

Lyle said something she barely heard. "What?" she asked weakly.

"Didn't I tell you? Bad things happen to good people, often for no reason."

"Lyle, but that's not true!" Didi exclaimed. "Bad things are not happening to me for no reason. They're happening to me because of you." Didi thought about it and said, "You must think bad things happened to *you* for no reason."

"Think?" he exclaimed. "They *did* happen to me for no reason." Lyle didn't look at Didi. "I was a lonely kid. My old man and I never got along. When I met Mel, I thought my life had finally worked out. We lived an okay life. A nice, normal life. What do you think you would do, Desdemona, if your husband and kids were killed and you were left with nothing?"

**2 3 1**

"Do you think I would take my heartbreak out on you?" she exclaimed. "No. I might take my own life—"

He said, "You wouldn't. God-fearing people don't do that."

I don't fear God, only His silence, Didi thought. And I fear you, you piece of shit.

Another contraction was starting.

"Well, I might go crazy then or something!" she said shrilly, raising her voice in sync with the terrible pain of the contraction. "Ahh," she cried. "Ahh." The words came out plaintive, wailing, screeching. "But Lyle, why would I want to hurt you? You did nothing to me. I wouldn't want to hurt you."

"That's what you think," he said, turning left off the dark highway onto an even darker road. "And how would you know? Your life's been so easy—" He paused. "Till now. How do you know what you might do?"

Didi held her hands on her belly and half listened to him, half tried to stave off fear. "What can I do for you, Lyle?" she said. "Do you want me to go to Mazatlán with you?"

He didn't answer her, and then the car stopped. Didi peered into the trees illuminated by the headlights. The place looked as deserted as the cemetery. They had exchanged one graveyard for another.

"Get out of the car, Didi."

When they were outside, standing near a small picnic area, Didi asked, kneading the beer bottle neck in her hands. "Are we in Pfluger Park?"

"Yes," he replied as he quickly walked around. Didi assumed he was searching the area for people. He held a gun in each hand. God help anyone who's here, Didi thought.

Is he going to shoot me? I'll never even get close to him. Horrified at that moment of never getting her chance at him, she walked toward him, and he whirled around to face her. "What are you doing, Didi?" he asked hotly.

"Nothing, Lyle. Walking to you."

"Well, don't. I don't trust you anymore. My head fucking hurts because of you." He moved closer. "What were you hoping for? Were you hoping to kill me?"

"No," she said. "Just disable you long enough to get to the road."

"Then why did you run to the woods?"

"Because you didn't seem disabled and the road was a long way off."

He reached out and touched her chin. Didi willed herself not to move away. Her belly tensed, beginning another contraction.

"You're not stupid, are you, Didi?"

"No," she said in a small voice.

"Neither am I. I'm not stupid either. Despite your idiotic Desdemona hints. I thought out everything. I planned for everything. The only thing I wasn't planning on was that damn cop. Otherwise everything would have gone so smooth."

Didi was caving over. Thank God it was dark by the side of the car and Lyle couldn't see her pain-distorted face.

"Lyle?" Didi said. "I'm not feeling so good—"

"How do you think the handcuffs felt against my head?" he retorted malevolently. "You deserve worse."

"I've been getting worse," Didi said loudly.

Lyle looked at her, almost surprised. "What's the matter with you?"

She took one step toward him, fiddling with the bottle. "I'm so big and pregnant," she rasped. "What could I possibly do to you?"

He took one step back. "I was thinking of tying you to the tree. Would you like that better?"

Shaking her head, Didi said she needed a bathroom.

She knew there were no bathrooms. What she wanted was to lie down. Lie down at the bottom of a freshwater lake. Drink, give birth, die.

The thought of dying made her slightly less thirsty.

"I'm going to go sit down on the bench right there, okay?" Didi said as she turned away, making her way down to a picnic table close to the car. She heard Lyle following her. "You're limping," he said. "You're walking kind of funny. What's wrong with you?"

"I'm just tired, Lyle. Very, very tired, and nine months pregnant."

Didi sat down. Lyle sat a few feet away from her. "Are you cold? I'll make a fire."

"The air is standing still, it's so hot. I'm not cold, Lyle. Where would you get that idea?"

He reached over and touched her forehead with his fingertips. "You feel clammy. You're wet with cold sweat."

She sat still, not moving away from him. That's nice, she wanted to say. That's real nice. Come a little closer. She squeezed the bottle neck between her hands. A little *closer*, Lyle.

He took his hand away. "I'll make a fire."

Shrugging, she tried to adjust her eyes to the dark. The car's headlights shone, but they were pointing away from them and into the trees. If it were lighter, she could have made out a road somewhere, other trees. But aside from the headlights, blackness surrounded her. She thought making a fire was a crazy idea in this stupefying heat, but a fire was something someone would see. Someone might come over, ask if they were out of their minds making a fire.

Lyle came back and sat next to her again. "You know, Mel and me made a fire here the first time we came to the park. It was summer and dark, like it is now. It was hot but we didn't care. We had a really nice night."

Didi said nothing.

She saw Lyle peering intently into the trees. "What are you listening to?" asked Didi.

"Shh. I want to hear if they've found us. Don't speak."

Didi huddled in the far corner of the table, while Lyle sat on top of the table with his feet on the seat and loaded a cartridge into his Colt. Then he sat with both guns cocked and listened. After a few moments he uncocked the guns, placed the police revolver on the table, and turned to Didi. "It's quiet. That's what I love about Eden— you can hear everything. Crickets, cars, police sirens. They aren't here. We'll wait for a little while longer and then we'll go. It's not far from here."

"What's not far?"

"It's only half a mile through the woods—you just have to know which way to walk." Lyle seemed to be watching her carefully, and then he moved over and touched her face. "I used to like touching Mel's face," he said.

How did she feel about it? wondered Didi.

Lyle said, "What do you think your husband is feeling now?"

"Must be scared shitless," said Didi without hesitating. "Much like me."

"If you were to die, how do you think he'd feel?"

There was no answer to his question. Certainly no answer she wanted to give him. They weren't talking about an abstract notion. They were talking about her dying.

"Maybe what I want," said Lyle slowly, "is to make him feel how I felt when Mel died."

"I don't know why. You don't know him at all. Why would you want to hurt him?"

"Why would God want to hurt me?"

"God knows you," Didi said. "He's the only one with answers for that one."

She thought. "Besides, that's bogus, Lyle. You didn't know I was married. I could have been a single mother on welfare, really unhappy and very alone."

He shook his head. "You looked really happy, Desdemona."

People had said that to her before. They said she radiated marriage.

"Tell me, Didi, if your husband came just in the nick of time to rescue you and saved you from me and shot me dead in cold blood,

tell me, would you . . ." He seemed at a loss for words. "Would you—
cry for me?"

"Yes, Lyle, I would." She couldn't tell if she was lying. Couldn't *feel*
if she was lying. I'd cry for me more, though, she thought. Cry in relief
for my beloved life.

"Would you go back home, back to your life, and forget me?"

"Forget you? Are you kidding me? No, I wouldn't forget you."

"No," he said. "I don't suppose you would. I'm going to make it
very hard for your husband to ever forget me. Kind of the way I myself
stopped believing in God, but I haven't forgotten Him."

Didi shook her head mournfully. "Yes, you have, Lyle," she said.
"Yes, you have."

"No, Desdemona," said Lyle, almost gleefully. "God has forgotten
you."

Our night isn't over yet, Didi thought, helplessly clutching her lousy
bottle.

"A fire sounds nice," she said.

"Does, doesn't it. But I'm not going to build it. Don't want any
curious teenagers coming to visit us, do we?"

"Don't we?" Didi said wanly. Her eyes were glazing over. She was
having another contraction. "Ahhh," she moaned, and he saw and his
eyes narrowed. "What?" he said. "You're in pain?"

"My eye hurts," Didi said. "It's just throbbing. I need to get it
stitched up."

Ruefully, Lyle smiled, stroking her face. "Don't worry, Desdemona.
It will be all right soon."

She screamed and it hurt worse. "Stop it!" she screamed. "Stop
threatening me!" She nearly fell sideways onto him, catching herself
only at the last second, holding back, the broken bottle neck shifting
in her twisted hands. She was at such an awkward angle. She would
have succeeded only in hurling herself off the bench, possibly swiping
him as she fell to the ground.

He said, "I'm not being kind enough."

"Kind?" she gasped. And then the contraction was over. She calmed down. "No, Lyle. You aren't being kind enough."

"Let's pretend to make that fire, Didi," he said. "It will make you feel better. We'll take a little walk, we'll talk about your life if you like. We have a little time, but not much." He seemed to be listening to the silence again. "I think I have more faith in your husband than you do. We don't want any surprises." Getting up, he extended his hand to her.

Didi didn't take the hand and got up off the bench by herself.

The two walked back to the car. He reached into it and turned off the lights. At first they were left in near darkness. Then Didi's eyes adjusted to the night. She made out the shapes of trees, the moon up above, and Lyle as he approached her.

Didi's handcuffed hands were intertwined together in front of her. She thought, I don't care if I have to dislocate my thumb or break it off, but I must free one of my hands.

Lyle took her by the upper arm and said, "Walk with me. Walk with me into the woods."

No, she thought. No. I can't go with him anywhere. I have to stay near the car. He is not Winnie-the-Pooh, and I'm not Piglet. This is not the Hundred-Acre Wood. I have to stay right here. "Lyle—"

She was almost glad he was holding her arm when the pain gripped her. She doubled over and moaned.

Lyle let go of her, and she fell to her knees on the gravelly road. For a minute she moaned on the ground in front of him as he stood and watched. Then it was done.

"Get up," he said.

He didn't help her. Didi got up with difficulty, pressing her hands against her knees to steady herself.

"Okay, what's wrong with you?"

"I just have a little stomachache. I haven't eaten, haven't drank,"

Didi said, in a voice rasping with thirst. Her throat felt as if it were bleeding. "I'm not feeling great."

He looked tense and suspicious. "Are you having those . . . baby pains?" he said uncertainly.

"No, no, nothing like that. Believe me, you'd know those," Didi managed to say in a calm voice. "Can't hide those. They're vicious." She was not going to tell this man she was in labor.

*Baby pains,* he had said. Didi's head tottered. When is this all going to end? When is it all going to end badly. It was not a question. Something inside Didi was ready to part with life. Oh, but

*baby pains*

She moved her right thumb deep into her palm to make her hand narrower—narrow enough to slide through the cuff. Without letting go of the bottle neck, she tried to move the right cuff off her wrist with her left hand. It wasn't working. When she almost dropped the broken glass, she stopped attempting to get the handcuffs off. Without the bottle, she was unarmed. She might free her hands, but she'd be unarmed.

They walked a little deeper into the stand of trees.

"Let's sit here, Lyle," said Didi when she saw the outlines of another picnic table. "Let's sit here and talk a bit. Want to do that? How would that be?"

Lyle's shadowy face smiled at her. "Sure, Desdemona."

She gratefully sat down on the bench several feet away from him. "Sit closer to me, Didi. We've been through a lot together."

"That we have," she said, moving closer to him. She didn't want him to see her fiercely trying to free her right hand while the left hand hung on to the beer bottle.

Lyle looked into her face. "I can see you were once beautiful."

"Thank you," she said softly, thinking, bastard, bastard, bastard. Get off my hands, get off my hands, she thought to the handcuffs. But they wouldn't come off and then

*baby pain*

She closed her eyes and began to count. She forgot about the cuffs for sixty seconds. The middle thirty seconds were the worst. She tried not to move, and only her bitten and bloody lip spoke of the baby's desire to leave her.

Lyle didn't look at her until the contraction was over.

"What do you want to know about me, Lyle?" Didi asked in a weak voice.

"About you?" he repeated, sounding surprised. "Nothing. I know about you already. I asked you about Desdemona. Did she have a hard life?"

Didi nodded. She figured she had about three minutes before the next contraction to tell him about Desdemona. "Desdemona was Othello's wife."

"Did he love her?"

"Very much," said Didi, wanting to cry again. No time for crying. Only minutes before *baby pain*. "He adored her. Then he found out that she might have cheated on him—"

"How did he find out?"

"Iago told him."

"Was Iago telling the truth?"

"No, of course he wasn't. Desdemona was a faithful wife."

Lyle smirked. "Like you, Desdemona?"

Nodding, she said, "Like me, Lyle."

"And then?"

"Then Othello went crazy and killed Desdemona."

"How did he kill her?"

"He smothered her."

"And the story was over?"

"No," replied Didi. "Othello found out Iago had been lying, so he killed himself."

Lyle studied her face. "He did?" Shrugging, he asked, "And Iago? He went scot-free?" Lyle asked with hope.

"No," said Desdemona. "He was found out and sentenced to be tortured to death for his crime."

"Ahhh," said Lyle. "A just punishment."

They were silent.

Turning to Didi, Lyle asked, "What punishment would be fitting for me, Desdemona?"

"None," she said instantly, "if you let me go."

"I see," he said, half smiling. "And if I don't?"

"Death by torture would be okay, then," Didi said, failing in a half smile of her own.

"Didi, I'm sorry," he drew out, "but you know I can't let you go now."

Didi mustered enough fortitude to ask, "So is that what you want? You want me to come to Mazatlán with you?"

"Well, no, you see," said Lyle softly, "that would be a bit like always keeping a wolf at the door, now wouldn't it? A pretty wolf, but a wolf nonetheless."

"I don't understand—" She closed her mouth to hide a moan of pain. He glanced over at her and said nothing. He must have thought she was reacting to him.

"Wouldn't it, Didi?" Lyle repeated. Didi was having trouble keeping her eyes open. The pain was becoming measurably stronger. The *baby pain* was here. There was no return to the state of her pregnancy where every once in a while Didi would feel the Belly benignly contract in a Braxton Hicks. There was only one way to go, and that was out of the pregnancy, and she was headed into that unknown now, and she was headed there with a beast. She and the beast together would enter the tunnel, and she would close her eyes and hope for the best, and pray for some good luck, even some mediocre luck, any luck, as long as it wasn't the terrible god-awful luck she'd been having lately. She'd close her eyes much as she did now and pray for ice to fall into her throat. When she would open her eyes again, she would have a baby and not be pregnant anymore.

But she might be dead. The baby might be dead.

No.

No.

## 9 : 4 5 P. M.

Using the landing lights, the pilot set the helicopter down on Wyona Road, right in front of the Blecks' house. Scott and Rich were the first to arrive, followed quickly by the four SWAT cars, followed by six more. By the time they got Scott's gear out of the helicopter, there were four black vans and a posse of sheriff's cars, nineteen cars in all on Wyona Road.

Scott asked the policemen to turn off their lights. Then he asked the sheriff of Eden for the map of the area that Scott had called him about earlier.

The sheriff, a portly, sweating man, finally admitted he didn't have one in his possession. Apparently the city hall office had one, but it was closed. Short of breaking in, there was no way to get it.

The Blecks' house was dark, except for the porch light and the single light in what was probably the living room. It looked as if the Blecks weren't home.

"They're not home?" said Rich incredulously. "How can they not be home?"

"I don't know, man. It makes no sense," said Scott.

"What about this day does?" said Rich.

Scott wasn't fooling around. He had his Glock in hand and his Heckler & Koch by his side, and he didn't take his eyes off the house. He called in for more reinforcements from San Angelo. Scott said they were not leaving Eden without Lyle Luft, dead or alive.

Rich thought it was ironic that they had been in San Angelo over two hours ago, so close to Eden, and yet so far. But even in Eden, what did they have? As they sat, Didi's life hung in the balance somewhere.

"Maybe there's nothing here," said Rich. "Maybe it's just another dead end."

"Nothing's been a dead end, Rich," Scott said. "Every single thing has led us to him, and I'm telling you, he's here. His Honda is here. He thinks we don't know about his car, but he won't be able to drive it anywhere, not in Texas, not in New Mexico, nowhere."

"Where is the Honda?"

"I don't know. Most likely parked somewhere. I thought he might be stupid enough to park it in front of the in-laws' house, but he's obviously not such a moron. He's parked it where there are a bunch of other cars, like a garage, repair shop, gas station, someplace like that."

"Well, this place's so small. How many gas stations can there be?"

"I'm on it, all right?" Scott said. "Me and you are waiting here for the Blecks. My boys and the sheriff's men will look for the Honda."

Rich said, "You know, he could have taken it already. Dumped the cop car, taken his Honda, and driven out of town."

Scott shook his head. "I'm pretty certain it didn't happen. He was only a few steps ahead of us. He's got business here, and we're going to find out what it is. If he just wanted to put Didi into his Honda and drive off, he could have parked it in a million different places in Dallas. It's very easy to park a car there. But in a city of a thousand people? Fifteen hundred? It's much harder to stash, but worth the risk for Lyle to leave it here. My guess is, he's hiding out right now, waiting to get it later. He doesn't want the abandoned cop car to alert the police. He'll wait, swap cars, and then head on out in the middle of the night. If we find the Honda, we're in like Flint."

Rich sighed. "Nice speech," he said, "but where's my wife?"

"The Blecks will tell us," Scott said. He paused. "Listen, don't look at this as failure, all right? But I'm afraid you've driven me to this." Opening his wallet, Scott pulled out a crumpled cigarette.

Rich sighed. "The day has gotten to you."

"Yes." He smiled. "I picked the wrong day to give up smoking."

"Do you have a light?"

"Do I have a light?" Scott chuckled, reaching into his load-bearing vest. "How do you think we set off all those bombs?"

He took a deep drag on his cigarette and looked measurably calmer. "God, that's good. I blame you," he said. "You came into my life, and look at me."

Rich said, "You can't have just one, they say."

"Don't I know it," said Scott, pulling out a pack of Marlboros from his load-bearing vest.

Rich smiled. "Some quitter," he said.

"Don't let anyone say I'm a quitter," said Scott, jumping off the car to pick up a photo that had fallen out of his vest.

"What's this?" Rich asked.

"My son." Scott showed Rich the laminated picture. "I don't want to be shot in the middle of boondock, Texas, and have the last face I see before I croak to be that of a total stranger. I want to look at someone close to me."

"What'd you have it laminated for? Don't want to bleed all over your kid?"

"Exactly right," said Scott.

Rich was quiet. "The last face you'll see will be mine," he said at last.

"Hey, I could do a lot worse," said Scott.

They waited.

Scott said, "Maybe, after this is over, we can play a round or two of golf?"

"I don't think so," said Rich, and saw Scott sink into himself a little bit. "After this is over, we're going to need a drink."

They waited.

"Why did you go into the FBI, Scott?" Rich asked.

"You know why I went in?" Scott replied, rubbing the machine gun. "Because there are bullies in this world, and I knew a bunch of them. Take you, you look like a nice man, a good man. Your wife is a good woman, and yet someone out there wants to do her harm—hurt her, maybe kill her. And I want him to know that I represent a force equal to or greater than him. I'm here to stop him. And I take my job very seriously. I don't like bullies—hurting helpless people. I don't like being helpless myself. I come prepared for him. I'm here to protect your wife against the bullies."


Neighborhood people came out to inquire about the commotion. Scott politely told them to go back inside, there was nothing going on, the police just wanted to talk to the Blecks. Yes, everything was fine, no, there was nothing anyone else could do. Except maybe tell them where the Blecks were. But no one knew.

"How can no one know? What kind of nosy neighbors are these?" Rich whispered to Scott as he sat back down on the hood. "Where we live, our neighbors from across the street have nothing better to do but to look out of their kitchen windows and see how many times the UPS truck comes to our house."

Scott was quiet. Then he asked, "Does it come often, man?"

Rich nodded. "Come to think of it, my wife is on a first-name basis with the UPS man," said Rich. "She calls him Benji."

"That's really special," said Scott, smiling.

"Every time she buys something for herself or the house or the kids, she buys something for me, too. That makes it okay."

"Of course it does."

Rich smiled. *I love my wife,* he thought. I don't care if she buys out the entire fucking Spiegel catalog as long as I get her back.

# 1 0 : 0 0  P.M.

I have a story to tell you, Lyle," Didi said. "Are you listening?"

"I'm listening, Didi." He seemed morose. "We don't have a lot of time," he said.

Didi's throat became dryer. "Don't we?"

Shaking his head, Lyle said, "No, uh-uh. We don't."

Didi was quiet. She had managed to move the cuff off her wrist and now it was firmly lodged on the bone at the base of her thumb.

Water. If only she had a little water. And a tiny bit of soap.

"Tell me your story, Didi."

There was no time. Her baby pain was in her belly again. Through this pain Didi tried to move the cuff farther down her hand; there was no feeling anywhere in her body except in her belly. She could have cut off her hand and not felt it.

The cuff stayed put, and when the baby pain was over, Didi felt liquid pain in her hand. She must have cut her wrist with the cuffs.

She watched him carefully. He had his left hand on the cop's revolver, and his right on the Colt with which he'd shot the officer. The dead officer's uniform looked awkwardly and unevenly pasted to his body. He sat still.

"Once," Didi said haltingly, "there lived an old woman who hadn't done anything nice in her life for anyone."

"Is this someone you know?" Lyle asked.

"No," said Didi, fingering the broken glass, holding it tighter to make sure she didn't drop it. "When the old lady died, she headed straight to hell—"

"Naturally."

"But the archangel Gabriel wanted to spare her an eternity of damnation, so he went to God and pleaded for the old woman's life. And God said to him, 'If you can find one good thing that she's done, then I will spare her and let her ascend to heaven.'"

"God is so charitable."

Didi squeezed her right wrist between the handcuffs, but the wrist hurt and wouldn't move any farther. She continued quickly, "So Gabriel searched through the old hag's life and finally found one kindness: the old woman had given an onion out of her garden to a hungry man. And God said to Gabriel, 'Take that onion and hold it out to the old woman. If it's strong enough to pull her out of hell, then she shall rise to heaven.'" Didi felt the rumblings of a tightening stomach. She held herself together. "Lowering himself into the firepit, Gabriel extended the onion to the old woman and said, 'Hold on, and I'll pull you out.' She grabbed the onion, and he started pulling. However, when the other sinners saw one of their own being saved by Gabriel, they grabbed on to the old hag's skirts and arms and legs, hoping the onion would pull them out too."

Lyle laughed. "That's exactly what I would do," he said. "Wouldn't you?"

Didi moaned and went on, "The onion was strong and the onion would have pulled them all out. Except the old hag started cursing at the other sinners, prying their fingers off her and shrieking, 'It's my onion, it's my onion, let go, vermin, it's my onion.' "

"She is so selfish," Lyle commented.

"That's when the onion broke, and Gabriel, with great pity, watched the old woman and the other sinners fall back into hell for eternity."

Didi couldn't hear Lyle respond, as she panted heavily, trying to work her way through baby pain, through the tunnel.

Then Didi heard Lyle laugh softly. "Did you hear me, Didi?"

"No, Lyle, I'm sorry. What did you say?"

"The park is so quiet. No one but me is talking. How could you not hear me?" His voice sounded petulant.

"I was trying to swallow. My throat is hurting. I really need a drink. Sorry. Could you say it again, please?" *You bastard.*

"I said," Lyle repeated impatiently, "that I don't see how that story relates to me. Unless you're talking about yourself as the old woman. Which I don't think you are. Am I right?"

"You're right. I'm not."

"Didn't think so. Well, *I've* done plenty of good things in my life. See, that's the whole problem. I've been a good person all my life. I don't see why God had to punish me."

"I don't see why *you* have to punish *me.*"

"I'm not punishing you. God is."

"God is too busy to be punishing me. And I don't deserve to be punished," said Didi, shifting on the bench. Her legs were falling asleep from sitting in one position.

"I didn't deserve to be punished, either," said Lyle.

"But you weren't punished by me, Lyle," Didi exclaimed. "What did I ever do to you?"

"Nothing. That's my point. What did *I* ever do to God? I wasn't that old woman."

Oddly, that had been precisely what Didi had been thinking. *What did I ever do to God?* Then she felt—resigned? No, but a feeling of failure began to wash over her, and failing a discovery of meaning in these old woods, Didi, struggling to believe in something, began to believe in her own death.

"And Didi, don't fool yourself. God led you into my hands. It wasn't a coincidence that it was you I found today. It was fate. It was divine providence, yours and mine, that our lives became tangled. Why didn't I find another pregnant woman—"

"What does being pregnant have to do with anything?" Didi said, desperation in her voice.

"Don't interrupt!" Lyle shouted, and she fell quiet immediately. They were unevenly matched—she pregnant and handcuffed, and he with two guns, a knife, and an agenda.

"Why did I go to the NorthPark Mall, the richest of all the malls, and why was the first thing I spied with my little eye as I got out of my car your belly in the yellow dress? I saw you and I said to myself, bingo. Bingo. Why didn't I find another pregnant woman?"

"I don't know," she said. "Because God wasn't looking after me."

"Damn right. Because it was your fate. When our fate comes calling, the only thing we can do is follow limply along."

"Well, Lyle, isn't it so convenient for you to be so fatalistic when it comes to my bad fortune and so rebellious when it comes to your own?" Didi said sarcastically.

He was quiet a second and then said, "What are you talking about?"

"Why do you think it's my fate to have met you but not your fate to have your wife and child die?"

"Because that was not fate. That was God's way of saying 'Screw you.' "

"Oh, for heaven's sake!" she exclaimed. "And this isn't God's way of saying 'Screw you' to me? If this isn't, Lyle, I don't know what is," she added. "My point is, bad things do happen. They happen to every-one—"

"Except you—"

"Now, even to me," Didi retorted. "This awful thing had happened to you, but instead of healing and coping and going on, you decided to turn on me. And what if you kill me, Lyle? And then my husband goes nuts and kills someone else? Some poor innocent fool who never knew what was coming to him? And what if the wife or husband of Rich's victim kills someone else? Think about it—it all started with you, Lyle. All with you."

"Not with me," Lyle said. "With God."

"No, Lyle, with you. God was testing your faith, or looking the other way. But you actively *sought* me out to hurt me."

"He had sought out my wife and son—"

"Oh, my God. No. Your wife got sick, and your son was too small to save. Think of how many small babies God saves—"

"Think of how many He doesn't. Mine He didn't."

Didi stood up in her agitation and said, "First you say you don't believe in Him, then you say He wasn't looking your way, then you say He actually tried to hurt you. Well, which is it, Lyle? It can't be all three, you know."

Lyle said, "Sit down, Didi. I don't like you to get so excited near me. You might hit me again."

Sitting back down, Didi continued, "That was my point, that was my whole point about the woman and the onion. With one good deed, she could have saved so many people. But you with one bad deed can harm just as many. You've already got the blood of two people on your hands, Lyle. One of them a police officer, probably with a wife and a couple of kids. That's what you did to his life and to her life, and to the life of his kids. You single-handedly ruined all of them forever. That's your legacy—"

"Shut up!" he screamed. "Shut up, shut up, shut up!" And he jumped up, ran up to her, and smashed the Colt hard into her face. Didi's nose felt as if she had run full force into a concrete block. "Shut up," he said, much quieter, "or I swear I will kill you now."

She choked on her blood, which flowed freely into her mouth from her nose, and started to cough, but she felt nothing, except another baby pain that wouldn't stop for a broken nose, for a gashed head, for lacerated fingers, for a murdered cop. For nothing.

When the contraction was over, she wiped her nose with the top of her hand, hiding the broken bottle underneath. She tried to hold the nose between her fingers to stop the bleeding, but it hurt too much. So she bent forward and let the blood drip on the ground. At that moment Didi knew her dying wasn't going to stop her baby from forcing his way into the world.

"What do you want with me, Lyle?" Didi whispered, spitting blood out as she spoke. "What do you want with me?"

**R**ich was in a frenzy. "I can't believe we're just sitting here, sitting here doing nothing. What if the Blecks are away on vacation? How long are we going to sit here before we realize we're too late, or they're not coming, or they don't have any answers? How long?"

"We are the ones just sitting, Rich," Scott said. "The rest of my men are all over this town. They're not sitting, and they will find him. Maybe Lyle and Didi are eating dinner somewhere, maybe they went to the movies. The cops are looking everywhere." Scott's face was drawn, but Rich observed fierce resolve. "We'll find him, Rich," Scott said. "And we'll find her."

"Don't you feel helpless sitting here waiting for something?" Rich said in a broken voice. "I thought she needed me to take out the garbage and to help with the kids and to get the jars off the high shelf and to speed her up a little when she crossed the street, but I see that she needs me to save her life, and I can't do it."

"I know, Rich." Scott said. "Today I hate my job."

"Today I hate my life," said Rich.

"Why don't you call home? Talk to your kids. It'll make you feel better."

Rich looked at his watch. "You're kidding me, right? The kids are in bed, and my mother is sitting at the kitchen table chain-smoking and picking up the phone every few seconds to see if it's still working. What am I going to tell my mother?"

"She must be worried sick. Just call her."

As Rich shook his head, Scott's cell phone trilled. Scott flipped it open and listened intently.

"Rich," he said, "they found the car! The Eden deputies found it."

"Oh my God," said Rich, feeling ready to collapse. "Is she there, is Didi there?"

Shaking his head, Scott said, "No, just the car."

Rich leaned against the hood.

"This is good news," Scott said. "We've got the bastard's car." Into the phone, Scott said, "I want you to take the car away from there. Get a tow truck and tow it. Tow it here. I want to see it. Oh, and leave ten men to wait for him to come get his Honda." He hung up and said to Rich, "Tony's Body Shop, off Eighty-seven. They found it in the back, in mint condition near some wrecks. The vehicle ID number matches up. It's the right car."

Rich couldn't think anymore. "What does that mean, that we found the Honda?" His brain was candy. "What does it mean?"

Scott gently shook Rich in a show of support. "It means," he said, "that Lyle Luft is still in Eden. And if he's still here, we'll find him. We'll get him when he comes to collect the car, or we'll get him after we talk to the Blecks."

"The cemetery!" Rich exclaimed. "His wife—the cemetery!"

"What? What?" said Scott. "I don't follow."

Rubbing his face with hands sweaty from heat and tension, Rich said,

"Does it make sense? His wife is probably buried in her home town. Eden must have a cemetery. I bet he went there."

Scott threw open the phone. In thirty seconds he dispatched three police cars to the Eden cemetery.

"You're smart, Rich," Scott said.

"No, I'm not," Rich replied. "I love my wife." He paused, struggling with his thoughts. "I know if my wife died, that's where I'd go—her grave."

"Why?" said Scott, listening to Rich, unblinking. "Why would you go there in the dark?"

Shrugging, Rich said, "Maybe when he went there it wasn't dark yet. I don't know. I'd go to visit. Or to say good-bye or to kill myself." His insides hurt so much, he felt as if blood were draining away from his heart and into the street. He felt light-headed. Lyle Luft wouldn't be killing himself until *after* he had killed Didi. Rich stood up, but his knees were weak.

Scott must have seen Rich's anxiety, because he said, looking up at him, "You can cross that out. Lyle is not killing himself."

"How do you know?" Rich said, unrelieved.

"Because," said Scott, "he wouldn't be needing a second car, would he? He could kill himself at his wife's grave, but after that, he wouldn't be going anywhere in his Honda, would he?"

Rich felt better.

A few minutes later the tow truck drove up the street, pulling along a white Accord. After the car was lowered off the hoist, Scott and Rich glanced in. It was too dark on the street for detailed observation, but the car looked clean. It was also locked. Scott popped open the door with a thin metal band and smiled at Rich. "I'm also a pretty good pickpocket in a pinch. What? Do you think I'm in the wrong business?"

"I'll tell you after you get my wife back."

One of the other police officers had sprung open the trunk. "Scott? You'd better come over here and take a look at this."

Rich and Scott quickly walked around. They looked inside the trunk. Rich staggered back. "Oh, God," he said. "Oh, God. Oh, Didi."

........................................................................
........................................................................
........................................................................

# 1 0 : 1 7  P. M.

........................................................................
........................................................................
........................................................................

What do I want with you, Didi?" Lyle said, keeping a polite distance away from her on the picnic bench. He was measurably calmer, and he smiled. "You haven't figured it out yet?"

"I haven't figured it out yet," Didi said tiredly. The fight was oozing out of her. She swallowed blood. All propriety gone, she lifted her dress and held the hem to her nose. It was quickly saturated with blood. Didi thought that soon there would be no hiding her contractions even from him, dense as he was. The pain was now overwhelming. When it came, there was nothing to do but grit her teeth and try to get through it. How could she put herself in labor at his mercy? She didn't by now expect him to run and get help.

Didi wasn't thinking much past getting away from Lyle. The fact that there was a baby on the way and she was in a place called Pfluger Park hadn't fully registered. The coming of the baby hovered behind thirst and fear and Lyle. It hovered back in Dallas, in a hospital bed, with Rich next to her, saying, *hush, baby, hush, wanna see what's on TV?*

"Haven't figured it out yet, huh?" Lyle said. "You can be a little slow. Is it the heat? Want to play our favorite game? Guess."

Didi drew in her breath, her body throbbing, shifting down on the bench. She propped herself against the back of the picnic table and said, "I see you're not done torturing me yet, Lyle. I thought after you killed two people and brought me here, we might be through playing. But I guess not. Okay, let's see. You mean you didn't just pluck me out of a crowd randomly like picking numbers in Lotto?"

Lyle shook his head. "No."

She asked uncertainly, "Did you know me, Lyle? Did you know who I was?"

He shook his head. "No, nothing like that. I didn't know you. I never laid eyes on you until this afternoon."

This afternoon? Surely not this afternoon. She had spent a lifetime with Lyle. Hers, the baby's, the girls', her husband's lifetime.

"Okay," she whispered. How long were they going to sit here at a picnic table in the middle of a park at night and pretend they were lovers, pretend they were future husband and wife, falling in love in Pfluger Park under the stars?

"Not much longer, Didi," said Lyle, "Two more guesses."

"You took me because I looked like your wife and you wanted to relive her through me?"

Again Lyle shook his head. "Melanie was small and blond. She was also careful with money. Nothing like you."

"I'm running out of ideas, Lyle," said Didi.

"One more, Desdemona. One more."

"Because I was shopping in NorthPark, you were under the mistaken impression I was rich and you wanted money from my family?"

"Having spent all day with me, you gotta know that that can't be it.

So why even say it? When my wife died," he said, "I received a small settlement from the hospital. Mel's parents threatened to sue, and the hospital was only too happy to give us a little dough. I got some and they got some."

"So if you have money, why did you sell my ring?"

"Just for the hell of it. Wanted some cash in hand."

Heavy-hearted, Didi thumbed the bottle neck, still between her fingers, and said, "I'm done, Lyle. I'm sapped dry. Not another idea in my head. I lose."

"You lose," said Lyle. "Let me tell you what I want."

He stood up and came up to her. She struggled to her feet.

And then Lyle whispered intensely, "*I want your baby, Didi.*"

## 1 0 : 2 0 P.M.

**R**ich and Scott stared mutely into the trunk of Lyle Luft's Honda. The two cops shined big black flashlights inside. Rich saw a white plastic baby bath, and inside that a patterned infant car seat. He saw two paper shopping bags filled with baby clothes. He saw a large Winnie-the-Pooh, and a small Mickey Mouse. There were six cases of ready-made bottles of Enfamil and six cases of size 1 and 2 diapers, all neatly stacked.

An unmarked car pulled up and two FBI men got out. Coming up behind Scott, one of the men said, "We've looked for them everywhere. They're not here."

"Of course they are," Scott barked. "Look at the trunk! You've got to find them, and fast. He's hiding out. He's here, in a private place. Maybe he's got an apartment or a room somewhere. Don't come back till you've found them."

The FBI man sighed and shrugged. "Will do my best, sir," he said and got back inside his car.

Rich stumbled away from the Honda. Scott followed him, H&K in hand. "Rich—"

Whirling around, Rich exclaimed, "And I thought we were helpless before! All of you guys, all of you, can't do anything. Not a single one of you. God!"

Scott lowered his head, and the black bandanna slipped over his forehead. Rich saw it and was angered enough to pull his own bandanna off his head and fling it to the ground.

Scott was silent a moment, and then pulled his bandanna off too.

Rich grabbed Scott by the shoulders. "We have to find her," he said intensely, shaking Scott and not letting go. "We have to find her right now."

As they were talking, a dark sedan pulled up. Two people got out and started walking toward the house.

**D**idi didn't wait for Lyle to continue. She pushed him as hard as she could, raised her hands high above her head, and, aiming for his eye, thrust the ragged edge of the bottle neck into his face. He dropped his gun and stumbled back, the glass stuck deep in the flesh of his cheek.

Screaming, she ran around the picnic table. Lyle jumped up on the table, ran across it, jumped down, and lunged at her. She moved quickly away, and he fell on the ground. Raising her foot, Didi kicked him hard in the ribs. While he was down she kicked him again, aiming at his groin. She missed and connected with his thigh instead. In frenzied frustration, she wanted to scream, but all that came out was something throaty and unnatural, like the dying breaths of a half-eaten animal. He's still here, and I am too, she thought. I am never going to get away from him.

Didi tried to kick him in the head, but Lyle caught her foot, tripping her. She fell hard on her back.

P A U L L I N A   S I M O N S

Wildly, she wriggled her foot free, leaving her sandal in his hands. She scrambled up, and he attempted to get up too, moaning. A quick thought ran through Didi's head—*Can't believe the bastard is moaning*—and just then she heard a pop, *felt* a pop, like a water-filled balloon at a town fair, POP and hot liquid gushed down between her legs, through her underwear, down her calves, onto her feet and to the ground.

Ahh, Didi let out an anguished breath, *ahh,* to let go, to relieve her heartbreak.

The water was here, the worst was here. Her baby was not waiting another hour to come into these woods and into Lyle's bloodied hands. Her throat was mute and her eyes didn't cry because her womb was crying hot water, crying right down her thighs.

Ahh.

She stepped away from Lyle and in a defenseless, useless gesture put her hands between her legs. The handcuffs pressed against her thighs. She immediately leaned down to Lyle and raised her arms to hit him.

He was quicker. He grabbed her legs, yanking her toward him, and she fell. He turned her over and fell on top of her.

"You bitch," he whispered. "Look what you did, look what you did to my face." Supporting himself on one hand, he grabbed the neck of the beer bottle and with a piercing yell yanked it out of his cheek. "You bitch," he said. "You gonna die." He flung the bottle away.

"Get off me," she hissed into his sweating, bleeding face. "Get off me."

"I'm not going anywhere," Lyle panted back. "Why are your legs wet? Have you wet yourself?"

"Get off me!" Didi's arms were pinned between her breasts and Lyle's chest. Her cuffed hands were pinned between them. There was nowhere for her to go. She whispered, "You're hurting the baby."

Lyle was not moving. "Scared, Didi?" he said into her face. "I

**2 6 2**

haven't gotten to kiss you properly—" And he roughly pressed his lips on hers.

She spit into his mouth, and a clump shot out far into his throat; he choked. "Goddamn, what was that?" he yelled. Didi hoped it was her half-dried blood.

She tried to move her face away from his. He pulled up, and she screamed. Lyle shoved the palm of his hand against her mouth and nose.

Didi fainted, or she thought she fainted, because she didn't hear Lyle for a while. She didn't hear herself either, screaming or crying or whispering. When she came to, he was still on top of her but had relaxed a bit, seeing the fight had left her. Though he was still on top of her, he didn't feel as heavy. Then she felt him, oh, what is he doing, is he unzipping his jeans? Oh, no, and then the Belly made her forget even Lyle, forget everything.

"Oh Christ," she whimpered. The pain was intolerable. "Please, please help me, please help me, please, please . . ."

On top of her Lyle laughed.

Then the baby pain was over. Didi needed to move her hands above her head. They were stuck and digging into her abdomen. Getting them out of the cuffs looked impossible.

"Desdemona," Lyle said, fumbling with her dress, touching her thighs, "your legs are so wet."

"Let me touch them, Lyle, let me touch them," she said.

"I'm not letting you move, pretty fucking Didi. You can't be trusted. It's a good thing I have the cuffs on you."

"Let me bring my hands up above my head," she whispered. "You're hurting them like this, let me just move them—"

He ground against her—against her thighs, against her stomach. His movement helped her to free her hands from his chest.

The baby pain was slamming her belly again. She screamed, with her cuffed hands just above her head.

All that time when she was holding the bottle neck she had been hoping for a miracle, but the miracle had turned out to be just a little black magic. He got close and she sliced him, she scarred him for life, sure, but that was it.

She was moaning uncontrollably. *The baby, the baby, you're hurting Mommy, you're hurting me, please, please help me . . . please . . .*

His hand cupped her mouth again. "Shut up!" he screamed at her. "Will you shut the fuck up?"

Didi thrust her hands forward and hit him with the rim of the handcuffs. She thought she hit him on the top of his head as he nuzzled in her neck, but he was barely hurt.

Lyle lifted his head and said, "What the hell are you doing?"

"Get off me, get off," she begged. "Help me, please, please, dear God, Lord Jesus, help me now, help me, please."

Fumbling with her underwear, Lyle said, "Do you hear me, Didi? Stop screaming, or I'll have to kill you that much sooner. Live a little longer, even if it is with me. But live, Didi."

When she wouldn't stop, he ripped her wet panties off her. Didi didn't give a shit about anything. She needed him off her instantly.

"Lyle, let me get on top of you," she pleaded. "You want me, Lyle?"

"Yes, Barcelona," he said. "I don't want you to be chaste when your husband finds you. I don't want him to think you died without sin."

"Then, Lyle, let's do it well instead of badly," she said feebly. To get him off the baby, she would have taken him standing.

He laughed and kissed her again, or licked her, or brushed his mouth on hers. She didn't give a damn anymore and couldn't believe he would want to touch her blood-covered body, couldn't believe he wanted to, to—with the broken holy water of her baby.

*The baby's holy water.*

She could barely breathe, and the pains came again. He ground against her. She tried to move from under him. It was no use.

He's going to squeeze the baby out of me with his weight, oh God he wants to take my baby—

Then she felt something sharp at her throat. She thought it was thirst at first. Her eyes were closed. Or was it just dark?

She opened her mouth to speak and felt pain at her throat again. "Didi?" he said softly into her face. "How long do you think it will take you to bleed to death if I cut you?"

"I'm not dying, Lyle," she said hoarsely, her world darkening.

"Open your eyes and look. Open them."

So they *were* closed. She opened them.

In front of her face she made out the shape of his knife. The same knife that had slid across her fingers earlier when all she had been fighting for was her ring.

Didi closed her eyes.

She felt an awful pushing sensation inside her groin. It was an insane baby pain—his head pressing against her pelvis.

"What are you going to do, Lyle? What are you going to do, you worthless piece of shit?" she hissed at him between her moans through her gritted teeth. "Because you'd better do it now. You're hurting the baby. You say you want it? Then get off it, get off the baby!"

That seemed to make an impression on Lyle. Still holding the knife in his right hand, he propped himself up on his arms as if he were about to do push-ups. His body came off hers. Holding himself up, he pushed her legs open.

Didi's mouth opened and her head moved from side to side. This is how my life—*deliver me, protect me from the violent, keep me, keep me, Lord God do not strip me of my life*—

She felt his penis trying to find her.

"God, you're wet," he whispered. She felt the knife at the inside of her thigh. "You know what I plan to do, Didi? I plan to fuck you, and then I'm going to cut the baby from you. I will take the baby from you, and then I will cut the cord, and then I will leave with it, and I will go to Mazatlán. I would have taken you too, but I see that you don't love me and you never will. Don't worry," he panted. "Your last deed in this world will be a good one, Desdemona, don't you worry. You lived to give life, you will die to give life to your child. It's a good deed, and you will go to heaven. Maybe God won't forget you then, when the good angel Gabriel will come to Him—" Lyle's breath assaulted her face—"to show him the onion of your good deeds—"

Didi uttered a breathless cry. The baby pushed against her insides, and his penis pushed against her crotch.

"But Didi," Lyle said, bringing the knife down to the ground and holding himself up above her. "But Didi, tell me," he whispered gleefully into her face, "when you're being lifted out of hell by Gabriel, tell me the truth—will you let me hang on to your soaking yellow dress, so that I might be saved too?"

Didi felt life seeping out of her.

Lyle laughed. "I thought so," he said.

He was thrusting into her, but still not finding her. Her big belly and his angle were making it difficult for him. Didi felt another gush of water flow out. "Wait," she whispered, suddenly getting an idea. "Wait, let me help you. You can't find me. Let me help. Lift up a little."

He lifted his pelvis higher. The knife rested on the ground under his right hand. He wasn't holding it; he was holding himself up.

"Wait, Lyle, wait," Didi said. With a superhuman effort, she lifted her head and chest off the ground. Without her hands to help her, she was nearly paralyzed under him. "Wait," she moaned. "I can't—can't push off the ground. My hands are no help." She stuck both hands between her legs, right into her own wetness, and she rubbed them back and forth, all the while muttering, "Wait a second, wait, where are you, where are you?"

"Here I am," and he thrust himself into her cuffed hands. He shouldn't trust me so much, thought Didi. Her fingers went around his balls—

Instantly he brought the knife to her throat and screeched into her face, "Let go, let go right now."

She let go. "Let me help," she said. "Some men like that, you know."

"Not this man," he said, relaxing a little and supporting himself on his hands again.

He senses so many things about me, thought Didi.

*Though not all things.*

Didi thought, here we are. He's rubbing his dick against me and I am rubbing myself on my blood and water. God forgive me.

Crying out in pain, she fell back on the ground. She pulled up her hands from between her legs, twisting her left wrist, slippery with blood, out of the cuff.

*That's it. I got it out! I got it out. All I needed was a little blood and water!* She nearly wept.

"Can't hold myself up anymore," Didi whispered.

"Don't need to," he said and rammed himself inside her.

She felt him slamming into her body. She heard him moan and felt rage: how dare he moan? How dare he? And he told her how he dared. "You're so wet," he said. "How can you be so wet?" And she was going to tell him she was about to have a baby, to stop, but all that came out of her was a hacking "Please." *Please, please.*

*Please don't hurt me.*

*Anymore.*

*Please—*

Lyle stopped moving for a moment, saying, "Too good, too good. Wait. I'm gonna wait, just a second." And she felt the fury fighting thirst in her throat. He bent his head down to hers to kiss her. Then he stopped.

"You don't taste so good," he said.

"No?" she croaked. "Must be the blood."

In the dark, she saw him look at her distastefully.

He said, "Desdemona, should I suffocate you?"

She moved her head slowly from side to side. She lay very quietly, her hands close together above her head.

"How would you like it, Didi? I thought you would like Desdemona's death." He was breathing into her mouth. "Listen," he said. "Don't worry about your baby. It will be safe with me. In Mazatlán. I'll rent a house by the ocean. Our baby will like it. I promise."

Didi's face was turned away from him. She was barely listening. Her attention was focused on his right hand and the knife.

She felt him bend down and kiss her cheek. He moved inside her. She willed herself to keep her eyes open. "Desdemona," he said. "I like you, you know. A lot. You're feisty. If it's a girl, I will name her for you, all right? I will name her Desdemona. Would you like that?"

She did not answer him.

"It will be all right." He was starting to breathe heavier. "I just want to—" He groaned. "Just one thing, and then I am going to—" He could barely keep talking. Keeping himself up and moving against her was taking all his strength. "It will be all right, pretty Didi."

Labored breathing. His? Hers?

No, she wasn't moving at all. Her energy was waning, but her gaze was riveted on the knife under his right hand.

She was right-handed, but she would have to be ambidextrous for the first time in her life. Yes, she couldn't throw with her left hand and she couldn't cut meat with her left hand. Now she would have to try.

Lyle was on guard and wary of her. Even this close to climax, he wasn't letting the knife go. Didi decided to help him. "Come on, Lyle," she whispered. "Come on. Feels so good, doesn't it? Come on, move, move harder, more," she moaned, her belly tensing into the grip of agony. "Come on, Lyle, it'll be so good, I like it too, move, go on, go on, go on."

As he moved harder, she groaned, screamed maybe, she couldn't tell.

She heard him yell out, "Ahhh, yes, yes, yes." Quickly she turned her head to look at him. His eyes were closed.

In the next second, Didi turned her head to the left and slid her freed left hand from above her head down in an arc to Lyle's hand. He had let go of the knife and was clutching the grass. The knife was free.

In one motion Didi grabbed the knife handle and then turned her head to see Lyle's face. His eyes were still closed, but his brain had belatedly realized something was wrong. Didi could tell, because even now, in the throes of coming, he tensed. Didi knew half a second more and all would be lost.

There was no time for him to open his eyes.

Didi screamed and rammed the blade into the side of Lyle's neck.

Lyle opened his eyes.

His mouth went slack in stunned surprise, his throat gurgled, and blood poured out. He collapsed against her, and his hand grabbed her elbow, then her forearm. Didi whimpered. She tried to break free of his hand but did not let go of the knife. The blade continued to pulse back and forth inside his throat.

The only sound coming from Lyle was the sound of a backed-up, sloshing sink. He was convulsing on top of her, burbling. Didi felt wet all over.

Get off me, she thought. Get off me, get off me! But she couldn't move him.

Terrified because he seemed so alive, Didi thought, it's all over for me. I couldn't kill him, he's laughing at me, I grazed the back of his head, or his ear, and he's pushing against me, into me, he's trying to crush me with his weight, with his laughter, and when he stops, that's when I'm done for, God, one chance, one chance to see that my baby didn't end up in Mazatlán, and look what I've done, scratched Lyle with his own knife, we're all sweating, I'm sweating from him, from the baby, these are my last sweats, I didn't need to stick my handcuffs into myself to make my hands slippery, feel how slippery my sweat is, and his too, the pig is sweating too.

Didi wasn't letting go of the knife, and Lyle wasn't asking her for it. She wanted to tell him he was too heavy, but she thought he knew that. He wasn't about to help her.

She tried to move the knife away from him, but the knife wouldn't move. Was it stuck in Lyle? She was still grasping it, so she twisted it up and down with all the force she could muster.

And then Lyle stopped moving.

Didi still felt a twitch here and there, but it could have been her own body. She wasn't sure, but Lyle seemed to have stopped moving completely—

*But he hasn't stopped sweating*, Didi thought with disgust. God, how can he be this wet? Or is it me? Am I wet?

Get off me, she said. Or thought she said. Or felt. Or prayed.

No. She didn't pray.

"Get off me, you revolting bastard," she said, her raw throat hurting. "Can you hear me?"

Lyle's head slipped off her shoulder and hung down to the ground.

Didi moved slightly out from under him, and breathed. Lyle's heavy body felt flaccid.

And Didi thought, *I didn't miss.*

Ahh, she breathed. I didn't miss.

"Get off me, you bastard," she said, louder.

There was no movement from Lyle.

Didi grabbed his shirt with her right hand and yanked him hard enough to slip half her body out, then the rest of it. She slapped his forehead with the palm of her right hand. The cuffs hit him, and his head bobbed back.

He was dead.

His eyes stared out at the moon and at Didi. His mouth was open in the same stunned surprise.

That's the face I'll remember, she thought, gritting her teeth. The relief left her. She felt pain start up inside her, rev up, and grip her. Moaning, she let go of the knife, closed her eyes, and clutched at the ground and her dress and her leg. When the contraction was over, Didi opened her eyes.

The right side of Lyle's throat was torn open. Even in the dark, Didi could see the ragged wound. Didi grabbed the handle and pulled the knife out. The hole gaped bigger, blacker, more exposed.

Didi realized she was too weak to stand up.

She touched her dress. It was wet. She looked at it. In the moonlight, her once yellow dress looked black. She felt her face. It was sticky.

Her arms, her chest, her entire body were covered with his blood as it drained out of him and down onto her.

She didn't care. He was dead.

"You're dead, you pig," she whispered, lying next to him on her right side, holding her belly. It was a bit more comfortable if she lay on her side. She dropped the knife, and with her left hand grabbed him by the hair, lifted his flopping head, shook it, and let it fall hard to the ground. She liked the sound. She let it fall again.

"Now I'd like to torture you, Lyle," she said, turning to him. "I'd like to torture you for a day—" And she started to cry and clutch at the ground. "Please," she whispered into the ground. "Please, somebody, help me." She clawed at the ground, tried to grab on and hold anything until the pain was over. With her water broken, Didi felt the contractions slam at her.

There was no time between contractions. It was the end, and she knew it. She had hoped it wasn't so, but now was the time to press her chin to her chest and bear down.

Maybe I can move next time, in the next thirty seconds when I'm feeling no pain.

But Didi couldn't move in the next thirty seconds between contractions either. The need to push did not abate. It was blinding, even when she lay on her side.

She rolled over, looking for the car, and then rolled back to Lyle and muttered, "I'd like to stay and make you cry, Lyle. But I'm tired of looking at your stinking face, and I have a baby to bear. A baby that's not going to end up in Mazatlán. I wanted to ask you something, but never got the chance. Did you become whole through my suffering? Did my humiliation heal you, make you one with God, you filthy piece of shit?"

She rolled away from him and cried through another contraction, pleading into the ground for someone to help her.

*Lyle, I know how you died and you had a bad death, but it was the death you deserved. You once asked me this and I answered you, but I lied. I'm not going to cry for you, and if my baby and I are going to be okay, I'll never think of you again. But if something should go wrong, if I'm never going to be able to have children after this, or if I lose my vocal cords or my rotted fingers, or if my septum leaks for the rest of my life, daily reminding me of you, then I'll remember that you're burning in hell, your immortal soul having gone through reliction, and I will feel better. Either way, you should have killed me quick instead of torturing me, because I wasn't going to go silently.*

*Lyle, you didn't know me at all.*

She picked up the knife and wiped it on her dress. The knife remained slick and bloody. She let it fall to the ground.

*I'm leaving you, and you'll have to have the Lord Jesus Christ ask for your eternal soul.*

Didi Wood couldn't stand up or leave him.

Lying on her side, facing him, she folded her hands together and prayed. *Give rest, Oh Christ, to Your servant, where sorrow and pain are no more, neither sighing nor life everlasting.* She meant to say *but life everlasting,* but went on without correcting herself. *Into Your hands we commend Your servant, we humbly beseech You, a sinner of Your own redeeming, receive him into the arms of Your mercy. Amen.*

At last Didi staggered up and limped to the car, handcuffs at her right side, water trickling down her legs.

Unforgiving gravity was pressing the baby down. Gravity's help was the *last* thing she wanted.

To stand and walk was unbearable.

When she got inside the car, she sat down.

That wasn't much better.

So she lay down on her side again, her head at the wheel, and tried not to push.

One thirty seconds.

Two thirty seconds.

Three thirty seconds. She couldn't open her eyes now. She was nearly done. The pressure in her groin intensified.

"No," she whispered. "No. We're not ready. I'm not ready. We can't be born yet, darling. Mommy needs to sleep just a little bit. Please . . . please help me."

Four thirty seconds.

She had to do something.

She pressed on the horn. It blared harshly and briefly in the darkened park.

## 1 0 : 3 5   P. M.

**W**e didn't do anything," was the first thing Bernie Bleck said.

"No, nothing," his wife said.

"That's good," said Scott. "Glad to hear it."

"If this is about the taxes from 1995—"

Scott cut him off. "How much do you owe?"

Rich nudged him.

Bernie said, "I don't know." Turning to Mrs. Bleck, "How much do we owe, missus?"

Maureen Bleck started to talk. "What, altogether? See, we meant to pay, but Bernie here, he came into a little bit of money, we sold one of our houses—not that we have so many or anything, no, we just had two, and we sold one of them, and we meant to build us a nice house in Naples, Florida, you know where that is? It's a real nice area, real warm, and the people are real nice, anyhow, we meant to build us a house, but things came up—and we never did go ahead and do it." She shook her head and stared at the ground.

Rich saw that Scott was about to let go his short-leashed temper. Yet something stopped him. Rich knew what made him stop gritting his teeth. He too felt fleetingly sorry for poor old Maureen Bleck, who had lost her daughter and grandson.

"Mrs. Bleck," said Scott, "that isn't why I'm here."

Bernie Bleck sucked in his breath.

"Don't worry, Mr. Bleck, sir," said Scott. "No matter how efficient you think the U.S. government is, not all branches communicate with each other. Believe me, this is not my jurisdiction. I do not do the dirty work of the Treasury. Well, not today anyway. No, I'm here because we want to know if you've seen your son-in-law lately."

"Son-in-law?" Bernie exclaimed. "Lyle? No, we haven't seen him since—" He caught himself. "Since a few months ago."

"No," said Maureen, hanging on to her husband. "Not since a few months ago."

Clinging to each other, they were inching their way to their porch.

Scott went around and stood in their path. Reluctantly they stopped.

"Have you seen him today?"

"Today? No, of course, not," said Bernie. "Why would we see him today?"

"He hasn't stopped by? He hasn't called?"

"Not as of seven o'clock," said Bernie.

"Maybe he called since then," said Maureen.

"I doubt it," said Bernie. "Why would he?"

Scott asked, "Where did you go?"

"To San Angelo. To the movies," Maureen said.

Scott said, "Mr. and Mrs. Bleck. Lyle Luft kidnapped this man's wife. A pregnant woman. This is a matter of life and death. He has come to Eden to pick up a car and then disappear. We found the car, but we haven't found him. We need to know where he may be hiding out. Lyle has killed a police officer and stolen his vehicle, so he has to be in a place where he can hide the car. Do you have any idea where he might be?"

The cell phone rang. Scott listened, grunted, then hung up. "Somewhere *other* than the Eden cemetery," he said. "Because he's not there."

Deflated, Rich stood spiritlessly at Scott's side.

"Gee, we haven't seen him in a long time," said Mrs. Bleck. "Where could they have gone, Bernie?"

Bernie wasn't listening. "God, I knew he was crazy. I told you and told you," he snapped. "Told Mel too. Don't marry him, I said. He is unstable. He'll make you unhappy." Bernie Bleck shook his head miserably. "Now look what he's gone and done."

Scott said sternly, "We need to find him right away. Is there any place at all that Lyle and your daughter hung out, frequented, liked? Any place here that meant something to him?"

"They used to go to the movies a lot," said Maureen, sniffling. "But the movie theaters are in San Angelo." She turned to Rich, "I'm real sorry—"

"Where else?" Scott interrupted her.

"Where else, Bernie?"

"How the hell should I know where that maniac liked to go? I told her not to marry him!"

"Try to stay focused, Mr. Bleck. Where else? He's not in San Angelo. He's here in Eden. He's someplace where he can hide a large Crown Victoria police car."

"Maybe Tony's garage?" offered Bernie Bleck. "He was kind of friendly with Tony."

"My men have searched the whole place. They're not there. That's where his Honda was, though, so you're on the right track. Can you think of anyplace else?"

"Not really," said Mrs. Bleck. "This is a real small town, you know. They met in Abilene, where Mel worked as assistant manager of a Taco

Bell. But here there really wasn't much for them to do. They went to the park a lot when they were here."

"Park?" Scott became rigid. "What park?"

"Pfluger Park. They used to go and have picnics there on Sundays—"

"Where is it?" Scott said, backing away and gesturing violently to the black vans and the cars.

"It's a few miles down Eighty-seven. There's a sign. Pfluger Park. It's kind of woodsy back there, and there are a couple of picnic areas, so I don't know—"

Scott was dragging Rich by the arm. "Thank you!" he yelled. "Let's go, let's go, let's go!"

Rich ran.

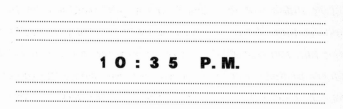

# 1 0 : 3 5   P. M.

**S**he didn't have the strength to keep pressing on the horn. No one was going to come anyway.

On the floor of the car, Didi saw her shopping bags from the mall. She wanted to get up, but she couldn't move. She lay in a fetal position, her right hand gripping the underside of the seat, holding on, riding the contraction down. She was in too much pain even to scream. All her energy was fighting the inevitable. She was too afraid to bring a baby into the world by herself. Yet every ninety seconds, her belly was telling her push, and every ninety seconds Didi was biting her lips in an effort not to.

Where are the keys to the car? Maybe I'll start the car up and drive to the nearest gas station, the nearest anything. I'll drive as long as driving somewhere doesn't take longer than thirty seconds.

It was too late to drive at this hour.

*They'd missed the ride to Mazatlán.*

No one to call. No radio, no phone. It's dark. I have no water. Don't they always tell you to have water nearby? Is that to wash the baby? It's a good thing I don't have any water. I'd drink it anyhow. The baby wouldn't get any.

Her body shattered through another contraction.

*Come on,* Desdemona. *Your hour has come.*

*No. I'll just lie on my side till help comes. I'll lie on my side and wait.*

*And the baby will die, stuck for an hour or two or four in the birth canal. Lyle didn't kill it, couldn't kill it, you wouldn't let him. You wouldn't let him. Why? So you could kill the baby yourself? So you could let him run out of life out of your womb but not into life yet? Somewhere in that tunnel, where you are and where the moon shines bright as your only light and where the trees are dark and the crickets cry, he's stuck with you, and you aren't getting up, Desdemona. Come on, get up,* she groaned, clasping the wheel. *GET UP, DIDI.*

She sat up, and felt the exploding pressure in her pelvis. *Push me, it said, or I will tear you from side to side. I will shred you.*

*Wait,* she breathed. *Wait. I have nothing to catch you with. I have nothing to tie you with, when you come. Just wait.*

Unbearable tremors overran her body. Her legs, her arms were shaking uncontrollably. In the hundred-degree heat of the night, Didi felt very cold. When the contraction was over, Didi ripped off her bloody dress. *I don't want my baby lying on Lyle's blood. He's not going to feel the pig anywhere near him.*

*Again.*

That motivated her. Disgusting bastard, she thought, leaning into the Victoria's Secret bag and pulling out her silk robe, silk nightgown, silk bra, and silk panties, all in the color of a nice burgundy. Didi took off her blood-soaked bra, but she had neither the stamina nor the coordination to put on the clean one. She hung on to the door handle and cried, breathing shallowly, breathing the baby back inside her.

In the next twenty seconds, she tried to put on the nightgown, and failed. Her shaking was too severe.

Didi finally managed to throw on the robe, ripping off one of the robe ties. Where's the knife? I need the knife. She had left it near Lyle. She moved the seat back as far as it would go, opened the car door, and screamed, "Help me!" Her voice rang through the trees. "Help me!" Didi didn't recognize her voice. It didn't belong to her. It belonged to a man, or a woman with no vocal cords. It barely registered out of the car. "Help me," the voice hoarsely whispered. Swinging the door shut, she laid the nightgown under herself. I have nothing to push against. I have no midwife to put my feet against, I have no stirrups, I have no Rich.

Who?

*Rich.*

"Help me," she whispered. "Dear God, help me."

*Still calling for God, after everything.*

Didi moved the seat closer to the dashboard.

The dashboard would have to be her Rich, her God, her midwife, her stirrups.

Putting her feet up on the dash, she gripped the door handle with one hand, the seat divider with the other, and rasped, "Okay. Let's go." And pushed.

She pushed as hard as she could. She felt as if she were being ripped from the inside out. Then it stopped. Panting, she let go of the door handle and lowered her hand between her legs. She felt a squishy, wet softness.

That's it, she thought. That's my baby. He's been there all along, just waiting for me.

Her teeth chattering, Didi remembered the cries of the nurses during her last labor. She put her chin on her chest, grabbed on to the door handle and the seat divider, and pushed.

And pushed and pushed. And then thought fleetingly, wait—

Here I am, pushing away, holding on for my life, shaking. But who's going to catch this baby?

And the answer came back to her in a rasp. You, Didi. You. Let go and guide your baby out.

She let go of the door handle, slumping against the seat and unable to hold herself upright any longer. The handcuffs were still attached to her right wrist. She could have found the keys, but they were with Lyle, and she'd be damned if she would touch that bastard again. Unless it was to kick him.

She put her fingers between the baby's crowned head and her own torn perineum and pushed. She pushed hard at first. If it hurt, she couldn't tell, she was numb, she was her own Darvocet, her own epidural anesthesia. She pushed hard, then remembered she was to push slow. At first it was just the squishiness, but then more came through, and for a second she became terrified that there was something wrong with the baby, because the head was so soft and pliant, and then she thought, *are the cuffs digging into his head,* and then, *no, that's not the head, it's his behind,* and before she had a chance to push again, the baby forced its head into the world. Didi held it in her hands. The little head was so slippery and she was shaking so badly, Didi thought, *I could drop it without meaning to, without wanting to. And where's the body? Do I have to push again? No, no.* Her legs were falling off the dash. Didi couldn't keep them up, couldn't keep them open. Grunting like a weight lifter, she pushed one more time, and then the body of her baby slipped quietly into her hands. She saw its back and behind. She turned it over.

It was a boy.

He was dark and still. *Oh, my God,* she thought, *he's not breathing.* She pried his mouth open with her fingers and a glob fell out. She didn't know what it was and wouldn't care to find out. She touched the baby's nose, his wet throat, opened the mouth a little more, held the head down for a few seconds. No sound was coming from him. Didi went deaf trying to hear her son's first cry.

Ahh, she breathed out, tears running down her face, ahh, come on, come on, darling. Taking him with both hands, Didi held him to her, and then lifted him up and turned him upside down and shook him a little. *Come on, come on.* She heard him croak and choke and splutter like an old car, and there was a little sound. Then it stopped.

*Oh, God! Come on, dear one, come on.* The baby coughed again, and suddenly let out a bellow, and even in the night, she saw his color change—from dark to something lighter. Didi put the baby on her naked belly and chest and realized she had been holding her breath. Grateful, she breathed out.

He cried. She saw his face. He was blue and his little face was all scrunched up and he was crying. "Wah, wah."

It was the best, the dearest sound.

Didi stroked his sticky head. His face was little, and his eyes were closed. His lips were very big, like Mick Jagger's lips. She didn't know where those lips came from. They were just enormous. Her throat made a noise. "My little one, my dear one, cry, my darling, cry."

And then she cried herself. "You're a sweet boy," she whispered. "You're a dear boy, you're Mommy's boy, and we've made it. Me and you, you and your mommy, we're here, and we're going to be okay. We didn't make that trip to Mazatlán, thank God. Thank Mommy. Thank you. You did very well," Didi said, stroking her baby's tiny face. "You did very well. What a brave one you are. Wanted to see your mommy, huh? Well, here I am."

Leaning back, Didi closed her eyes. "Today is the day God and I gave birth to my son," she whispered. "And his name is Adam."


Didi had nothing to cover the baby with. He was under a flap of her robe, but they couldn't both fit under it if Didi was going to try to find the highway.

The baby was still attached to her. There was nothing to cut the cord with except *the knife* near Lyle. She looked out of the car. She could see his silhouette on the ground. The cord would have to stay uncut.

There was no more pain. All pain had stopped when the baby was born, but her left wrist felt weak, and Didi thought she might have broken it trying to get free from the cuffs. Also there was a vague stunned feeling to her body. Parts of her felt swollen and numb. She was sure that tomorrow she would feel worse. It was a blessing she would feel anything at all *tomorrow*, Didi thought.

Her baby was crying.

"Dear Adam," she said. "I have nothing to wrap you in. All I have is the robe on my body and the nightgown that's all full of blood now, and my yellow dress, which is clearly unsuitable. Why don't you have some milk? And tell Mommy," she whispered, "what it's like to drink, Adam."

She put him to her breast, and it took him a few seconds, but he got the hang of it, and stopped crying, and opened his eyes. She looked down at him looking up at her, and muttered something to him, something sweet and simple.

Didi's eyes felt very heavy. She was about to fall asleep, but she suddenly became afraid that Lyle might still be alive. That he was just pretending to be dead, just so she could have her baby, and then he would snatch him, kill her, cut her throat, and escape to Mazatlán.

She had to get out of there.

Wearing only her wine robe, Didi gingerly stepped out of the car, holding her naked baby. She wobbled like a newborn giraffe and nearly fell over.

Didi looked to see where the road was. She was going to honk the horn, but then, thinking it might upset the little one, decided not to.

She found the road, and with the baby in her arms, began hobbling, clad in one sandal, to what she hoped was out of the park and onto the highway. After a few steps, she kicked the sandal off and continued walking barefoot.

If it hadn't been for the quarter-moon up above, she would have been lost in the dark.

Thank God for the moon.


Up ahead, she thought she heard a distant noise and saw bright lights. Is that God? Didi thought.

She saw a procession of cars with red and blue flashing lights turn off the main highway and rush toward her. Didi was walking in the middle of the road. The cars were coming up fast. Their lights were on her. The first car slowed down, then stopped. A man got out and ran toward her.

It's Lyle! thought Didi, turning around and limping with her baby away from the cars. She wanted to run, but couldn't run. She heard his voice: "Didi, Didi."

Oh, God, I knew it, I knew he was still alive, help me, and then arms grabbed her and a voice again said, "Didi," and a man was crying and holding her to him. She couldn't see his face. She wasn't dying yet.

"Didi," he said.

With one eye, she looked into a familiar face. The other eye felt as if it were closed forever. Was it Lyle? It was hard to tell. She hadn't seen another face in so long she'd forgotten what other men looked like. It wasn't the dead policeman. "Didi," the man repeated, looking at her with a horrified expression. "It's me, Didi, it's Rich."

Rich, she thought. Rich?

It wasn't Lyle.

The man was crying, and Didi mumbled to him, and he said, "What?"

She said it again, and he said, "I can't hear you! What?"

And she whispered, "Water. Water."

He started to go away, and she grabbed onto him with one arm. "Don't leave me," she said. "Water."

"Water!" Rich screamed. "Bring her some water!"

Someone ran out of the car with a bottle and gave it to Rich. Didi opened her mouth, and he put the bottle to her throat but didn't tilt it all the way up. He was trying to be delicate, but she grabbed it away from him and poured the contents of the bottle into her throat. Then she bent over and threw the water up without letting go of the baby.

"Let me hold the baby," Rich said, crying. "Is he alive? Let me hold the baby, Didi."

"No," she said, holding the infant tighter. "Water."

She was brought more. She continued to stand, then she sank down to the ground. She threw up the second time she drank and the third, but then some must have stayed inside her and she felt better.

Another man came up to her.

She looked up at him and he crouched down. He had a kind black face. She was leaning against Rich, who was holding her up in a sitting position. All Didi wanted was to lie down and sleep, so she lay down, holding the baby to her breast. The man leaned over her and said, "Didi, we're so sorry. We tried to find you. We really tried."

She nodded. She didn't believe them. God could have found her. He could have told them where she was.

"Where is he?" the man asked. "Is he out there somewhere?"

"No," Didi said. "He's dead."

The man stared at her and then nodded. "Good," he said.

She felt Rich hold her tighter. "Oh God, Didi. Oh, God, oh, God. OHGOD."

She said, "Rich?" and then forgot the rest. "I called for Him too. I called for Him the whole day."

"He came. . . ."

Didi looked at the man in front of her and saw understanding in his eyes. She whispered to him, "Lyle—he was going to kill me and take my baby. I had to kill him. I stabbed him with his own knife."

The man said, "Good."

She saw Rich staring at her from the side and then staring at the man dressed in black with an expression Didi could best describe as disbelief. The man nodded to Rich, and said comfortingly to Didi, "Shh, shh, don't worry. You're safe. You're all right. The ambulance is right here. We're here to help you. You don't have to worry about anything."

No, she didn't suppose she did.

And then in the ambulance she stretched out. Her baby slept next to her. "The baby is alive," she said.

"The baby is alive," echoed Rich.

"You know," Didi said, after the paramedics cut the cord and set up an IV drip, "I don't feel too bad, considering I've just had a baby."

Rich groaned.

"Really," she said. "Listen, this labor, though, must have been harder than I ever imagined. I think I went into delirium."

"Really?" he said, kissing her head. "Why do you say that?"

"I must have been in tremendous pain. I dreamed—no, it's just too silly. I dreamed—will you believe it—that I was kidnapped, and beaten and cut, and had my nose broken, and was nearly killed, can you believe it?"

Rich couldn't look at her.

"I was right, Richie, wasn't I?" she said, taking his hand and squeezing it. "Karma came knocking. I was right."

Through his tears he shook his head and smiled crookedly. "Karma has nothing on you, my darling. Karma didn't know what it was dealing with when it picked you."

Didi almost smiled.

Rich was thinking about something. "What, Richie?" she said.

"Didi, we were both wrong."

Didi didn't have enough energy to be surprised. She let go his hand.

Rich took her hand in his and rubbed it gently. She was glad it wasn't the injured hand. "We were both wrong, and I'll tell you why. I just figured it out. He wasn't your karma, Didi. *You were his.* God didn't forget you at all. He didn't abandon you. He sent you to get that man out of His world, to put him out of his misery and out of our misery. And who better to send than you? God sent you because He knew you would do what you were meant to do—kill him and live yourself."

Didi closed her eyes. God had sent her to kill Lyle. "I don't think we should be second-guessing God, Richard," she said. "How did God know I would . . ."

"He knew," Rich said. "He knew."

They fell quiet. She reached out to him, touching his face. "Richie," she said. "Maybe after I've recovered from all this birth stuff, we can take a vacation?"

Wiping his face, he said. "Anywhere, Didi, anywhere." And then later, "Where would you like to go?"

Hoarsely, her answer came. "Anywhere but Mazatlán."

# EPILOGUE

**R**ich opened the car door for Didi. She slowly got out and squinted even though she was wearing sunglasses. The bright sun this Sunday reflected wildly off the water. The family had come to feed the ducks. The girls piled out from the back of the minivan, squabbling over who was going to hold the bag of bread.

Rich opened up the new hunter-green stroller and then gently lifted the boy out of his car seat and put him in. The baby twitched but continued to sleep, barely disturbed by the change of napping quarters. Didi came around to push the stroller. She walked slowly, favoring her right leg. A bone in her ankle had been fractured in the fall from the car.

In her heavily bandaged left hand, she held a bottle of water and every few minutes sipped from it. It was ten in the morning and still bearable outside. Didi knew that they could only stay out until noon because it would get too hot for the baby.

"I'll push, I'll push," Rich said to her.

"It's okay—"

"No, please. Let me."

She let him.

At the lake, they watched the girls feed the ducks. Rich stood close by Didi. She stood with her hands on the stroller, taking little sips out of her water bottle. Amanda and Irene were squealing as the white geese waddled over to them and the ducks from the lake scrambled up the embankment, squawking, *feed me, feed me*. The delight turned quickly to hysteria when one of the overzealous geese nipped Irene's finger. Rich picked her up, and for the rest of the feeding she threw the bread down while safely perched in his arms. Pushing the stroller, Didi went to sit down on the nearby bench. She adjusted the baby's hat and settled back.

Rich came over with Irene and sat down next to Didi. "You okay?" he said to Didi. Irene wiggled out and ran to Amanda.

"I'm great," she said, turning her face to him. "I just wanted to get the baby out of the sun."

When Rich said nothing, she patted his face. "Don't worry."

Nodding, he sighed deeply.

They were quiet for a moment. Didi felt hot.

She said, "About dinner tonight. What does Scott like to eat?"

"I don't know. We didn't get that far."

Smiling, she said, "I don't know why. You had plenty of time to chat."

"Yeah, but oddly, we were talking about other things," Rich replied.

Pausing, Didi said, "Well, I have to make him something. Does he like spaghetti?"

"I'm sure he does," Rich tried to assure her.

"Hmm. What about steak? Everyone likes a good steak."

"Steak is good," Rich agreed.

She thought about it. "What if he's a vegetarian? Then what?"

Rich studied Didi's face; her eyes were hidden from him by her wide sunglasses. "Scott put away a roast beef sandwich right in front of me. Make him a steak," he said.

"Steak it is, then," said Didi.

When they were finished feeding the ducks, Amanda put on her Rollerblades and, with Irene running alongside, skated ahead of Rich and Didi.

Didi had difficulty walking and stopped for a rest every few minutes. Two young women passing by slowed down near the stroller and looked in.

"My," said one, "what a cute baby!"

"Thanks," said Didi.

"How old?"

"Two weeks."

"Oh, he's a cutie. And look at that red hair!" The woman looked at brown-haired Didi and then at blond Rich. "Where's the hair from?"

Pointing at Rich, Didi said, "He's guilty. His dad's very red."

"Oh, so adorable."

The other woman, who had been standing quietly beside her friend, moved forward and said to Didi, "I'm pregnant myself. Thirteen weeks. My first. Scared to death. The whole labor thing." Lowering her voice, she asked, "How was it for you?"

Didi said, adjusting her sunglasses, "Oh, it wasn't bad." She paused. "Not bad at all."

The woman looked at her and said, "You got a bit of a sore throat, huh? Losing your voice?"

"Yeah," Didi said. "It's coming back though. You should have heard me last week."

Rich put his hand on Didi's back.

"Where'd you have your baby? I'm having mine at the Columbia Medical Center in Plano."

Nodding, Didi said, "That's a good hospital. I—I didn't have mine locally."

The pregnant young woman peered closer at Didi's son and said, "Hey, what happened to his arm? Is that a bandage?"

"Yeah," said Didi, reaching down to adjust the receiving blanket to cover her boy up to his neck. "He—I fell and he broke his arm when he was still *in utero*."

The women looked horrified.

"He'll be okay," Didi said. "Really."

"Come on, honey," Rich interrupted. "Let's go."

"Okay," Didi said, raising her hand in a wave to the two women. "Good luck," she said.

"Yeah, thanks," muttered the pregnant woman. "Good luck to *you*." The women sped up and passed them.

Rich and Didi slowly followed the girls. Didi was limping. "Girls, come back," she said hoarsely in a low voice, but they didn't hear her.

"Amanda, Irene! Listen to your mother! Don't go so far out!" Rich yelled.

The girls slowed down.

Rich asked, "Are you okay, honey? You want to go back home?"

"No, I'm okay," Didi said, taking off her glasses. The seven stitches over the left eyebrow had been removed last week and the dark, ragged wound was healing. The black-and-blue marks around her eyes were now turning yellow. The broken nose was still swollen and misshapen.

Rich said, "Women. They just want to know everything, don't they?"

"They mean well," Didi said. "And they don't know."

"I guess. I wish they would just keep going."

Didi took Rich's arm as he pushed the stroller. "Richie, people mean well. They're trying to be nice. It's okay."

"Yeah, but those questions, those questions. How do you do it?"

"It's easy," she said, smiling at him and putting her glasses back on as she saw a man and a woman with a stroller approaching them. "Watch."

They stopped again, and Didi and the other woman oohed and aahed

over each other's baby. When was he born? July 13? Wasn't that the
hottest day in seventy years? Yes, said Didi. It was. Oh, look how cute.
How big was he? Was the labor terrible? Oh, mine was the pits, said
the other woman. Mine wasn't too bad, said Didi.

Rich stood silently, with his arm around his wife.

The baby woke up and Didi carefully took him out of his stroller.
Rich offered to carry him, but Didi said, "No, that's okay. I'll carry
him." He remained in her arms for the rest of the walk.